PROTECTING WHAT'S MINE

JENNIFER SUCEVIC

ALSO BY JENNIFER SUCEVIC

Campus Heartthrob

Campus Player

Claiming What's Mine

Confessions of a Heartbreaker

Crazy for You (80s short story)

Don't Leave

Friend Zoned

Hate to Love You

Heartless

If You Were Mine

Just Friends

King of Campus

King of Hawthorne Prep

Love to Hate You

One Night Stand

Queen of Hawthorne Prep

Stay

The Boy Next Door

The Breakup Plan

The Girl Next Door

CHAPTER ONE

"You know, it's not too late to change your mind." Shoving his hands into the pockets of his khakis, Dominic watches me from across the wide expanse of the bright, sunlight-filled room.

Sucking in a deep breath, the edges of my lips slowly curl into a small smile as I gaze at the huge, floor-to-ceiling panes of glass lining the entire eastern wall of the living room. From this vantage point on the thirtieth floor, I can easily survey the deep blue vastness of Lake Michigan along with the skyscrapers that make up the Chicago skyline.

It's a stunning view.

Just as picturesque as I remember it.

Excitement thrums through my veins. It feels good to be back. Even though I've been gone for a decade, Chicago has always felt like home.

"I won't be changing my mind," I murmur, my eyes held captive by the sparkling water in the distance. "It's a gorgeous view, isn't it?"

He snorts, but I hear the affection he feels for me riddled throughout his deep voice. "It's a view that only two point nine million can buy."

"It's my view now."

I'm not sure it was the right decision to make, but I hope so. I've spent the last two years just trying to hold it together. Struggling to make it through life on a day-to-day basis. Feeling as if I were drowning in a bottomless well of grief and sadness. There were days when I felt like I would never find my way out of the labyrinth of despair that consumed me.

I hate to admit it, because it makes me sound weak and ungrateful for the life I have, but there have been too many nights when I've laid awake, sobbing, wondering why I was still here. Wondering why I hadn't died in the accident that stole my parents from me.

It would have been so much easier that way.

Instead, I'm here.

With no family to speak of.

Sensing the direction of my thoughts, my godfather closes the distance, coming to stand beside me at the window. For just a moment, we both stare silently at the lake. It's this particular view that sold me on the place. I wanted to be right smack in the middle of the hustle and bustle of downtown. Since I'll be starting a graduate program in Art History at Northwestern, I wanted to be close to the university. I'm not more than a stone's throw away from all the museums near the lakefront and all the great shopping on the Magnificent Mile.

What I need is to be in the thick of all the action. To be in a place where I can walk outside at two in the morning and find people. I need the pulse of the city to help bring me to life again. To revitalize me. It feels as though I've been in a deep hibernation since my parents died. I've spent the last two years living in a self-imposed isolation, unable to break free. But I can't do that anymore.

It's time to awaken.

And Chicago is the perfect place for that to happen.

The city streets all but hum with unrestrained energy.

I glance at Dominic, thankful for his constant guiding presence in my life. Without any words spoken between us, he seems to understand just how significant this moment feels. It's as if I'm on the cusp of a brand-new life. Sliding his arm around my waist, he tugs me close.

Several factors went into my decision to pick up and move, but Dominic topped the list. He's all I have left. Technically, he isn't my family. Not by blood, anyway. He's my godfather. Dominic is the one person I can call at any time of the day or night, and he'll sit silently on the other end of the line, knowing exactly how I feel. In a way, he feels it too. The loss of my parents has blown a hole in his life as well.

"Even though you have this place, you're welcome to stay with me. Anytime, Gracie. My house will always be your home."

His words have my lips tipping up at the corners. He has no idea what that means to me. Just how appreciative I am for them. For the sentiment behind them. No matter what happens, I will always have Dominic. He's my safety net. My rock. My de facto family.

As his deep blue eyes crinkle, his mouth curves into a smile.

He knows exactly how difficult this is for me.

Starting over.

Leaving the past behind.

Trying to carve out a new life for myself.

One my parents are no longer a part of.

That thought pierces my heart, making it difficult to breathe.

"I know." With thoughts of my parents and this move churning in my mind, I slowly lower my head until I'm able to rest it against the side of his arm. I can't believe I'm a few blocks from Lakeshore Drive. The views are as sweeping as they are breathtaking. I'm lucky to have found this place. "Thank you."

"Your graduate program doesn't start for another three weeks. You could always stay at the house until then. There's certainly no rush for you to be on your own. That way you can take your time and ease into your new life. Is there any reason you should be thrown into the deep end of the pool just yet?"

He's right. I could crash at his place for the next couple of weeks.

But I don't think I want to. I need to be on my own.

Well... I need to give it a try.

The last two years have been both emotionally, as well as mentally, crippling. I was two months into my junior year when my parents died. From what the police could tell, my father had been driving too fast for the weather conditions. They'd been hit with a terrible storm. Torrential downpours. I have no idea why they didn't just pull over and outwait the weather. Ultimately, that decision cost them their lives.

And made me an orphan in the process.

No parents.

No siblings.

No grandparents, aunts, or uncles.

My parents had been only children and their parents were now deceased, leaving me with no one.

Lost in a debilitating haze of heartache, I'd wanted to drop out of college. Dominic is the one who convinced me to stick it out and finish up the academic year. It hadn't been easy. I'd almost flunked out that fall semester. Depression. Grief. Sadness. I had been adrift in a sea of despondency that had threatened to swallow me whole.

Because Dominic had been close to my parents, he'd long ago been set up as my guardian if the worst ever occurred. He spoke with the school, asking for leniency when I'd been on the verge of getting kicked out. It took nine months before I started fighting my way back again. Retaking a few classes, I focused on graduating from the university and getting the hell out of there.

I applied to a few graduate programs and was lucky to get accepted at Northwestern. My essay and interview were enough to sway them into giving me a chance to prove myself. Before the accident, I had been a straight A student. Once I was finally able to emerge from my cocoon of grief, I was able to get back on track again.

"I need this," I murmur quietly. "I think it's going to be good for me." I don't know whether I'm trying to reassure him or myself.

But the words ring true.

Right now, in this very moment, I *need* them to be true.

I need to believe that life will continue to improve from here on out.

Gently he presses his lips against my temple. "It will be, Gracie. I have no doubt about that." He pauses for a moment. "I just can't help but wish you were staying at the house. At least for a little while. I don't want you getting overwhelmed. Moving, starting school, volunteering..."

I understand his concern. In a way, I have the same fears. But it seems necessary. As if I need to shock my system into living again.

When I don't immediately respond, he continues, "The last two years have been..." His softly spoken words trail off into nothingness.

We both know what it's been like. The sheer depth of my despair has, at times, frightened him.

Sucking in a breath, I force it back out into the world. "Difficult."

To say the least.

His arm tightens around me. "I'm happy to have you back again."

Both of my parents were born in Seattle, which is why we ended up moving back there when I was in seventh grade. At the time, my mom's parents had still been alive, and she'd wanted to be closer to them. To help them out.

My parents met Dominic while they were attending law school in Chicago. They had liked the city so much, they'd stuck around after graduating. Both of them took jobs with the district attorney's office. So, I was born in Chicago. Until moving to Seattle, this had been the only home I'd ever known. I loved Chicago. Loved everything about the city. The ties that I had here, the memories, and the happy childhood spent wandering around museums and zoos played a huge part in my decision to return.

No matter how many years have crept by, Chicago has always been where my heart was. It just felt like home. More so than Seattle ever had.

A feeling of rightness settles over me like a comforting blanket. "I'm glad to be here."

Even after my family moved to Seattle, we still spent a lot of time with Dominic. He visited for holidays. We vacationed together. He's been an ever-constant presence in my life. After my parents died, I spent my school breaks with him. There was always a plane ticket waiting for me. I never had to ask or broach the subject. I never felt unwanted or unloved.

Spending time alone in the Seattle house without my parents... I just couldn't do it. There were too many memories. A tidal wave of grief just waiting to suck me under when I least expected it always lingered in the background.

Our house in Seattle was massive. A five-bedroom rambling old Victorian with soaring ceilings and intricate woodwork that my parents spent four painstaking years refinishing in their spare time. As someone who appreciated architecture, I loved all the fancy molding and trim, gorgeous stained-glass windows, and glossy hardwood floors.

I haven't been back in almost a year and a half. I can't bear to walk through the front door. Mom and Dad's stamps are everywhere. There's no where I can go without a hundred different memories flooding into my mind.

And my heart.

As of right now, the house is closed up. Dominic pays a company to handle the upkeep and maintenance until we figure out what to do with it. There's no way I can rent it out to strangers. Nor can I bring myself to sell it.

How can I possibly sell all the memories that lay dormant within?

I suppose at some point I'll have to decide what to do, but for now it can wait. There's no hurry. My parents inherited a great deal of money from my mother's family. It's all sitting in a trust that Dominic manages for me.

Rising up onto the worn toes of my Converse sneakers, I kiss the side of his face. "Thanks for everything."

With his arm still wrapped around my waist, his eyes soften as he continues gazing down at me. "You don't have to thank me. We're family." He cracks just a hint of a smile as he says, "It's just you and me, kid. Against the world."

I can't help but return his easy affection. It may be just the two of us, but I consider myself fortunate to have him in my life.

Unlike my parents, who worked as prosecutors in the district attorney's office, Dominic decided to go the route of high-priced defense attorney. He didn't come from money the way my parents did. He would always wink, jokingly saying that he couldn't afford to be a bleeding-heart liberal like my parents. After practicing law for about five years, he opened his own office and bought a beautiful, old stately house on the Northshore. It's situated right on Lake Michigan.

Never married, there have been a slew of girlfriends over the years. There have even been a few close calls where we thought he might pop the question, but it never happened.

I remember my dad laughing and my mother shaking her blond head as she rolled her twinkling blue eyes at his quintessential bachelorhood. He has always seemed perfectly content to date one beautiful woman after another. Once I'd overheard my father mutter something about Dominic having a whole stable full of pussy.

I hadn't understood what that meant at the time and I hadn't wanted to figure it out either. All I cared about was that Dominic was great fun to be around. Always smiling and laughing, he was the life of every party. People naturally gravitated to his charismatic personality. Women especially. In fact, they still do.

When I'd been in high school, I'd secretly crushed on him.

Who wouldn't?

Dominic was tall and handsome. He had broad shoulders, a tapered waist, elegant hands, and thick blond hair. His bright blue eyes always seemed to be filled with mischief. He had perpetually tanned skin from taking his sailboat out on the weekends. Other than practicing law, sailing was his other great passion. He didn't have a thin build, but he wasn't overly muscular either. He spent the work week outfitted in expensive, handmade suits and the weekends in khakis, polos, and Sperry topsiders.

He reminded me of a walking Ralph Lauren ad, content to live the good life.

I pegged him to be somewhere around forty-five. He was one of those men who grew more attractive, more distinguished, with age. The little laugh lines bracketing his eyes made him more striking. Last year, when the two of us had celebrated his birthday, I'd teased him mercilessly because he wouldn't tell me how old he was. As a gag gift, I gave him a cane, denture cream, and a subscription to AARP magazine.

He had not been amused.

The recollection still makes me smile.

It's one of the few happy memories I have to hold onto in a churning sea of sadness and grief. So, I've held tightly onto those fleeting moments with both hands. They have been far too rare and much too precious to ever take for granted.

"In no time at all, this place will feel like home."

Giving him a smile, I say, "It already does." Leaning my body into his, he tightens his arm around my waist. "You're here."

CHAPTER TWO

Looking quite handsome, George, the doorman, is decked out in full regalia. From the smart looking cap on his balding head to the shiny black shoes adorning his feet and the red wool coat and black pants in between, he fits right in with the elegance and formality Lexington Place, the building I have chosen to call home, prides itself on.

What I really like about it though, is how seriously the owners take security. It's like Fort Knox around here. After setting up an appointment for a tour, I was immediately background checked. As I was shown around, the manager was quick to point out all the hidden cameras and panic buttons discretely placed throughout the building and inside the condos. The employees that were staffed twenty-four hours a day, seven days a week. And the fingerprint entry technology that was used for each door. I've never been overly concerned about personal safety, but the extra measures made me feel better since I'll be living on my own.

This morning I stopped in the lobby and chatted with George for a few minutes. Rather helpfully, he directed me to the nearest grocery store, which is a Whole Foods, about four blocks away.

That works out perfectly since I don't have a car. It seems like more of a hindrance when living in a city that is so walkable. Traffic is usually heavy, and parking can be a nightmare. There are always plenty of available taxicabs. Plus, the city has a subway and bus system. Since Dominic keeps a driver on staff, all I have to do is text him, and he'll send Henry to pick me up.

With my purse in hand and comfortable sandals adorning my feet, I take my time meandering down the sidewalk, simply enjoying the sights and sounds of the city. There's such a vibrant energy here. It's infectious. I look in shop windows, popping in one or two places to check out a few wares that catch my eye.

Once I'm at the grocery store, I grab a small cart and pick out what I'll need for the next few days. I try to be conscious that the walk back to my building is four blocks, I don't want to buy too much.

When I moved in a few days ago, Dominic took me shopping, and we filled up the fridge and cupboards. Unfortunately, a couple of things were forgotten. I buy just enough to fill two small bags, which feels manageable to carry, before retracing my steps again.

As I stroll back to Lexington Place, I can't deny that there is something thrilling about being smack-dab in the middle of downtown. I don't know if it's the noise. Maybe it's the people, most of whom seem to be rushing to get from one place to another. You can easily spot the ones who live here- they seem unimpressed by their surroundings, as if they've grown used to the chaos. They've got earbuds shoved in or are multitasking on their phones.

The tourists, on the other hand, are the ones with awe painted across their lit-up faces as they stare unabashedly around them, trying to take everything in all at once. The high-end shops. The exclusive hotels. The restaurants. They gaze up at the skyscrapers with bright eyes filled with wonder.

Excitement bursts within me like an overfilled bubble.

I love it.

I love everything about being downtown.

The sensory overload. The sights and sounds. The smells of different restaurants all blending together. The contrasting colors of the buildings and shops. The merchandise displayed enticingly in windows. Taxis and buses barreling down the street.

I feel more alive at this moment than I have since my parents passed away. In no time at all, I reach the building. I'm a little disappointed to have returned so soon. I could wander around the city for hours, just soaking everything up like a greedy sponge.

Right away, George grabs the door for me. "Found the store without any problems?"

"None at all. Your directions were excellent. Thank you."

"Just remember, you can always call us if you're unable to walk back with your groceries, Ms. Castile. It's one of the perks of living at Lexington place."

"Thank you, I'll keep that in mind." I can't contain the bright smile that blooms across my face. "It's just so beautiful out. Perfect weather for exploring the neighborhood."

Almost instantly an answering smile lights up his weathered face, and I know instantly that he's a cheerful, friendly man. I have a feeling that George and I will become fast friends. Other than Dominic, I don't know anyone else in the city.

"That it is, Ms. Castile."

Jostling around one of the bags, I push the call button for the elevator. After falling in love with the condo online while still living in Seattle, Dominic contacted the manager straightaway. He scouted out the building and surrounding neighborhood, making sure it would be a safe place for me to live.

I wouldn't say that Dominic fought me every step of the way, but he pointed out every disadvantage of living here. I know he hoped that I would stay with him for a while, taking my time to find new living arrangements. I wasn't averse to the idea, but after finding this place, I knew it wouldn't be necessary.

Visiting the condo in person was the first time in forever that I'd felt excitement pumping through my veins. I think Dominic could sense it as well, which is why he didn't throw up too many roadblocks.

Even though Dominic has a massive house, certainly more than enough room for us to live without being on top of each other, I craved my own space. I wanted to be close to school and The Art Institute of Chicago, where I'll be volunteering. I'm hoping that by the time I need to land an internship, their familiarity with me will give me an edge over other candidates vying for the same position. My dream is to one-day work for them as a curator. There are other art museums in the area, and I would be grateful to land a position at any of them. But I have so many fond memories of The Art Institute.

While most kids don't find strolling through the corridors of a museum and learning about art to be fun or exciting, it's always been one of my favorite pastimes. Even as a small child, I could stare in fascination at a landscape for hours at a time, studying every minute detail. I would curl up on a bench and try my hand at sketching replicas.

Right down the street from my building is the Field Museum, the Museum of Science and Industry, Shedd Aquarium, Adler Planetarium, and The Museum of Contemporary Art. Having all of these spectacular places no more than a mile or so from where I live leaves me feeling nothing short of giddy.

How could anyone be bored in a city like this?

I plan on filling my days with school, volunteering, and museums when time allows.

"Have a good day, George," I call before stepping onto the elevator.

"You too, Ms. Castile."

Pushing the button for the thirtieth floor, I wait for the doors to close. Just as they start sliding shut, a big, masculine hand shoots out and catches the metal frame in one palm. My eyes widen with surprise as the doors immediately slide open. A moment later, a man steps inside the cabin with me. Feeling just a bit uncomfortable, I shift, knowing that I should probably say hello and introduce myself, but there's something about him that makes me reluctant to draw any attention to myself.

As soon as that thought flutters through my head, he pins me in place with dark, velvety eyes. My breath stalls as his gaze continues piercing mine. At that moment, under his sharp scrutiny, I feel frozen in place. Unable to move a single muscle. The phone he's holding chirps, breaking the thick tension that fills the small, enclosed space.

Dismissing me at once, his gaze shifts. Once his eyes relinquish their strange hold over me, I'm able to force out a relieved breath.

I realize that my legs are trembling. It feels as though I'm moments away from sliding to the floor in a heap. Having those intense, espresso-colored eyes fixated on me had everything within seizing before quickly grinding to a halt.

Rather ridiculously, my heart continues to beat wildly against my ribs.

Now that he's preoccupied with the device in his hand, I'm able to stare unabashedly at him from beneath my lashes. Hands down, he's the most gorgeous man I've ever seen.

Thick, inky black hair hits the collar of the starched white shirt peeking out from beneath a gray suit jacket. I know next to nothing about men's fashions, but even I can spot quality when I see it. And this is definitely high-end, luxurious fabric that was hand-stitched specifically for him. I'd bet every penny of my inheritance that it wasn't bought off a rack.

It fits his well-built frame perfectly, molding flawlessly to the wide breadth of his shoulders and across his chest before tapering in at his waist. Gray suit pants stretch over his muscular thighs draping to shiny black wingtips.

I've spent the last four years on a college campus. I've been surrounded by handsome boys. But that's the difference here. The guys I'm used to are, for all intents and purposes, *boys*. They wear snug T-shirts, long athletic shorts, and slides on their feet.

They look *nothing* like this.

It's like we're not even talking about the same species.

Unable to help myself, I continue gazing at him in rapt fascination.

He's just so completely... *stunning*. That's probably the wrong word to use to describe this man, but it fits.

There's something powerful, almost dangerous, that radiates from him in thick, heavy waves. There seems to be a darkness within him. It's a little intimidating. Okay, *a lot* intimidating. A hundred butterflies take flight inside the confines of my belly. Even if I wanted to, I don't think I could look away from him.

Coal black brows pinch together as he continues staring at the phone. Using his thumbs, he quickly taps out a message. I'm tempted to inch closer, just enough to catch a glimpse of what he's so intent upon.

My eyes linger on his wide hands.

For just a moment, I wonder what they would feel like skimming over my naked body. I haven't been touched in a year and a half. Before the crash, I'd had a boyfriend at college. I had liked Eric well enough. He'd been nice in the goofy, immature kind of way that twenty-one-year-old boys are. We'd been together for just about six months when the accident occurred. After my parents died, he didn't know how to deal with me.

With my overwhelming grief.

Slowly but surely, we drifted apart. I retreated within myself as a comforting numbness set in. He was unable to penetrate my cool detachment. I can hardly blame him for not knowing how to help me or for not being mentally or emotionally equipped to deal with something so heavy and intense.

I didn't know how to deal with it myself.

Only now, two years later, am I beginning to thaw.

To awaken from a long, dark slumber.

So, to feel this kind of instant, over-the-top attraction for the opposite sex...

It feels... *good*.

Better than good.

Amazing.

Even though nothing will come of it, I wholeheartedly welcome this impromptu infatuation running rampant through my system. For just a sliver of a moment, I want to soak it all up. I want to bask in it.

It feels so good to *feel* something again.

And come on... Just *look* at him.

If you want to have a harmless little crush on someone completely unattainable, this is the perfect man to star in your fantasies.

He's just so impeccably put together.

Polished.

Right down to the massive silver Rolex around his left wrist.

Feeling very much out of his league, I automatically glance down at my own attire. My white shorts hit mid-thigh. A summery T-shirt hugs my breasts. Black sandals that I hastily shoved my feet into just before stepping out the door are strapped to my feet. A pair of tortoise shell sunglasses are perched on top of my head. I'd been so antsy to get out and start exploring that I'd thrown my long, blond hair up into a messy bun.

In hindsight, I should have taken a bit more care with my appearance. Much akin to Dorothy no longer being in Kansas, I'm no longer living in the dorms with a bunch of other grungy college students who don't give a damn. Maybe it's time to step up my game. It's something to consider, at the very least.

Unconsciously, my eyes gravitate back to him. Once again, I'm bowled over by his good looks. By the sheer size of him. I guess that he's somewhere around six foot three. Which makes me almost a whole foot shorter, since I top out around five foot four. Five foot five with heels.

In one smooth movement, he pockets the phone before looking at me with a strange intensity that leaves me breathless. If I were thinking properly, I'd drag my eyes away. But I don't. I can't. Even though the elevator continues climbing to the top of the building, it feels as if time is at a standstill.

One side of his mouth hitches.

Not a lot. Just a bit.

It's more than enough to send my heart somersaulting, though.

His complexion is olive in tone. Nothing like my pasty whiteness. If I had to guess, I'd say he was of Italian origin.

God, but he's beautiful. That one thought continues to ring throughout my head like a bell. I'm only partly conscious of the fact that I'm once again staring unabashedly. Heat slowly creeps up my neck until it reaches my cheeks.

Finally, the elevator chimes, signaling our arrival to the thirtieth floor. I should be relieved to escape his intimidating presence. Even though my eyes are still locked on his, I hear the doors slide open. Using his hand, he holds the metal frame so that they won't close before we exit the cabin. Somewhere in the back of my brain, I realize that we're both going to the same floor.

When I make no move to leave, one perfectly sculpted brow wings up as he continues watching me with something akin to amusement. When he'd first strode onto the elevator, he'd seemed almost dark and brooding. Or maybe his swarthy good looks just lent themselves to that description. There hadn't appeared to be any light or humor within him.

That being said, he looks oddly entertained.

At my expense.

Just kill me now.

Please.

As that jarring thought slices through me, my hands tighten around the reusable grocery bags I'm holding before I flee from the elevator as if the hounds of hell are nipping at my heels.

Now that I'm no longer staring at all that male perfection, I silently berate myself for acting like a complete idiot in front of the stranger who apparently lives on the same floor as I do.

Great.

You would think that I've never come across a handsome man in all my twenty-three years. I shake my head at my own ridiculousness. I'm willing to bet that my open adoration was the perfect balm to his already massive ego. A man like that obviously knows how good-looking he is. I bet women throw themselves at him on a daily basis.

Slowing before my door, I set both bags down. Even though I resist the urge to glance over my shoulder, I know he's about ten feet behind me. I'd hoped that he would head in the opposite direction after departing from the elevator, but no such luck.

A shiver skitters down my spine as he brushes past me on the way to his condo. I almost swoon as his spicy masculine scent wraps around me. Feeling out of sorts, I press my finger on the keypad before twisting the knob. Out of the corner of my eye, I watch him stop at the door next to mine. He doesn't spare me a glance before gaining entry into his own place.

Hauling the groceries inside, my entire body slumps as I lean against the door and close my eyes. I inhale one breath, then another, trying to calm everything racing madly within me.

I can't decide if I want to run into him again or not.

Probably not.

Obviously, I can't trust myself not to gawk at him like some kind of nitwit. How demoralizing is that?

So much for making a good impression on my new neighbor.

CHAPTER THREE

"What would you say if I throw a small party Friday evening?"

Bringing the glass of iced tea to my lips, I take a drink while contemplating him over the rim. "Exactly how small are we talking?" Because *small* in my book means roughly a dozen people. More of an intimate gathering of sorts.

Even though he shrugs all casual-like, his blue eyes sparkle with humor. Yep, he knows exactly what's running through my brain. "Maybe a hundred. Somewhere in that vicinity."

I almost spit my tea across the table. "*A hundred?* In what universe is that considered small?"

"Two-fifty would be large."

"I don't know one hundred people."

"After Friday night, you will. Which is precisely why we're throwing this shindig. We need a way to get you back out there again. And this does the job rather nicely."

From across the table, I make a face. I don't think I was ever *out there* to begin with. "Who would you invite?" Total strangers? Randoms off the street?

He shrugs as if the actual guest list is a non-issue. "Oh, some work colleagues. Friends of mine. People who knew your parents."

He must catch a glimpse of the shadows still lurking in my eyes when he brings up Mom and Dad. You'd think I would be desensitized to it by now, but I'm not. The pain still has the ability to slice through me at the most unexpected of moments. Softly he says, "I thought you might enjoy reacquainting yourself with some of their old friends."

I force a smile even though it feels like my throat is closing up. I appreciate what Dominic's trying to do and don't want to appear ungrateful. "That sounds nice."

He nabs my fingers and gives them a gentle squeeze. "I'm just excited that you're here. I think a party would help you meet some new people. It's not going to be a big, fancy deal. We're talking casual."

Although I have no desire to be thrust so quickly into the Chicago social scene, I can't say no. Dominic has been wonderful to me these past two years. I'm grateful for everything he's done. Without me asking, he swooped in and took care of all the responsibilities that should have fallen on my ill-equipped shoulders.

The funeral.

The house.

The will.

The inheritance.

The insurance policies.

Everything I had been unable to wrap my head around those first few months after the accident. Almost two years later, and he's still dealing with all of it. The sale of this condo went through him. And he's already settled my fall tuition bill at Northwestern.

Deep down, I know he's right. I may not want this party, but I need it. I need someone to force me out of the self-imposed hibernation I've been stuck in. It's not like I have any friends here. The few I had, I eventually lost touch with.

Like Chloe.

My childhood best friend.

It didn't happen right away. We continued texting and FaceTiming after I moved to Seattle. And up until college, we visited one another regularly. But after my parents died, even Chloe couldn't penetrate the deep fog that sucked me under. The yawning physical distance separating us was just too much to overcome. After a while, no longer able to put up a good front, I stopped responding to her calls and texts.

I allowed our friendship to fall by the wayside.

Now, almost two years later, I regret icing her out. Once I'm settled, I have every intention of getting back in touch with her. For right now though, I'm taking things one step at a time. Slow, deliberate steps that continue to propel me forward, closer to the life I envision myself living.

Which is what this party will help achieve.

I almost groan as that thought pierces my consciousness.

"Okay," I finally grumble.

Dominic squints as if he doesn't believe that I've agreed to his party proposal. "Okay? *That's it?* No cajoling? No begging? You're capitulating, just like that?" His eyes narrow further.

For some odd reason, his reaction lightens my heart. I can't help but chuckle. Slowly, as if it's painful to voice the words out loud, I say, "You're right. A party is exactly what I need. Meeting some new people along with a few old ones who worked with my parents will be good for me." I suck in a deep breath before pushing out the rest. "It might even be *fun*."

Not looking the least bit convinced by my sudden acquiescence, he scrutinizes me for a moment before saying, "All right, Grace Elizabeth Castile, what kind of sly trickery are you trying to pull? A little reverse psychology, is it? Or are you about to hit me with some outrageous bill and you're trying to soften the blow?"

I snort at the accusation. "I promise, there's no trickery at work here." An evil smile spreads across my face. "But there is a bill I need you to pay."

Wearing a smug expression, he folds his arms across his chest. "I knew it."

I chortle in response. "*Just kidding!* There aren't any bills right now." My eyes travel around my new condo, which has been furnished with a few antiques from my parents' house along with some new things I've picked up since moving here. It's a mixture of traditional and modern, and I love it.

As my eyes slide over each piece, I realize how *me* this condo is turning out to be. I spent the last four years living in the dorms with a roommate. It's nice to have a place all to myself. "I think I've spent more than enough over the last two months." I paid for the condo in cash with money from my inheritance. Plus, the school tuition bill. And some furniture.

I feel like I should be tapped out.

Changing tones, he quickly reminds me, "You don't have to worry about money, Gracie. You're fine. Quite honestly, you won't have to worry about money for the rest of your life. You don't have to work, if you don't want to."

After I graduated from college, Dominic told me that I could simply volunteer at a museum if that's what I really wanted to do. I don't need an income. Between the inheritance from my grandparents and the insurance policy money from my parents' death, I've got more than enough to sustain me for the long run. Especially if it's invested wisely, which is what I rely on Dominic for.

Don't get me wrong, I'm eternally grateful for that money. It's one less thing to worry about. I may be young, but I understand what a huge gift financial freedom is.

But I can't imagine *not* working. I've spent the last four years trudging through college. I've earned a bachelor's degree in art history and am now enrolled in a graduate program at Northwestern. I'd like to get my doctorate, with the end game being that I find a curating position at an art museum.

What's the alternative?

Spending my days being idle?

Shopping and lunching?

That's not the kind of life my parents envisioned for me. They never told me that I didn't have to work. Until Dominic went through their Last Will and Testament, I'd had no idea how much they were worth. I'd always known that we weren't lacking for anything. But I hadn't realized they were independently wealthy.

After they inherited all that money from my grandparents, Mom and Dad continued working. They were both so passionate about the law. Their lives held purpose and meaning because of it. That's what I want for myself. Even though I'm pursuing a different kind of career, it's no less important.

If anyone should appreciate the fact that I want a meaningful career, it's Dominic. He's been a workaholic for as long as I've known him. Putting in eighty-hour weeks is nothing to him. Sometimes, if there's an important case, he'll have his associates and paralegals work during the weekend at his house. He always compensates them generously, so there isn't that much complaining, but still...

"I want a career, Dominic. I love art. Eventually I want to find a position as a curator. I don't want to just be a volunteer. I want my input to matter. I want to be involved in the decision-making process regarding exhibits and displays. Not to mention, the actual art itself. That's all I've ever wanted."

He showers me with a smile full of pride. "I know, sweetheart. You could delay school for a bit if you feel overwhelmed. The option to start later is always a possibility. There's nothing wrong with taking a bit of time off."

I appreciate his concern. But still, I shake my head. I'm looking forward to delving into the art history program at Northwestern. I don't want to put it off. What would I do with all my time? Sit around? Think about my parents? Get depressed?

No, I need to throw myself into this new life. I can't take the chance of getting stuck in my head again. That's one of the reasons I moved here. Fresh start. New beginning. No more living in the past.

"I'm ready now."

"I want you to realize that there are options available to you even if you start the program and decide to delay it after a few weeks. I don't want you feeling like you have to continue with it, that you have to take a full course load so that you can finish up as quickly as possible. There's no rush for you to find a paid position. Your parents did extremely well for themselves. They were careful with how they invested your mother's inheritance. It's grown exponentially over the years."

I feel bad for admitting this, but I don't know how much I'm worth. It isn't a topic my parents openly discussed and after they died, Dominic handled all the finances so that I could focus on moving forward and getting through school. I want Dominic to continue managing everything, but I should at least have a working knowledge of what's going on. It seems... ignorant or, at the very least, oblivious to not know.

"I was thinking that maybe I should handle some of my own bills from now on." I wave my hand, encompassing my new residence. "Now that I'm living here and not in the dorms, I'll have to pay for utilities and necessities on a monthly basis. It would be easier for both of us if I didn't have to bother you all the time."

He gives me a look as if I'm talking nonsense. "Gracie, please, you could never be a bother."

"I know, but it seems like I should be doing this myself. I'm twenty-three years old and I don't know what I have in the bank."

"You're right," he concedes. "You should have more responsibility where your inheritance is concerned, but I think we need to take it slow. Give yourself time to get acclimated to Chicago, your new condo, and the program you're enrolled in. This move is a huge change for you. Everything about your life is different now. I hate the thought of you taking on too much. Your inheritance is a lot to manage. But at some point, you'll have to do it on your own."

Silently mulling over his words, I nod. He's right. Everything about my life is different than it was two short months ago. It's probably for the best that he continues managing everything monetarily until I'm able to get into a groove. Maybe six months from now, he can slowly start handing over the financial reins. I don't want complete control, though. I know what Dominic said is true. My parents' wealth is extensive. I don't want to make any bad fiscal decisions.

Sometimes it feels like I have very little say or control over my own money. I don't like having to ask permission for something that is mine in the first place. Yes, I'm young and I've been through a traumatic few years, but I'm ready to at least pay my own monthly bills.

Even though I was twenty-one at the time of the accident, Dominic was appointed as the estate executor for my inheritance. He's in charge of everything until I turn twenty-five. Honestly, I don't have anything to complain about. Whenever I ask for money, he never says no. He simply deposits the funds into my checking account. And he's always been generous with my monthly allowance.

"If you want to sit down and go over your portfolio, I'm more than willing to do it. I've told you that from the beginning."

That's true. He has offered. Repeatedly. I just wasn't ready before. Now, two years have slipped by, and I have no clue about my wealth.

"Okay. Maybe we can sit down in a few months and go over everything. But you're right, it's probably better if you retain control for the time being."

"It's what your parents wanted. They loved you very much and wanted to make sure you had someone trustworthy to look after both you and your assets."

It breaks my heart to hear him say that.

My parents loved Dominic. He might not have been blood, but he was family just the same. Without him, I would have no one. As soon as that thought takes root in my mind, I quickly shove it away. I hate dwelling on how alone I am.

Ironically, when it was just my parents and me, I never felt like that. My life had been full, brimming with love. But without them there's this huge, gaping hole. The only one capable of filling it is Dominic.

His brow furrows as he continues watching me. "What's wrong, sweetheart?"

Not wanting to talk about the thoughts crashing around within my brain, I push them away. "I just love you, and I'm happy to finally be here in Chicago. I don't say it enough, but I'm grateful for everything you've done for me."

Reaching across the table, he slips his fingers into mine and gives them a gentle squeeze.

"I will always be here for you, Gracie." Lightening the mood, he gives me a little wink. "It's just you and me, kid. No matter what."

Hearing those words, even though it's something he tells me often, has the rare ability to calm everything rioting inside me.

And for that, I'm grateful.

CHAPTER FOUR

Knuckles rap against the door. This has been my bedroom at Dominic's since I was a kid. If someone didn't know better, they would assume I grew up here. Books, knickknacks, pictures, and clothing fill the space making it look lived in.

"Come in."

The door opens, and Dominic's blond head pops in. A long, low whistle escapes his lips as his eyes sweep over me with appreciation.

Grinning in response, I hold up my arms before giving a little twirl. "So? What do you think?"

With a smile stretching across his handsome face, he shakes his head. "You look stunning, Gracie."

Glancing down at the dress, I admit shyly, "I feel like a princess. The gown is gorgeous. Thank you so much. How did you guess my size?"

Looking pleased with himself, he shrugs his broad shoulders as if it's no big deal. "I'm a man of many talents. Do you really expect anything less from me?"

I roll my eyes.

"All right, all right. I bought three different sizes of the same dress. The other two are hanging in my closet in case this one didn't work."

He gives me a playful wink before adding, "Tonight is too special to ruin by not having the perfect fit."

I laugh. "Well, thank you. I love it." Again, my eyes are drawn to the six-foot mirror leaning against the wall. The gown really is lovely.

And I feel beautiful in it.

The dress is a rich, deep blue crepe that matches my eyes perfectly. It's strapless, with a beaded sweetheart neckline and a long slit up one leg. Dominic also picked out strappy silver sandals that make my legs look long and lean.

I meet his eyes in the mirror as he moves to stand behind me. "Did you really pick all this out yourself or did someone help you?" I wiggle my brows, alluding to the possibility of a female friend that he has yet to introduce me to.

His smile broadens, making him look even more debonair than usual. "Fine. You caught me. I had a little bit of help."

Surprised by his words, I spin on silvery heels so that we face one another. I don't think I've heard him mention a woman in at least two years. "Will I get to meet her tonight?"

Almost immediately, he chuckles. "I had help from my personal shopper at Saks." One brow arches in question. "Were you thinking someone else?"

A sheepish smile settles across my face. "Maybe."

I think Dominic could use a steady woman in his life. He has a gorgeous house right on the sandy shores of Lake Michigan. Even though I've never gotten the feeling that he's lonely, I can't imagine that he wants to remain a bachelor forever.

Because I'm busy dwelling on his single status, I don't realize that he has slid a large rectangular box out of his pocket until he presents it to me. Surprised, my eyes instantly jerk up to his.

"You moving back home seemed like a special occasion that needed to be celebrated." A look of uncertainty flickers across his face as he slowly opens the case. "I hope you like it."

Eyes widening, my gasp is audible. Shaking fingers fly to my mouth in shocked awe. A stunning sapphire and diamond necklace lays nestled against a rich, black velvet backdrop. "Oh my God," I whisper, "I can't believe you did this!"

I can tell that this isn't cheap costume jewelry he picked up at a chain department store. No, this is the real deal.

Slowly, I shake my head. The piece is so spectacular that I can't bear to rip my gaze away from it. "No," I finally murmur, "I can't accept this! It's way too much, Dominic." Again, my wide, disbelieving eyes shift to his.

My response seems to delight him. He beams from ear to ear. "Gracie, you deserve this and so much more. The last two years have been terrible. I wanted to do something special for you. Something you would love." Again, uncertainty crosses his face as his eyes search mine. "You do love it, don't you?"

My gaze drops to the glittering diamonds and sparkling sapphires. They're practically glowing in the black velvet box. "How could I not? It's a gorgeous piece."

"Then I want you to have it. Enjoy it. There's been so much grief over the last two years. We both need to start enjoying life again."

Biting my lower lip, I hesitate, conflicted about accepting such an extravagant gift. I want to, but...

"This must have cost a small fortune."

He shrugs broad shoulders encased in a dark suit jacket. "I can afford it. It's not like I have a wife or daughter to spoil rotten. Just you. So, please, allow me to do this."

My eyes lift to his in question. "Are you sure?"

Sensing my capitulation, he beams. "Positive."

Dominic has always been generous to a fault with me.

"Okay," I whisper.

Not saying a word, he sets the black case down on the dressing table before picking up the necklace. It sparkles and shines as the gems catch light from the chandelier overhead. He moves to stand behind me before positioning the diamonds and sapphires against my neck.

My hair has been swept up and piled high on the top of my head. Dominic's fingers smooth over the stones, trailing gently across my chest before fiddling with the clasp in the back. For a silent moment, neither of us dare to move. His hands rest lightly atop my bare shoulders.

His eyes lock on mine in the looking glass. "You are stunning. And it has nothing to do with the necklace, dress, hair, or makeup. You have this light within you that shines so brilliantly. It's nice to see it again." He kisses the top of my head. "I've missed it."

"Thank you," I whisper through the thick emotion clogging my voice, "for everything."

I take in my reflection, barely recognizing the girl staring back at me from the silvery looking glass. The sophisticated hairdo, the flawless makeup, the lovely gown, the stunning necklace, and lastly, the silvery high-heeled sandals that make me look elegant and refined.

Dominic has done a better job dressing me than I usually do.

"You're welcome, sweetheart. Just remember to have fun tonight. This party is all about you." He kisses my temple. Stepping away, he holds out his arm, and I loop mine through his.

His black suit and crisp white shirt look exquisite on him. The top button has been left unfastened, so even though he's dressed up, there's still an air of casual refinement to his style.

My eyes run over the length of him. "You look pretty snazzy yourself."

He cracks a smile before inclining his head my way. "Then we make quite the pair, don't we?"

I trot out my best English accent, trying to sound as regal as possible. "We most certainly do, my lord."

His deep chuckle resonates as we leave the bedroom behind and head down the second-floor corridor to the staircase.

"Perhaps you should leave the British accent to the British."

I pretend to take offense even though I know he's right. My British accent is crap.

Sconces light the hallway as we walk to the curving staircase that leads to the first floor. Music from the string quartet set up in the living room near the baby grand piano fills the air. I didn't realize that guests had already begun to arrive. As the babble of dozens of voices wafts over me, my belly pinches. These people are nothing more than strangers to me. I don't realize that I've tensed until Dominic pauses, throwing a questioning glance my way.

"You okay, sweetheart?" As always, his words brim with concern.

My lips lift, and I give him a slight nod. "I'm fine. A little nervous, I suppose." I force out a laugh. "This party is for me, but I don't know a soul."

He pats my hand in a comforting manner. "I won't leave your side, Gracie. You have my word. No matter what happens, I'll be right there."

As if he can read my innermost thoughts, he adds in a quieter voice, "You won't ever be alone again."

His words have the exact effect they're meant to, which is reassurance that I won't be thrown to the wolves this evening. Just knowing that he'll stick close is enough to strengthen my resolve.

Not wanting him to worry, I paste a bright smile on my face as we descend to the two-story foyer where a few guests still linger. With a friendly smile, Dominic greets everyone warmly before introducing me-or reintroducing me in some cases-to his friends, some of whom were friends with my parents as well. To my surprise, it only takes a few minutes before I'm at ease and enjoying myself. As a passing waiter strolls by, Dominic grabs two crystal flutes full of bubbly Veuve Clicquot.

By the time I get a second glass, I'm laughing and have loosened up. I watch as Dominic charms all of his guests, drawing the more reserved people out of their shells by reminding them of stories about my parents that leave everyone laughing and remembering them with fondness.

Midway through the party, Dominic glances behind me, and his eyes light up. Before I can turn around to see what-or who-has captured his attention, his hands go to my bare shoulders, locking me in place.

"I have one last surprise for you."

My head spins with the announcement. What more could he give me? This party is already over the top. Waiters in tuxedos circulate the room with trays of fancy little canapes and glasses of Veuve Clicquot. There are at least a hundred and twenty friends and associates in attendance. For a hastily thrown together affair, everything is perfect.

Not to mention my dress, shoes, and necklace.

It's very possible that I'm in a fairy tale right now.

All at Dominic's orchestration.

Although most of the people surrounding me are strangers, I've thoroughly enjoyed myself this evening. True to his word, Dominic hasn't left my side. His arm has been casually draped around my waist most of the time. I've notice a few speculative looks aimed in our direction.

"You couldn't possibly."

Without any warning, he quickly turns me around. I'm hit with a wave of dizziness for a moment. The warmth of his hands burn into my shoulders, grounding me and squashing the nausea. For the second time this evening, I gasp. My hands fly to my mouth in surprise.

"*Chloe?*"

A huge grin spreads across her face before she gives a little squeal and flies toward me. I do the same. Colliding midway, we wrap our arms around each other, jumping up and down as we hug.

"What are you doing here?" I'm still shrieking and reeling at the unexpectedness of seeing her.

"Dominic invited me! *Surprise!*"

I can only imagine the sheer joy written across every inch of my face as I glance over at him and mouth, *thank you*. He grins and gives me a modest little shrug.

Bringing Chloe back into my life means more than just about anything.

And he knows it.

"Why don't you two head out to the terrace so you can catch up. I'll have some champagne and appetizers brought out for you to enjoy."

Unable to believe that she's standing next to me, I squeeze Chloe again, unwilling to let her go for even a minute. She looks amazing. Her strawberry blonde hair lays against her shoulders in thick, shiny waves. You'd think she would have a smattering of freckles across the bridge of her nose since her complexion is so fair, but there aren't any. Her skin is like porcelain. The short, forest green dress she's wearing skims her toned thighs and matches her eyes. Where I'm short and curvy, Chloe is tall and willowy.

"Thanks, Mr. Grimaldi." Her eyes flash and sparkle with barely suppressed mischief. We may not have been in contact for almost two years, but I know that look all too well.

Again, happiness bursts within me like an overinflated balloon.

Grabbing her hand, I tow my childhood best friend toward the French doors that lead to the terrace. The night is perfect for sitting and enjoying the lake breeze. The fire pit has been lit. It blazes, emitting warmth.

There's just so much I want to say, that I'm actually at a loss as to where to begin. An apology is poised on the tip of my tongue when Chloe leans into me and says in a sly tone, "Well, I see *Uncle Dominic* is still as handsome as ever." Throwing a sultry glance over her slender shoulder, she makes a little purring noise deep in her throat.

The apology brimming on my lips falls by the wayside as I burst into laughter. Same old Chloe. God, but I love it. I can't believe how much I've missed her friendship. Even though we've barely begun to talk, it already feels as if the two years separating us is slipping away.

Maybe that's because I moved during middle school, and we were forced to stay in touch for eight years. In a way, we were used to the separation, the yawning expanse of time that continually sat between us. Then we would get together and fall right back into the old patterns of our friendship.

As soon as I close the French door behind us, silencing the party inside, I wrap my arms around her, pulling her in for another warm hug. My apology immediately bubbles up to the surface again. "I'm so sorry, Chloe, for not staying in touch. For pushing you away."

When I'd needed my best friend the most, to hold my hand and tell me that everything was going to be all right, I retreated inside myself, refusing all offers of comfort. For a while, it had felt too painful to live and breathe. For my own sanity, I'd cut everything and everyone out except for Dominic. I regret losing touch with my friends now, but it was a save-yourself kind of situation back then.

Chloe tightens her arms around me until the very breath is pressed out of my lungs. Painful as it is, I don't want her to stop. "Listen, I can only imagine just how crappy everything was for you. I wish there had been something I could have done to help. Evelyn and Edward were like parents to me. I loved them. Maybe if we had lived closer to one another, it would have turned out differently."

Our colleges had been far apart- mine in Seattle, and hers in Chicago. There had been no easy way to visit for a weekend. It was too long of a drive, and plane tickets were expensive.

In all honesty, I hadn't been up to it. Even though I don't say the words, I'm not sure if us being closer would have changed the outcome. After my parents' deaths, I had been left reeling. Grief-stricken. And then depression set in. It's an emotional concoction I wouldn't wish on my worst enemy.

Dominic had been the only one capable of penetrating my despair. In a way, it was like we had been drowning together. We were the only two people who truly understood the grief the other one was feeling. When my roommate grew concerned because I was no longer getting out of bed in the morning, Dominic was who she reached out to. He dropped everything and immediately flew to Seattle.

He picked me up at school and brought me back to my parents' house until I was able to function like a normal human being. We lived there for about three months. He flew back to the office when necessary. Otherwise, he worked from the house, making conference calls and Skyping. He took care of all the nitty-gritty details I couldn't bring myself to tackle.

A fresh wave of grief washes over me as I remember the first few months after my parents died. Though there is still heartache, the pain isn't as sharp and piercing as it used to be. Don't get me wrong, it hurts. Losing them will always be painful, but it doesn't feel as though it's going to bring me to my knees the way it once could.

Sitting on chairs near the fire, Chloe gets right down to business. "So, Dominic mentioned that you've moved back permanently. He said you're now attending Northwestern." She looks impressed.

Pushing all those dark, heavy thoughts from my mind, I focus my attention on Chloe. On getting reacquainted with her. "Yes, I bought a place downtown. A few blocks from Lakeshore Drive."

She grins. "I'm so jealous! I work about a mile from there. Maybe we can grab lunch or dinner during the week."

My heart continues to expand. "I would love that."

Another impish look fills her eyes as she leans toward me. "So, tell me all about Dominic. Has some lucky lady finally tied his fine ass down?"

I burst out laughing at her question because Chloe has always had the hots for Dominic. Truth be told, when we were both fourteen, the pair of us would watch him with big cow eyes. He was either oblivious to our crushes, or he just pretended to be.

Either way, hearing her moon over him again makes me feel lighter. Younger. Freer. It's a great feeling, one I want more of.

Reaching over, I grasp her hand. "It's really good to see you, Chloe. I'm glad you were able to make it tonight."

Her eyes soften. "I wouldn't have missed it for the world. We have so much to catch up on."

Yes, we certainly do. And I'm looking forward to finding out every single detail regarding what she's been up to for the last two years.

CHAPTER FIVE

Dominic wanted me to spend the night at his place, but I decided to head home after the party. My ears still ring with laughter, chatter, and music. My cheeks hurt from smiling so much. Everyone was so warm and welcoming. Not only was it nice to reconnect with Chloe, but with others who'd also known my family before we moved to Seattle.

At one point, after many glasses of alcohol had been consumed, someone cranked up the sound system, and everyone started dancing.

To music from the eighties.

It's never good when people of a certain age start busting a move.

What am I saying? It was hilarious.

Even Dominic was out there shaking his moneymaker. Unable to resist, Chloe had dragged me out onto the makeshift dance floor as well. Chloe has never been able to resist the lure of dance music.

Everyone seemed to have a fantastic time.

Me, included.

Feeling tired, I stare out the window of the Range Rover as it moves through the city. I can't help but be enthralled by the lit-up buildings as we travel south. It's a captivating sight.

Listening to so many stories about my parents makes me feel nostalgic. I can't deny that my feelings are tinged at the edges with sadness. It's difficult to think about them without feeling sorrow. I enjoyed hearing every single memory their old friends and colleagues shared with me, but it's difficult because I know I won't ever see them again.

I'm finally ready to embark on a new phase of my life. One without them. They were there when I started college, but they didn't get to see me walk across the stage and graduate. Nor will they be there to celebrate any other milestone life has in store for me.

For that reason, there will always be something missing.

Before I realize it, we're pulling up to the front of Lexington Place. My new home. It doesn't feel like home yet, but it will with enough time. I scoot out of the SUV as Henry opens the door and head toward the building. George works the day shift. Someone else mans the door during the evenings. He's tall and gaunt-looking. With a smile in place, he tips his hat before allowing me inside. I call for the elevator, thinking about how good it will feel to take off all this finery and slide beneath the comfy cotton sheets I just purchased.

As I unlock the door to my condo, silence greets me. It's both a relief after the party, as well as a reminder that I'm on my own. No longer do I live with my parents. Nor do I share a dorm with a roommate. After two years of slogging uphill, trying to move past what happened, I'm finally moving forward again.

Slipping off the gorgeous silver heels, I hold them in my hand as I pad into the immense, open space of the living room. My sleek gray couch and two tufted chairs, along with a stylish glass coffee table, rest on a plush area rug. The long expanse of floor to ceiling windows remain unadorned. The glass is tinted. I'm able to see out, but no one can see in. It seems like a crime to cover such a gorgeous sight.

People pay millions for this kind of view.

The condo is over three thousand square feet, with three generously-sized bedrooms, a large, mahogany-paneled study, a huge gourmet kitchen with white cabinets and gray marble, a formal dining room with pillars and a coffered ceiling, and a living room with a tall, soaring ceiling. An ocean of dark, glossy hardwoods flow throughout the entire place and the ornate crown molding matches it.

I love it.

I can imagine myself being happy here someday.

As much as Dominic tried to cajole me into staying with him, he didn't have anything negative to say after touring this building. I think the heated swimming pool on the rooftop and gym on one of the lower floors impressed him. I feel incredibly lucky to have snagged this place.

I don't bother flicking on the lights. The illumination from the city shines through the windows. The view, even at night, is completely breathtaking. Every evening, around seven o'clock or so, I find myself gravitating to the terrace with a glass of wine.

It may be almost two in the morning, but I find myself drawn to the private patio. There's just something about the bustle of the city below. It never seems to sleep, no matter what time it is. I may be alone, but when I'm out there, watching the world unfold, I don't feel quite so lonely. I feel like I'm part of the irrepressible energy that is Chicago.

Even though I should be exhausted, I'm oddly restless.

Perhaps sipping a glass of wine on the terrace while enjoying the city is exactly what I need. I don't bother changing out of my gown. My hair is still piled on my head. The sapphire and diamond necklace shimmers against the paleness of my collarbone. Going to the butler's pantry, I pour myself a small glass of white. The need to feel the wind brushing over my cheeks pounds through me like a steady drumbeat.

Tonight feels like a turning point of sorts.

I moved in over a week ago and have done little things to make this place homier, but the party makes me feel like I really am moving on with my life. I think my parents would be proud of me. For graduating college, getting accepted at Northwestern, and pursuing my dreams of working for a museum.

Settling onto one of two chaise loungers I've recently acquired, I gaze out into the vast darkness. Although I'm right across from the lake, a long stretch of greenery separates me from Lakeshore Drive. Closing my eyes, I hear the churning of water over the sounds of traffic that never seem to stop.

There's something soothing about it.

Taking a sip of wine, I can't help but dwell on how far I've come in the past two years. There were times, especially during the first six months, when I didn't think I would make it. Times when I had wished I were dead and not struggling just to make it through another day.

Being on the other side, on the cusp of starting a brand-new life in a city that I've always considered to be my home and reconnecting with my best friend feels like a victory.

Life, I muse silently, *goes on.* No matter what happens, no matter how horrific the aftermath, it continues to unfold. That, I suppose, is the only thing that can be counted on.

As I sit, contemplating what the future holds and all of the infinite opportunities that suddenly feel exciting and possible, I hear the French door from the condo next to me open before closing with a resounding thud.

For just a heartbeat or so, my ears are met with silence.

I suspect that my neighbor, the attractive man I couldn't stop staring at in the elevator, has come out to enjoy the balmy evening as well. Summer will soon be over. Within a matter of weeks, the weather will begin to turn cooler. The cold crispness of autumn will be ushered in.

I can't say that I'm not looking forward to down jackets, Ugg boots, cashmere gloves, and colorful scarfs. Believe it or not, I've missed Midwestern winters. Seattle is more temperate. It has rain and gray skies rather than brilliant sunshine and glittering snow on bare tree branches.

I haven't seen Mr. Tall, Dark, and Ridiculously Handsome since making a fool out of myself by ogling him like a lovesick teenager. Trust me, I've been on the lookout. I'm a little embarrassed to admit that I've loitered in the lobby. Naturally I couldn't just come out and ask George about my sexy new neighbor. Privacy is of utmost importance here at Lexington Place. But that doesn't mean my eyes didn't dart to the thick glass door every time George opened it.

Nevertheless, it was a fruitless endeavor.

There were no sightings of my neighbor.

Closing my eyes, I inhale a deep, calming breath. As the sound of the lake and the traffic continue washing over me, I hear the long, keening moan of a woman.

My eyes widen as my mouth opens to form a small, round *O*. Every muscle in my body tenses. I sit completely still, wondering if I really heard what I think I just heard. But now, as I listen harder, all that meets my pricked ears are the sounds of the city beneath me. Just as I begin to relax on the thickly padded teak lounger I'm sprawled out on, I hear it again.

Only louder. Deeper. Throatier.

Feeling slightly amused, I press my lips tightly together to stifle my laughter.

Yep.

That is most *definitely* the sound of a woman being pleasured. I bite my lower lip, wondering if I should sneak back inside to give them a bit of privacy. Although, if they had wanted privacy, they wouldn't be out here where their closest neighbors could overhear them.

Her moans, soft and breathy at first, grow increasingly more guttural. More vocal. More frenzied. As if she's deeply aroused by whatever is going on over there. I hate to admit it, because it makes me feel like a huge perv, but I'd be lying through my teeth if I didn't confess that I was getting turned on just listening to her. I can't imagine what the attractive man next door is doing to elicit such a response.

Well, that's not altogether true.

It's not like I haven't had sex before. I have. The caveat is that I don't remember ever sounding like *that*. Which, if I'm being perfectly honest with myself, seems like a real shame.

Somehow, I just *knew* that the man in the elevator would be an amazing lover. I don't know what made me think that. Maybe it's his dark, swarthy good looks. Or the width of his palms. Or the full sexiness of his mouth. Perhaps it has more to do with his commanding presence. There was just this undeniable... *vibe* emanating from him. The simple act of staring at him had my belly prickling with wave after wave of sexual tension.

Then I hear him.

The slightest hint of an accent in his deep, gravelly voice arrows straight through me, hitting my clit. I shiver with need, which is a reaction I've never experienced before.

You like that, baby?

Oh God...

I stifle the whimper of desire that tries to fall from my lips before shifting my body ever so slightly on the lounger. I clench my thighs, but it does little to alleviate the ache. My entire body feels strung tight with thick, sexual tension as desire blooms within me like a flower. Closing my eyes, I lift my arms high above my head, stretching as her breathy moans continue washing over me.

The slap of a palm against delicate, bare flesh rings out.

A loud wail pierces the night air.

A low, insistent pulse thumps to life in my core.

I can't believe how turned on I am. There's no ignoring it anymore- I really am a pervert. Or perhaps it's been too long since I've been with a man.

Sex with Eric, my college boyfriend, was... pleasant. It's not like I didn't orgasm. Half the time. But they were all low on the Richter Scale. Nothing explosive. Or cataclysmic. I certainly didn't scream my head off like I was auditioning for the starring role in a porno. I just assumed stuff like that only happened in romance novels.

And, more obviously, pornos.

How many times have I rolled my eyes when I get to the part where the woman climaxes, sees stars, and nearly passes out?

Too many times to count.

Can't say I've ever come within striking distance of *that* happening to me.

Biting my lower lip again to stifle a low moan of my own, I can't deny that whatever is going on next door sounds exactly like something out of a book or porno.

Then again, am I surprised?

The man in the elevator looked like sex personified. He reeked of it. Hot, dangerous, and sexy. With him, there wouldn't be any slow love-making where you stared into each other's eyes while whispering *I love you* before finally orgasming together.

Nope.

The man next door *fucked*.

Hard, dirty, and with a vengeance.

You only need to be trapped in the stifling confines of an elevator with him once to sense the sexually charged energy he exudes like pheromones.

I chastise myself again for not giving the amorous couple on the patio next to me the privacy they obviously think they have. Yet- I still don't move a muscle. I'm much too turned on to leave now.

I want to hear how this ends.

Actually, I *need* to hear how this ends.

Which is exactly why I decide to wiggle out of the silky panties I have on before dropping them to the floor. I'm surprised by how drenched they are. Maybe I shouldn't be, though. I can't remember the last time I was this amped up.

Reclining on the chaise, I hike up my gown so I can spread my thighs. A thrill zips through me as the breeze hits my naked flesh. Closing my eyes again, I listen as the man next door fucks the woman he's brought out to the patio. Her moans swirl around me, escalating in both pitch and intensity.

Breathy words full of need punctuate the thick night air.

Yes!

Oh God!

Please!

Mmmm, right there!

Once in a while, I hear the sharp, stinging slap of flesh hitting flesh as if he's using his hand in a lightning quick stroke. Not to hurt. She certainly doesn't sound pained. It sounds like she's enjoying every delicious moment of contact. I can't help but wonder what it feels like to have a man spank you in the most intimate spot imaginable.

Another thick sliver of need slides through me like warmed honey.

I'm astonished to realize that I just might enjoy a few smacks.

My mind conjures up an image of my neighbor. Dark, muscular gorgeousness poured into a frame that easily tops six foot three. In my head, he isn't screwing a beautiful, faceless woman. He's fucking *me*.

He's whispering those oh-so-dirty words to *me*. Laying those wide hands on *me*. Relentlessly driving *me* toward orgasm.

My core pulses and throbs as I continue listening. My fingers stroke over my own hot flesh.

How much do you want to be fucked?

God, so much...

Yes, I feel *exactly* the same way.

I want to be fucked by *him*. He clearly knows how to push a woman toward untold pinnacles of pleasure. I want him to awaken everything that has lain dormant within me for the last two years. Maybe my entire life.

Hearing the woman next door forced closer and closer to the edge makes everything within my body tighten up like a taut bowstring. I couldn't hold in the soft moans that are falling from my lips even if I wanted to.

Which I don't.

At this point, I'm mindless of everything except my own pleasure. My throaty desire mingles with the cries from the woman being fucked not more than forty feet from me. An orgasm hovers as my fingers continue stroking away. Arching my back, I circle my clit with a little more pressure.

Yes!

Oh God, I'm going to come!

Those words could be my own.

I'm right there.

Hovering on the precipice.

I want to hold on to this feeling for as long as I can. I want to dangle here, enjoying all this delicious pleasure as it continues to wash over me. Just when I can't hold on a moment longer, I hear her scream.

Past the point of caring, I let go as well.

My moans mingle with hers.

He grunts.

I imagine his firm, muscular body hovering over hers as he thrusts into her with hard, demanding strokes.

I can't help but wish she were me. Wish that he was filling me with all that thickness. Little spasms of pleasure rack my body as I continue stroking my pussy with gentle fingers.

I haven't felt this blissful in years.

Finally opening my eyes, I stare into the velvety darkness as the breeze hits my now feverish cheeks. Like a contented cat, I stretch lazily before straightening my dress. Scooping up my panties, I tiptoe inside to find my bed.

CHAPTER SIX

When I wake the next morning, the blazing sun streams in through the unadorned windows. As the rays slant across my face, I roll over, clutching the pillow to me.

I feel... absolutely marvelous. Which is surprising, because I drank my fair share last night.

The party was fantastic. I make a mental note to call Dominic later and thank him again for everything. I don't think the evening could have been more perfect. And I really enjoyed meeting all his friends and colleagues.

Maybe he'll be able to set aside a little time this week to meet for lunch. We've always been close, but since my parents died, we've become even closer. It's nice living near him again. Nice to know that if I want to drop by at a moment's notice, I'm only forty-five minutes away.

Just as I'm about to snuggle into the blankets and go back to sleep, my eyes shoot open as I remember in vivid Technicolor what transpired on the terrace last night.

Oh my God!

Did I seriously do that?

I pull the pillow over my face before screaming into it.

Laughter mingled with disbelief spills from my lips. The masturbation itself doesn't bother me. It's not like I haven't done that before. But touching myself while listening to another couple having sex is certainly a first for me.

In all honesty, I don't care.

No one but me knows what happened. It's not like those two were cognizant of anything but themselves.

Clearly.

If anyone should be embarrassed, it's them.

Not me.

Pushing thoughts of last night from my mind, I roll out of the king-sized bed and step in front of the windows. It must be around ten or so and the weather looks fabulous. Not a cloud in the bright, azure-colored sky. My eyes fall to the street below. Traffic is heavy, which is normal. Even on a lazy Saturday morning, everyone has somewhere to be and are in a hurry to get there. For a few minutes, I watch a couple of joggers on the sidewalk that winds along the edge of the lake.

A pang of longing shoots through me as I follow their progress.

Once upon a time, that used to be me.

I haven't run in so long.

I guess I lost the drive to do it.

When my life fell apart, running fell by the wayside. For the first time in years, a spark of desire to feel my feet pounding against the pavement flows through me. To feel my lungs burn as I gasp for breath. To feel my muscles sting as I push them past their limit.

Without thinking, I go to my dresser, pulling out a sports bra, shorts, and a hot pink tank top. I dress quickly and gather my long blond hair into a ponytail. I don't give myself any time to reconsider my decision as I grab my phone and a pair of earbuds before heading toward the door.

I don't have to run far.

I can walk part-way if I need to.

The point is to get back out there and do something I've always enjoyed. Something that makes me happy. My dad encouraged me to run when I was in middle school. He ran every single day of his adult life, rain or shine. I think that's one of the reasons he enjoyed living in

Seattle. He could be out on the streets in January or February instead of running laps on an indoor track. Once I worked up enough stamina and could run a couple miles, we started entering 5K's together. A year before he died, we ran a half marathon. A framed picture of us with our arms wrapped around each other after the race sits on my dresser.

It's one of my favorite photos.

Stepping onto the elevator, I stick my earbuds in before scrolling through the playlists on my phone. I need music that will get my blood pumping. I'm just about to reach over and press the lobby button when someone beats me to the punch.

Not expecting anyone else in the enclosed space, my head jerks up, and my eyes collide with espresso-colored ones. I suck in a breath as my neighbor's dark gaze stays pinned to mine.

The way he's staring at me...

It's like he knows...

No.

There's no way in hell that he's aware of what I was doing out on the balcony last night.

Or that I was even out there in the first place.

I was quiet. Like a mouse.

He can't possibly know. I'm overreacting. This is paranoia getting the better of me.

Even though it's Saturday morning, he's wearing another dark suit and crisp white button-down shirt. The top button has been left unfastened, and he isn't wearing a tie. A smattering of dark, crinkly hair is visible at his neckline.

Slowly, he lifts a hand, and I find myself mesmerized by the movement.

God... those hands!

My insides shudder with pent-up longing.

Oh-so-slowly, he swipes his thumb across his lower lip. My mouth waters.

Holy hell.

What am I doing? What's happening to me? This isn't a normal reaction.

My gaze abruptly jerks back to his. My mouth tumbles open as his eyes slide down the length of my body. My nipples-damn them-tighten under his intense perusal, which feels like a physical caress.

I stifle the whimper of need poised on the tip of my tongue. I realize that I'm wearing nothing more than tiny running shorts, an athletic bra-which does *nothing* to hide my arousal-and a thin tank top.

When his hooded gaze flicks up to mine, heat radiates from every pore of my body.

If the hungry look in his eyes is any indication, he knows that I not only sat there like a perv while listening to him screw another woman, but got off on it, too. Literally. I *literally* shimmied out of my panties, spread my thighs, and stroked myself until I came just as hard as the woman he was pleasuring.

Good Lord, even though I thought I'd been quiet, he still heard me.

Kill me now.

I can't take the way he's staring at me. Like he's already stripped me bare and is on the verge of fucking me the way he did that woman. I'm ashamed to admit, even in the privacy of my own head, that I'm conflicted.

Because I want it.

I want him.

And yet...

Before the elevator doors fully open, I squeeze through, shooting out of the car like my ass is on fire. George barely has enough time to open the front door before I fly through.

"Have a good day, Ms. Castile!"

I imagine that by the time my sexy, next-door neighbor reaches the sidewalk, I'm already halfway down the block. I'd also be willing to bet that a satisfied smirk mars his darkly handsome face.

It's amazing how the hot burn of humiliation can spur you into running three miles in less than thirty minutes. But it does. I guess I'll have to thank him for making my first run in two years a good one.

Ha!

Not going to happen.

If I never see that man again, it'll be much too soon.

CHAPTER SEVEN

Smoothing over my short skirt, I step away from the taxi and glance around, trying to find Chloe in the thick crowd of people gathered on the sidewalk in front of the club.

But I don't see her.

Nervousness settles in the pit of my gut.

Sucking my bottom lip between my teeth, I gnaw on it as indecision sets in.

What if I can't find her?

There's no way I'm going inside solo. If worst comes to worst, I can catch another cab home. No big deal.

Everything immediately settles as I catch sight of her rushing down the street in sky-high heels. For a moment, I was worried that maybe she'd forgotten about me. Chloe may be the oldest friend I have, but our friendship has been on hiatus for almost two years.

Maybe she's changed.

I don't know yet.

We're still trying to find our way back to the friendship we once had. It takes a few moments before I notice the group trailing behind her. It looks like Chloe has invited about six other people to join us. I'll get a chance to meet some of her friends tonight.

Ever since the party at Dominic's, we've been texting back and forth, getting reacquainted. Chloe works at a law office about eighteen blocks away from my building. She's a paralegal. They must have a lot going on, because she hasn't been able to get away as easily as she thought she would for lunch. Or maybe her boss is just a demanding jerk. Which is kind of what she's implied in our conversations.

I've spent the last week walking around Northwestern and ordering the books I'll need for class. I bought a few more things for the condo. And I took Dominic out for lunch. I wanted to foot the bill as a thank-you for the wonderful party, but he wouldn't allow it. I also spent the last week skulking around the building, hoping I wouldn't run into my neighbor.

I haven't.

The man seems to have disappeared.

Again.

Chloe rakes over my outfit with a critical eye. "You look amazing!"

I grin in response, feeling even more at ease. "I love your skirt!"

She's wearing a very short red skirt paired with a black halter top. It's a simple outfit, but she wears it well. Chloe is tall and thin. She can wear just about anything and rock it. Her thick strawberry blonde hair has been left long and wild around her shoulders. A pair of black high-heeled sandals completes her look.

Taking a moment, she quickly introduces me to her friends. Four girls and two guys. Everyone seems friendly.

With a smile on her face, she loops her arm through mine. "Ready to have some fun?"

I glance over at the long line of people winding around the side of the brick building. Are we really going to spend half the night waiting to get into some exclusive club? "Maybe we should go somewhere else. This place looks packed." The bouncer hasn't let one person in since we've been standing here.

"No worries. I know people here." She gives me a little wink. "Come on."

En masse, we move toward the brawny bouncer standing guard at the front entrance. It's quite clear that no one is getting past him. Big, beefy arms are folded across a barrel-like chest. It's ten o'clock at night, but he's wearing black sunglasses that hide his eyes. Plus, there's a no-nonsense expression on his face that looks like it's been carved from granite.

I slant a dubious look in Chloe's direction. She looks strangely self-assured regarding the situation.

Suddenly she shouts, "Hey, Lucas! Miss me, baby?"

I hold my breath, waiting for Lucas to laugh in her face before telling us to beat it to the back of the line.

But, in a shocking turn of events, that doesn't happen.

He stares at her for a heartbeat before a big smile spreads across his face. Two muscular arms shoot out, grabbing Chloe and hauling her sandaled feet off the sidewalk. She squeals and slaps him on the chest.

"You better believe I did, sweet cheeks."

Once he sets her down, she loops her arm through mine before making introductions. I'm still somewhat flabbergasted that this mountain of a man can smile. "This is my best friend, Grace."

His head swivels towards me. Since he's wearing dark shades, I have no idea if he's giving me the once-over. I kind of feel like he might be.

"Hey, best friend Grace. Nice to meet you."

I give an awkward little wave in response.

Without further ado, he unclips the black velvet rope in front of the door, allowing us entrance. As we walk inside the club, he firmly whacks Chloe on the ass. She doesn't seem to mind.

"Let me know what you're doing Sunday night."

"Will do," she calls over her shoulder.

I glance back at the people who are now loudly complaining because they've been waiting in line and still haven't been allowed inside. If I were Lucas, I'd be worried that they might decide to storm the door.

"Is he your... *friend?*"

Catching my meaning, she smirks. "Sure, you could say that."

That comment has my eyebrows rising, but I don't ask any further questions. It's not because I've lost interest in the kind of relationship they have, but more because I'm now scanning the night-club we've just walked into. From the outside, this place looks unassuming. In fact, I wouldn't have even known it was a club, except for the long line of people outside.

My eyes widen as I continue taking everything in.

I feel as though I've fallen down the rabbit hole.

It's like sensory overload.

On steroids.

This place is crazy!

Craning my neck, I glance toward the ceiling. It must be four stories high. On the ground level, there's a huge dance floor with tables scattered around the periphery. A long, sleek glass bar stretches across the far wall. Hundreds of bottles of liquor line glass shelves. Lights flash and fog creeps low to the ground.

Three levels of balconies ring the dance floor. People stand one, two, or three stories above, watching what's going on below. Platforms with scantily clad women dancing on them are scattered around the first floor.

I squint.

At first glance, it looks like they're wearing colorful swim-suits. Or maybe lingerie. But the harder I stare, the more certain I am that my first impression isn't correct.

I think their bodies are painted.

Music pumps from a DJ booth high above the dance floor. The women on the platforms twist and twirl around poles. One lifts her leg, and I'm half afraid of what I'm going to see. It's like a horrific car crash. One I can't look away from.

Chloe chuckles. "They're wearing thongs."

Skepticism laces my voice. "You sure about that?"

"Yup." She waits a beat or two before announcing, "I've been working here for three months now."

Eyes darting to hers, my mouth drops open.

She's joking.

Maybe.

I level a disbelieving look her way. "No, you have not."

I can't see her working in a place like this.

Or maybe I can.

Chloe has always had a larger-than-life personality. And she has a fantastic body. When we were kids, Chloe spent countless hours in ballet and jazz classes. In high school, she was on the dance team. The girl knows how to move. I guess the idea of her working here isn't as far-fetched as I originally thought.

Her eyes glitter. "We have a lot to catch up on, don't we?"

"Yeah," I admit, still feeling floored by the disclosure, "I guess we do."

"Should we get a drink?"

That sounds like a good idea since my senses are still overloaded.

Strobe lights throw different patterns and colors across the floor. The beat of the music practically reverberates off the walls. It's not obnoxiously loud, but you can feel it vibrating in your bones. Maybe other places as well. The pulsing seems to have settled in my lower region. I shift uncomfortably, needing that drink.

Slowly, the group makes its way to the bar. This place is packed. I notice that the bartenders, all women, have been painted alike. Kind of like a uniform. You'd think it would be obscene, but it's not. The paint covering their bodies is beautiful. There's an artistry to it that intrigues me. I can only imagine how long it takes to get ready for a shift. I make a mental note to ask Chloe.

"The money here is amazing," Chloe says. "Totally worth it."

One of the bartenders saunters over to greet us. She has a build much like Chloe's- tall and willowy. "Hey, beautiful, what can I get for you?"

Ummmm... is she talking to me?

When I pause, her ruby red lips quirk before her eyes shift to Chloe. "A newbie? Aww, how sweet. I love club virgins."

Chloe laughs before rattling off a drink order. I hate to admit it, but I can't stop staring. I'm totally fascinated. She looks as though she's wearing a shimmering gold swimsuit. But obviously, it's not.

"Honey, you keep looking at me like that, and I'm going to take you home at the end of the night and have my way with you." She gives me a wink.

I think she's just teasing.

I am definitely out of my element right now.

But, surprisingly, it doesn't feel like a bad thing. I'm enjoying myself.

After two rounds of some fruity concoction the bartender whips up for us, we all move to the dance floor. Two songs later, my eyes are closed, and my hands are sliding through the air. The low pulse of the bass thumps deep inside me. It feels almost sensuous. I'm not drunk, just pleasantly buzzed. I'm having the best time. I'm nowhere near the same caliber of dancer that Chloe is, but I love to shake my booty. It makes me feel lighthearted and free.

It's the best feeling in the world.

I'm not thinking about my parents, the last two years, or all the unknowns I'll face in the future. The music continues to wrap around me, insulating me in an alternate reality. One without a past or future. At this moment, I'm nothing more than loose limbs and body parts moving to the rhythm of the music.

Feeling more relaxed and carefree than I have in ages, I open my heavy-lidded eyes to gaze at the sea of strangers surrounding me. My hands twirl above my head.

I look up at the girls dancing on the platforms, and then higher, to the balconies wrapping around the floor. People crowd around the edges so they can watch what's going on below.

There's an eclectic mix of people present.

College-aged kids. Young professionals. Hipsters. Socialites. A crowd of edgier, alternative-looking guys. Men in suits. The only thing they all seem to have in common is that no one looks to be over the age of thirty. I'm wondering if Lucas, the bouncer at the door, has strict orders to keep anyone who looks middle aged out. This must be where all the young, beautiful people come to cut loose.

Again, I'm blown away that Chloe works here. As she mentioned earlier, we need to find some time to sit down and talk.

Really talk.

I'm about to close my eyes and give myself over to the pulse of the music again when the fine hairs at the nape of my neck rise. A chill sweeps over my entire body, which is ironic since I'm a sweaty mess.

I have the strangest feeling that someone is watching me.

There are three different levels with balconies. Someone could very well be staring at me from up above. Glancing around, I try to figure out if the feeling that has settled in the pit of my stomach is a simple case of paranoia or if I'm being watched.

It's dark, and the strobe lights make it difficult to see, but I feel the moment my eyes collide with his. A jolt of electricity zips through my body, and just like before, I can't look away.

My next-door neighbor's eyes pin me in place. Even from this distance, they never release mine. I can do nothing more than stand in a mass of writhing bodies, my gaze held captive by his. His inscrutable expression never falters.

I'm so intently focused upon him, that I don't immediately realize he's here with someone. It takes a moment or two before I become cognizant of the woman clinging to his side.

I watch as she trails long, elegant fingers down his chest. Her mouth is at his neck, kissing and licking. But that's a guess because her long, straight hair curtains the view.

Lord knows that if I were her, I would do the exact same thing.

He's not paying her any attention, though. His eyes are still boring into mine. There's a tumbler wrapped in one big hand. Not breaking our stare, he brings it to his lips and takes a drink. My heart pounds almost painfully against my ribs.

His lips are so full and sexy.

The music is still thumping, but I'm no longer aware of it. It's drowned out by the deep, rich voice in my head.

How much do you want to be fucked?

God, so badly.

Do you like that, baby?

Yes!

My panties flood with heat as I continue staring at him. His husky words, laced with dark sensuality, ring throughout my head.

When someone shakes my shoulder, I rip my eyes from his.

"Grace, are you all right?"

A small frown mars Chloe's face.

When I say nothing in response, she continues, "You were just standing in the middle of the dance floor like a statue. I'm not going to lie, it was weird. I think you need some water. Too much dancing."

It's not the dancing, I want to tell her.

But I don't. I keep what happened to myself.

When I glance back toward the balcony, the spot he's just occupied is empty. For a second, I wonder if he was ever there to begin with. Did I conjure him up?

Have I finally become unhinged? Maybe Chloe is right about needing something ice-cold for my parched throat. I'm sweaty and probably dehydrated.

Not waiting for an answer, Chloe grabs my hand, and we weave through all the gyrating bodies. When we arrive at the bar, the same bartender makes a beeline for us. There's a raw sexuality and confidence about her that's almost impossible to ignore. The fact that she's wearing nothing more than body paint just ups her hotness factor.

I've never been attracted to a woman before. And I certainly would never consider experimenting now. But I'm beginning to think I have a harmless girl crush here.

"Two waters, please," Chloe says.

When the bartender turns to grab our drinks, I'm able to see that she truly has no clothing on. The dancers wear thongs, but the bartenders apparently don't. Spinning back around, she catches me staring again and gives me another flirty wink before grinning.

"That'll be six bucks."

Chloe is just about to dig through her pockets when I say, "I've got it."

Pulling out a ten, I slide it toward her. She grabs it. Before I can tell her to keep the change, she hands four singles back to me.

"Keep it."

A roguish smile curls her red lips upwards. "You want to give me a tip?"

Leaning against the bar, she beckons me forward with one elegant finger. Her eyes turn seductive. "Come here, newbie."

Not quite sure what's going on, I lean toward her. I expect her to whisper something in my ear, but when our faces are scant inches apart, she says, "Give me your tongue."

Surprised by the request, I blink in confusion.

The edges of her lips tilt up further. "Stick out your tongue for me."

Maybe it's the drinks I've had or just plain curiosity. Or maybe it's what just happened on the dance floor, and my brain still isn't functioning properly. I don't know.

But I do as she commands.

Almost cautiously, I stick out my tongue. My pulse continues to hammer under my skin. Chloe stands at my side, not saying a word. Very slowly, the bartender moves closer until she's able to draw my tongue into her mouth.

Her eyes are locked on mine the entire time she sucks.

It's not a rough action. In fact, it's unexpectedly gentle. Soft, even. No more than fifteen seconds slip by before she releases me. Instead of backing away, she places her lips to my ear and whispers huskily, "Now imagine that's your clit."

Those five words reverberate throughout my entire body.

Especially my clit.

CHAPTER EIGHT

The late August sun beats down on me, but the wind rolling in off the lake cuts through it. It's the perfect time of the day for a run. I try to get out here every morning. I've quickly become addicted to the endorphins pumping through my system. Until I started running again, I never realized how much I missed it and the connection it gives me to my dad.

Once I hit Lakeshore Drive, I continue along the wide path until reaching my halfway point. I started out doing three miles a day. Now I've pushed it to four. I don't have to walk anymore. I'm running the entire distance. Silly as it sounds, it feels like an accomplishment.

The past couple of months and all of its changes- moving back to Chicago, being accepted to graduate school, and gaining some much-needed control over my life- make me feel like everything is falling into place again.

I stop for a moment and survey the rich blueness of the lake. It's so vast. When you're standing at the shoreline, it seems as big as an ocean. The white-capped waves continue rolling toward the shore as the breeze cools my heated cheeks.

During the move, I wasn't sure if I was making the right decision. Change can be scary. Difficult. And I've had more than my fill these last couple of years. But right now, everything seems to be working out better than expected. School starts in a week, as does my volunteer position at The Art Institute of Chicago. For twelve hours every week, I'll be able to walk through the corridors and soak up everything on display in the museum.

And then there's Chloe.

Now that she's back in my life, I can't believe I ever pushed her away. What was I thinking? When I needed her the most, I retreated, because protecting myself felt like the safest option at the time. The pain was just too intense. Too overwhelming. After a while, I couldn't handle all those people patting me on the shoulder, constantly checking in to ask how I was doing, and giving me sympathetic looks and hugs. All it did was remind me of everything- all the goodness and all the love- I'd lost with one bad decision.

Sucking in a breath of fresh air, I tilt my face toward the brightly shining sun. The heat stroking over it makes me feel alive again.

When my heartbeat finally slows, I turn toward Lexington Place, ready to head home.

Home.

Slowly but surely, that's what it's beginning to feel like.

I do a few quick stretches to keep my muscles loose. Just as I'm pulling my knee to my chest, another jogger catches my eye. A few things about him register all at once.

Tall, athletic body.

Dark hair.

Deep olive complexion.

Power, potent and intoxicating, radiates from him in thick, heavy waves. Even from this distance, I feel it. A shiver snakes down my spine as I stare.

I'd know him anywhere.

He has, since that first elevator ride, played a prominent role in my thoughts.

Even though I haven't moved a muscle, my heartrate kicks back up.

Silently, I prod myself to turn, to run as fast as I can. But I don't. I feel ensnared by the dark eyes trained on me.

This is the first time I've seen him in anything other than a suit.

He's wearing long, black athletic shorts today.

And no shirt.

My greedy eyes travel over perfectly sculpted shoulders before sliding down the smooth muscles of his chest and abs. A smattering of hair swirls across his chest. His waist is narrow. Defined. Loose shorts hang from lean hips. Powerful thighs and strong calves complete the picture.

The past times I've run into him, I could tell he was built. Muscular. Not in an overdone way, but it's obvious that he works out.

Somehow, he's more delicious than I allowed myself to imagine. Trust me when I say that I've let my wicked thoughts run wild where he's concerned. It wouldn't surprise me in the least to find out that he's a model. He's way too scrumptious-looking. The man is pure male perfection. Every time I'm around him, it feels like my brain leaks right out of my ears.

He has to notice the way he affects me. It's embarrassing. The only thing that makes me feel remotely better is that it must be the same for most women.

The ones with a pulse, anyway.

How could it not be?

Quite honestly, I hope he won't recognize me and just jogs on by. We've never had a conversation. I'm just the weird chick who lives next to him, the one who got off while he screwed some other woman out on his balcony.

When he's less than twenty feet away, he dashes my hopes by slowing his pace and eventually coming to a complete standstill. His eyes stay locked on mine.

My breathing hitches, but I don't say a word. I'm afraid that if I try to speak, all that will come out is a pathetic squeak. The man is too handsome for his own good. It's like being blinded by the sun when you look at him.

Up close, I notice beads of sweat dotting both his forehead and chest. His inky black hair looks as dark and shiny as a raven's wing.

I wish I could rip my eyes away from him. Maybe then I would be able to hold a semi-intelligent conversation that wouldn't further the poor impression he already has of me.

After another moment ticks by with us simply staring, the edges of his lips slowly bow upward.

Damnit!

Why does this man have to be so ridiculously sexy?

It's unfair.

If he's a ten, I'm a seven.

I've never been one to complain about my looks. I've always been content with my blond hair and blue eyes. Sure, I'm a little on the short side. And curvy. I've been told countless times that I look like the wholesome girl next door.

I almost snort.

In this case, I really am the girl next door.

This guy, on the other hand, is exotic-looking. If someone picked him up and plopped him down on a fashion show runway in Milan, he would fit in perfectly.

"You're Thirty-A, right?"

He has a deep, melodic voice. His words are lightly accented. My girly parts roll over in response.

I'm sure he's waiting for me to jump in and introduce myself. When I remain silent, his brows lift. "You just moved in a few weeks ago?"

All I can think about is the elevator ride down to the lobby after the balcony incident. Just *thinking* about it has my entire face going up in flames. I want to melt into a puddle on the concrete and disappear between the cracks.

"Yes," I murmur, "that's me." I have no other choice but to brazen this out. Stepping forward, I thrust my hand toward him. I wish I'd had the good sense to wipe my sweaty palm on my running shorts, but it's too late now.

"I'm Grace. Nice to meet you."

His voice washes over me like a wave. "Nice to finally put a name to such a pretty face. Matteo."

My brows quirk. *"Matteo."* Like everything else, his name fits him perfectly.

The intensity in his obsidian eyes deepens. "Yes, Matteo. Are you heading back now?"

I glance toward Lexington Place, which is about two miles away. The building is barely visible in the distance. "Yeah, this is my halfway point."

"We can go together then."

I grimace and shake my head. Is he crazy? I'm barely holding myself together right now. "No. You should probably go on without me. I don't want to slow you down. I'm just getting back into running after a bit of a hiatus."

His dark eyes slowly flick over my legs. "You suffered an injury?"

Matteo's gaze feels like a physical caress. It makes my heart stutter. "No. Nothing like that."

His eyebrows rise as if he's waiting for an explanation. When I remain silent, he says, "I don't mind slowing down."

In that moment, I realize that he isn't going to take no for an answer. I nod my head, accepting that we will be running back to the building together.

True to his word, he slows his pace, and I do my best to pick mine up. Otherwise, he would be speed walking beside me. If the man is trying to get a work-out in, what he's doing isn't going to cut it.

Even though I'm focused on my breathing, I'm still hyperaware of Matteo at my side. How could I not be? He's tall, muscular, and strikingly handsome. The man certainly has a presence.

By the time we reach the glass doors of our building, George is there to open them for us. I'm huffing and puffing. My face feels heated. Those two miles were done in record time. For me, anyway.

Matteo barely looks as though he's exerted any effort at all.

George tips his hat to us as we head into the wood-paneled lobby. If he's surprised to see us together, it doesn't show. We call for the elevator before stepping on and riding up to the thirtieth floor. Before I know it, the doors are sliding open. I can't help but release a sigh of relief. Sharing the same space with Matteo makes me tense.

Opening my door, I turn to meet his eyes. "Bye."

His dark gaze rakes over me with no smile in sight. Again, I'm struck by the feeling that this is not a man who makes slow, sweet love to a woman.

No.

This is a man who likes to fuck.

Hard.

The words he uttered and that woman's cries of pleasure from that night on the balcony ring throughout my head as our stare continues to hold.

I know *exactly* what's going through my mind, but I haven't the faintest idea of what's going through his. Matteo's gaze is shuttered, yet still piercing. I feel all but slayed by it. Much more breathless than when I was running to keep up with him.

"Goodbye, Grace."

I acknowledge his words with a jerk of my head, turning away to escape the impenetrableness of his stare. He has a way of making me feel as if I've been stripped bare.

I'm not used to that.

Nor am I sure how much I like it.

Just as I'm stepping over the threshold, on the cusp of freedom, he says, "I'm sure we'll see each other around."

My eyes dart to his. Another bolt of electricity surges through me as our gazes reconnect.

"Yes," I force out the rest of the words, "I'm sure we will." That being said, I quickly slam the door. The way he affects me is unnerving. The worst part is that as attracted to him as I am, part of me wants to run and hide. I wonder if it's too late for that.

For some reason, I think it might be.

CHAPTER NINE

When I head downstairs to go for a run the next morning, Matteo is waiting for me in the lobby. I'm not going to lie, it kind of throws me off. Being around all the gorgeousness isn't easy. It takes some getting used to, and I'm not there yet. He makes me feel self-conscious and awkward in a way I've never experienced before. He has this way of watching me that sets my already frayed nerves on edge. I feel tongue-tied when we're together.

I don't think we've exchanged more than a handful of words.

And yet...

I can't say that I don't enjoy having him at my side. He may jack me up inside, but I like being around him. It doesn't make the least bit of sense.

What I find most amusing is the way women instantly perk up when they see him. I'm talking every female we pass on the street. It doesn't matter if they're pre-teens or middle aged, they all rubberneck. And the looks they shoot my way after getting an eyeful of him are hilarious.

I can't resist smirking back at them every once in a while.

See?

It's not just me. He has this effect on all of womankind. I can't take it personally.

An hour later, we part company at my door. This time he doesn't stop to chitchat. Matteo gives me a wave before continuing to his own door. That casual behavior makes me suspect that us running into each other in the lobby is nothing more than a coincidence.

But then I come down the next morning, and Matteo is waiting in the lobby again. This time, I figure we're either on the same schedule, or he's decided that I need a running buddy. Again, we don't talk much. A few pleasantries are exchanged and a little bit of banter.

It takes everything I have to keep pace with the man. His legs are much longer than mine which gives him a longer stride. I can tell that he's trying to slow down, and I hate it.

So I push myself harder.

And I run faster.

By the time we run five miles and make it back to the building, I'm on the verge of stroking out. I don't think Matteo realizes it. I try not to collapse into a Jello-y mass of limbs until after I'm inside my condo.

Matteo.

Is that the sexiest name ever or what?

By Friday morning, a pattern is set. By unspoken agreement, we meet in the lobby of our building. We run five miles along the lakefront and return after about an hour.

There is no *same time, same place, see you tomorrow.*

To be honest, I'm not even sure if he enjoys my company because we barely talk. I don't know what I'd say if he were to strike up an actual, in-depth conversation. Every time we converse, I get tongue-tied. So I keep my mouth firmly shut and focus on keeping pace with him which requires all of my attention.

I find it difficult to believe that he has any interest in me. I saw the woman he was with at the club the other week. I didn't get a good look at her face, but she was definitely all... slinky.

And sexy.

In other words, she was the perfect compliment to him.

I, however, am not.

After our Friday morning run, Matteo leaves me in the hall again as he continues toward his place. I'm tempted to ask if he'll be running tomorrow morning, but I don't. After showering and changing for the day, I get a text from Chloe asking if I'm up for a night out at Covet.

That was one crazy place.

A Technicolor dream world.

That being said, I had an amazing time.

So... why not?

School hasn't started yet. And neither has my volunteering opportunity at the museum. I still have quite a bit of free time on my hands. And I haven't met any other people my age. All the residents I've run into in the building so far, other than Matteo, are older.

In their thirties and forties, at least.

I think Matteo is in his late twenties, possibly early thirties. We haven't swapped life stories. And I'm okay with that. I like the fact that we've been running together and just keeping it light.

I don't expect anything more than that.

Much like last time, we skip the long line and are ushered inside the sumptuous walls of Covet. This isn't my first time here, but I feel just as awed by the spectacle around me. The girls dancing on platforms, the DJ spinning records in a balcony high above the dance floor, the thumping beat of the music, the multi-colored strobe lights, and the fog rising off the floor. Not to mention all the beautiful people writhing en masse and lining the balconies.

Just walking through the door makes me feel sexy. I haven't been here for five minutes, and already my body is moving to the music.

"Maybe we should get you a job dancing on a platform." Chloe wiggles her eyebrows at me.

I almost laugh.

I can't imagine walking around in nothing but body paint and a smile. I shake my head. "Not going to happen."

She jerks her chin towards the bar. "I think Sasha would enjoy it."

My eyes slide in that direction, taking notice of the same bartender who had been flirting with me the last time I was here. I doubt she'll remember me. Hundreds of people must pass through here each night.

"Please."

Elbowing me, she grins. "Trust me, she wants you. My advice is that if you've ever been, shall we say- *curious*, Sasha is definitely the one to experiment with."

My brows skyrocket up my forehead. "And exactly how would you know that?"

Her grin turns mischievous, as if she has a delicious secret she won't be sharing anytime soon. "Let's just say I've dipped a toe in the lady pond and leave it at that."

My mouth pops open. *"You did not!"*

"Just once!" Pausing, she nibbles at her lower lip before admitting with a smile, "Okay, twice."

"What?" I screech in disbelief.

Inching closer, she whisper-yells to be heard over the music, "Trust me, that girl gets a lot of pussy. And she knows *exactly* what she's doing with it, too."

The way she gently suckled the tip of my tongue last week flashes through my mind.

Now imagine that's your clit.

I gulp.

Before I can pepper her with any more questions, Chloe pulls me alongside her as we make our way toward the bar. She waves to almost everyone we pass. As soon as Sasha sees Chloe, she makes a beeline for her, ignoring other waiting customers in the process.

"Hey, baby." Her dark eyes flash before shifting. As soon as they land on me, her smile turns wicked. "I see you brought the newbie back." She gives me a sexy little wink. "Couldn't stay away?"

I shake my head.

"Good. That's what I like to hear." She flicks her heavily made up eyes towards Chloe. "The usual?"

"Please."

She turns, grabbing several bottles before expertly pouring and combining different kinds of liquor. Unable to stop myself, my eyes roam over her painted body. Instead of a gold bikini like last time, her toned flesh is decorated with brightly colored flowers. The artwork is impressive.

I don't know how she can stand in front of a huge, raucous crowd as if she's fully dressed. I don't have the confidence to pull that off. But she does. She totally owns it. Turning back to us with a drink in each hand, she slides them toward us. I notice that each of her breasts is painted to look like a flowering bud with an unpainted nipple in the center. When I finally lift my eyes, remembering that I shouldn't stare at this woman's body, there's a knowing smirk on her face.

Busted.

Again.

Instead of blushing and feeling embarrassed, I simply smile. "I like your flowers."

She gives me another sassy wink. "You let me know when you're ready to get up close and personal, honey."

Grabbing our drinks, we turn away from the bar, each of us taking a big sip before surveying the crowd on the dance floor. The friends Chloe showed up with tonight have already disappeared into the throng.

Once we've finished our cocktails, Chloe grabs my hand and pulls me through a mass of gyrating bodies until we locate her friends. And then, just like before, I happily give myself over to the pulsing beat of the music. The DJ continues spinning records, one upbeat song bleeding into the next. I have no idea how long we stay out there. After a while, one of Chloe's guy friends gets between us, and the three of us dance together. His hands are on my hips. Chloe is behind him.

Grinning, he pulls me closer and grinds against my backside. I raise my arms above my head and twirl them in the air. Chloe continues to flank his other side. We stay melded together for the next two songs before he leaves to dance with someone else. Thirty minutes later, I'm dripping with sweat and could use a breather.

I let Chloe know that I'm heading to the bathroom and that I'll be back in a bit. I'm thinking about stopping at the bar and grabbing a water because I could use something to drink.

I'm having so much fun.

I feel light and carefree.

It's the best feeling in the world.

I don't want it to end.

It takes nearly ten minutes before I'm allowed inside the chrome and glass ladies' room. Glancing at myself in the mirror, I inspect the damage. Thankfully I brought a small silver purse that crosses over my chest. It's big enough to hold my phone, money, lipstick, and mascara—the essentials. I freshen up and head to the bar to grab a bottle of water.

Sasha immediately takes care of me, and I leave her a ten-dollar tip.

From beneath thick eyelashes, she gives me a loaded look. "You know that's not what I'm after, sweetheart." The woman has gorgeous, almond-shaped eyes. They're a rich, sable brown that matches her hair. There's something exotic about her appearance.

Unable to help myself, I grin over my shoulder before blowing a little kiss in her direction. A gurgle of laughter escapes from her lips.

What I like most about this place is how easy it is to lose yourself. There's so much going on. It's a sensory overload bonanza.

As I circle the crowded dance floor searching for Chloe, a pair of hands grab me from behind, quickly pulling me into the shadows. And then a hard, unforgiving body presses against me.

For one stunned moment, my mind goes blank.

Oh my God, I've heard about things like this happening!

I'm reminded of the movie *Taken,* where Liam Neeson's daughter gets snatched up to be sold on the black market as a sex slave, and he has to fly to France and rescue her.

Blind panic fills me at the thought of being kidnapped.

I suck in a shaky breath, ready to scream my head off, when I hear a familiar voice in my ear say, "Calm down. It's me."

Recognizing the faint accent, the adrenaline pumping through my system dissolves, leaving my knees weak and rubbery. I sag against Matteo in relief. A muscular arm snakes around my rib cage. His fingers fan out so that they graze the underside of my right breast. His other hand is at the base of my neck, lightly resting against my throat. Strangely enough, I don't feel trapped by the hold he has on me.

If I wanted to break free, I could.

The question is, *do I want to?*

"Who's the guy?"

My eyes almost roll up into my head as his warm breath feathers across my neck. Which is... I know.

Okay?

I know...

I shouldn't have this kind of reaction to him. It's just plain stupid. And yet, here I am, practically swooning.

"The guy?"

I have no idea who he's talking about. Despite the loud music and the thumping base, I'm only aware of him. Of his fingers caressing the underside of my breast. The way his lips nuzzle my ear. I feel every inch of him as he holds me tightly against his hard body.

Lust and desire consume me in the blink of an eye.

"The one you were dancing with earlier."

Oh.

Jason. Or Jack. I can't remember his name.

"He's just a friend."

"Are you sure about that?" His tone is teasing, but there's a flinty edge to it.

"Yes, he's a friend of a friend. I met him last week."

As those words escape in a rush, I frown, wondering why I'm explaining myself to him. I don't owe Matteo clarification for my behavior.

Exactly who does this guy think he is?

Trying to regain some semblance of control, I tense my muscles and stand a bit straighter.

"What are you doing here, bella?"

Bella?

What am I doing here?

Excuse me? Am I not allowed to be here? Why is he questioning me? "I came with a friend. We're here to dance and have fun."

He purrs against the delicate shell of my ear. "Are you?"

"Well, I was before this."

Inhaling deeply, I turn my head until I'm able to meet his obsidian-colored eyes. There's an intoxicating promise of hedonistic pleasure in them. Another thick slice of desire slowly lances through me. We're standing so close together and his large hands are on my body, once again pressing me against him. His mouth is no more than an inch away from mine.

Questions roll off my tongue before I can stop them. "What about you? Are you here with someone?"

Breaking eye contact, he lifts his head and gazes out onto the fog covered floor, nodding toward a woman dancing about twenty feet away from us. Feeling as though I've been sucker punched, the breath catches at the back of my throat as I reluctantly study her.

Long, dark, straight-as-pin hair cascades down a lithe back. Slender, toned arms twine sensuously in the air. A tiny black dress covers her body. Her slender legs start somewhere under her armpits. And her face is stunning.

Am I surprised to find him with someone who looks like this?

No.

I would be more surprised if he wasn't. But I can't deny the disappointment surging through me.

If he's here with *her*, what's he doing lurking in the shadows with *me*?

I'm proud of how snappy the words coming out of me sound. "Then maybe you should get your hands off me and rejoin your date."

"She's not my date." He chuckles. It's deep and low and scrapes at something buried within me. "I don't *date* women."

My eyes stay riveted to the woman he's here with as his words echo through my head. I jolt when his lips glide over the column of my throat.

"I fuck them," he says in the same husky voice.

His words make something curl tightly in the pit of my belly. The vileness of them should be off-putting. Their effect should be like a bucket of cold water dumped over my head. They should douse the fires within.

But they don't.

"And you're going to fuck *her* tonight?" I almost cringe as those words slip out of my mouth.

A shiver works through me as his hot breath brushes over the delicate flesh of my neck. There's a sharp contrast between the scrape of his stubble and the softness of his lips as his mouth drags across my skin.

"I haven't decided yet. Would you prefer that I fuck you instead?"

Oh God... his words are so dirty.

I refuse to admit that I want him.

Although I'm willing to bet he already knows. From the first moment I saw him in the elevator, I'm sure he knew that I was his for the taking. I'm like a puddle of goo around him.

Even when I should resist him, I can't.

Trying to salvage a few scraps of my pride, I lie through my teeth. "No, I don't want that."

Even though I can no longer see his face, I hear the amusement in his voice. "Is that so, bella?"

There's that endearment again.

He's so sure of himself.

His confidence shouldn't be such a turn-on. Using all my willpower, I free myself from his arms and step away from his warm embrace.

I hope the distance will help clear my head.

His arms drop to his sides as I spin toward him. As always, his beauty knocks me off-balance. He's so tall that I have to crane my neck to look him in the eyes. A deep sensuality shimmers in them. They all but scream sex. Everything about him does.

I feel myself drawn to the power he so effortlessly exudes. A low hum fills the pit of my belly.

Matteo thinks he can have anyone he wants. He thinks he can leave one woman on the dance floor as he drags another into the shadows to seduce her.

Without his hands and lips on me, rational thought prevails.

"No," I say with a little more force, "I don't want you."

Of course I'm lying.

And he knows it.

With a hint of a smirk, he cocks his head to the side. "Are you sure about that?"

"Positive."

Before he can do anything else to break my resolve, I spin on my heels and walk away to put as much distance between us as possible. Not once do I glance back to see if he's following. Matteo doesn't strike me as the type of man to chase after a woman. He's much too used to women pursuing him.

Although I find him ridiculously sexy, this is not a man I should get tangled up with. He's just... *too much*. Plus, we're neighbors. It's not like I can have a one-night stand with him and then just disappear, never to see him again.

He would be right next door.

And he'd still fuck women on his balcony for me to overhear.

That thought settles like a heavy stone at the bottom of my stomach.

Shoving through the crowd, I crane my neck in search of Chloe. But there's such a crush of people here. Covet seems even more packed than it was before. After about ten minutes, I still can't find her. For all I know, she and her friends have moved to one of the upper balconies that ring the dance floor.

After the run-in with Matteo, I'm ready to call it a night. I want to get out of here. I decide to head to the bar. Maybe Sasha has seen Chloe. Out of the corner of my eye, I catch a glimpse of long strawberry blonde hair. No one other than Chloe has hair that particular shade and length. The sight of her settles me.

I'm still calling it quits, though. I've had my fill of Covet. And I don't want to chance another encounter with Matteo either. Especially if he's here with another woman. He's managed to suck all the fun out of this evening.

Making my way toward Chloe, I realize that she's involved in a heated exchange with a man. By the time I reach her side, she looks like she's on the verge of blowing her top.

"Hi, is everything okay?" My eyes dart cautiously between them.

Pasting a smile of her face, her green gaze meets mine. "Yep, just fine." Her teeth are clenched so tightly that they seem in danger of shattering.

I take another glance at the man standing next to Chloe. Actually, it seems more like he's hovering over her. I notice his hands are fisted at his sides.

When she doesn't explain the situation, or who this guy is, I ask, "Are you sure?" I can feel the thick tension swirling between them.

"Mmm hmm. Flynn was just about to take off." Her expression turns steely. "Right?"

His jaw ticks as he locks it. His eyes burn into hers. He never glances in my direction. I realize with a rush just how good-looking he is. "I guess so."

She smiles brightly, but there's a hard-edged look in her eye. "Okay then, bye!"

Looking as though he wants to argue-or maybe throttle her-he says through gritted teeth, "Fine. I'll see you on Monday."

Her eyes flatten as if she's not looking forward to continuing the conversation at that point. "Yes... Monday."

With that, he stalks away. The strange drama unfolding between them almost takes my mind off what just happened with Matteo.

Almost.

But not quite.

"What was that all about?" I ask. "Do you know him?"

Staring moodily after the dark haired man, she mutters, "It was nothing. Just a dude I ran into from work."

My eyes continue tracking him as well. "He's kind of hot.

There's no *kind of* about it. The man is *definitely* hot. He has thick, chestnut brown hair, deep blue eyes and dimples which I usually think are adorable and endearing. But that wasn't the vibe I got from him.

If he works in Chloe's office, he could be a lawyer.

Her gaze shifts to mine, and she snorts. "Trust me, he's more than aware of it." Changing the subject, she asks, "So where've you been? You were gone forever." Arching a brow, her expression relaxes and she seems more like her usual, good-natured self. "I thought you might have taken off with someone."

Would I have left with Matteo if he hadn't been here with another woman?

I suppress a sigh because I already know the answer to that question. If I didn't know what kind of man he was before, there's no mistaking it now.

Since nothing significant happened, I keep the run-in with Matteo to myself. "Hardly. There was a long line at the bathroom, and then I couldn't find you."

"Yeah, I probably should have taken you to the employee one in back. We would have been in and out and back on the dance floor."

"Next time."

Chloe's eyes wander down the bar to where Flynn now stands. He's staring at her. Another stormy look clouds her face. "I need a drink."

Even though my frayed nerves have been smoothed over, I'm still ready to call it a night. I rub my temples and tell a little white lie. "I feel a headache brewing. You don't mind if I leave, do you?"

Surprise mingles with disappointment that our evening is being cut short. "Of course not. Want me to come with you?"

I shake my head. My evening may be over, but hers doesn't have to be. "No, I'll be fine."

"How are you getting home?"

"I'll catch a cab, no worries."

"Are you sure you don't want me to go with you?"

Her eyes drift to the tall, dark-haired man watching her from the other end of the bar. It's obvious that something is going on between them. I wonder why she isn't telling me what the real story is with Flynn. When we were younger, we confided everything in one another. I knew all of Chloe's secrets. And she knew mine. But then again, there's more to my trip to the bathroom than I've shared as well.

I wave off her concern. "No, stay and have fun with your friends. I'll text you when I make it home."

She nods. "Okay, if you're sure."

"I am."

Chloe pulls me in for a quick hug. I make my way to the front of the club. Once I'm outside, a cool breeze sweeps across my cheeks. Inhaling deeply, I savor the fresh air filling my lungs.

I glance up and down the street, looking for a taxi with its light on, but there are none in sight. They're usually crawling all over the place. It's not even that late- only one in the morning. The sidewalks are still crowded with people.

As I continue to look for a cab, a shiny black limo glides up to the curb. Before I can move out of the way, the backdoor swings open. I peek inside, wondering who is about to get out. It could be an actor or an athlete. Many television shows and movies are filmed in Chicago. And there are sports teams aplenty- the Bears, Blackhawks, Bulls, White Sox, and Cubs.

Imagine my surprise when I see Matteo.

My breath rushes from my lungs in an annoyed sigh. He's the last person I want to see. I left the club in hopes of avoiding him.

His next two words send my temper skyrocketing.

"Get in."

CHAPTER TEN

"Excuse me?" I don't move a muscle.

Eyes still fixed on mine, Matteo enunciates the words more carefully as if I don't speak English. "I said, *get in*."

The man is delusional. That's the only rational explanation I can come up with. My spine straightens, and I imagine smoke pouring out of my ears as I stand on the sidewalk outside the club.

When I don't make a move to follow his directives, he sighs loudly in exasperation. Even when I'm pissed, his accent still has the ability to make me weak in the knees, which irritates the hell out of me.

"Get in the car, Grace. We're both going to the same place. I'll take you home. There's no reason for you to be on the street alone at this hour."

A shiver scuttles down my spine at the commanding tone.

I'll take you home.

Prying my eyes away from him, I pray for a taxi to come barreling down the street so that I don't have to get in the car. One heartbeat, then two slip by. And still there's nothing.

No taxi-cabs in sight.

Feeling desperate, I admit, "I don't want a ride home from you."

The man is dangerous. He makes me lose control. His dark eyes roaming over me and his big, masculine hands searing me with their heat make me feel so much more alive than I've felt in the last two years.

"Bella."

He coaxingly murmurs the endearment, but it still rings with authority. A steely determination that will not be denied and cannot be ignored. Bossiness should not be an attractive quality.

But with Matteo...

It is.

Feeling the pressure of his demand beating down upon me, I start to fidget.

How does he do that?

How is he able to make me feel as though I need to follow his edicts when we're barely acquainted?

It's maddening.

I'm tempted to walk away, but something deep inside me demands that I respond.

Demands that I... oh God... *acquiesce*.

Which only pisses me off further. I'd rather walk home at this point. My eyes flick to the heels I'm wearing. Clearly, those will have to go. Looks like I might be hoofing it home barefoot tonight.

"You have approximately thirty seconds before I get out of this limo."

My eyes jerk to his in surprise. He doesn't finish the threat. But then again, he doesn't have to. My mind cartwheels with possibilities.

I may not know him well, but I understand that he's not a man who throws out idle threats.

Making a snap decision, I stalk toward the long, sleek black car. I just want to go home. It doesn't escape me that he's the reason I cut my evening short in the first place, and now I'm going to be locked inside the cabin with him for the duration of this drive.

As I climb into the limo, he slides across the plush leather to make room for me. Because I'm wearing a short dress, I carefully lower myself onto the seat before a driver comes around to close the door.

I avoid looking directly at Matteo as the vehicle pulls away from the curb, maneuvering through late night traffic. Worrying my lower lip, I'm keenly aware of the distance between our bodies. It's not nearly enough. I can't get any closer to the door. I'm practically smashed against it.

Perhaps he's tired as well, and we can just ride together in companionable silence.

Instead of allowing that to happen, he snakes an arm across the back of my seat. His fingertips graze the top of my shoulder. Every single one of my muscles locks up. It feels like my flesh is being singed. I do my best to ignore him, but I can feel his dark gaze burning into me.

The cologne he's wearing wraps around me until I'm dizzy from the heady scent of it. Until something settles in my core, making it impossible to sit on the plush leather seat without clenching my thighs in an effort to alleviate some of the pressure building within me.

"Grace..."

My name rolls off his lips like a seductive caress. That slight Italian accent makes me want to swoon.

I stay still. At this point, I'm barely breathing. Maybe he'll give up if I continue to ignore him. We'll arrive at the building soon, and I can bolt out of the car as if the hounds of hell are snapping at my heels.

One long finger slips under my chin, and he slowly turns my head. A slight smirk quirks his lips. His eyes are heavy-lidded. At half-mast.

"Tell me, what *exactly* are you trying to accomplish with this behavior?"

The strange question makes my brows jerk together. My words come out sounding hoarse. "Excuse me?"

He doesn't release my chin as I continue holding his hypnotically intense gaze. "Are you trying to stir my interest? Because it's not necessary, bella. It's already been stirred."

My eyes widen as his meaning sinks in.

Good Lord, no!

Is that what he thinks?

That I *want* him chasing after me? That this is some sort of game on my part?

I don't want that at all!

This man is *way* out of my league, and I know it. I'm under no illusions as to how something between us would end.

Instead of setting him straight, I ask a question of my own to remind him that he wasn't at the club alone tonight. Maybe I need some reminding as well. "What happened to the woman you were with?"

My words come out sounding petulant. As if I'm jealous.

Which I'm not.

At all.

Okay, maybe a teeny bit.

His eyelids lower as he continues to study me.

He murmurs, "I'm not as interested in fucking her as I originally thought." Releasing my chin, he trails his fingers down my neck and chest before caressing the outer curve of my breast. His slight touch makes my nipples tighten.

"Turns out there's someone else I'd rather fuck instead." His voice dips lower, growing more seductive. "I could make you feel very, very good." His fingers travel downward, grazing the side of my belly before settling on my hip. Giving a little squeeze, his hand skates along my outer thigh. Shifting toward me, he closes the distance between us. "Wouldn't you like me to give you another orgasm?"

All of the oxygen is sucked from the cabin of the limo. It leaves me gasping in shock.

His dark eyes sparkle as his lips curve mischievously. "Only this time, I'll actually be touching *you* when it happens."

His fingers slowly glide toward my inner thigh before stroking upward.

Oh God... I need to stop this madness immediately. I need to still his fingers before they go any higher.

But I don't.

His low voice is like warm, decadent honey. The way he watches me from behind the fringe of thick black lashes makes me feel like a fly trapped in the silken web of a spider. I can't break free from the trance holding me immobilized. The way he strokes my flesh leaves me breathless.

And wanting more.

"Did you think I couldn't hear you?"

I say nothing.

I can't.

He growls. His eyelids continue to lower as if he's remembering, savoring the noises I'd made. "Your breathy little moans made my cock rock hard."

Using his wrist, he pushes against my thighs, widening them until he's able to touch my panties. Then he draws delicate little circles against my clit.

One touch.

That's all it takes.

I knew it would be like this with him. Moaning, my head lolls against the butter-soft leather.

"Take your panties off, bella. *Now.*"

The words don't faze me as much as they should because I'm operating on autopilot. I don't think about the harsh demand. Because that's exactly what it is. He's not asking. He's telling. Without weighing the consequences of my actions, I shimmy out of the underwear. He waits with his hand stretched out in expectation.

Why is that so sexy?

I set the wispy scrap of lace in his palm, and he immediately stuffs the material into the pocket of his suit jacket. His eyes never leave mine.

I fleetingly realize that I won't see them again.

Then his fingers are back on me, stroking up my inner thigh. This time he doesn't have to pry my legs apart. They're already spread, eagerly awaiting his touch. I hold my breath as he inches closer, pushing my dress up as he moves.

Higher.

Higher still.

Until it's bunched across my lap, and I know that my pussy lips are on full display when the cool air in the limo hits them. His eyes slowly lower to my spread legs.

"Beautiful."

He touches me with strong, sure strokes. Ones that leave me trembling on the seat, desperate for more. I can't stop a moan of pleasure from escaping when his blunt-tipped fingers dip inside my warmth.

It's been so long since I've had a man touch me.

"Did you enjoy listening to us fuck?"

I bite my lower lip to stifle another moan. I don't want him to have my sounds of pleasure. He's already taking what he wants from me. I don't want to give him anything more.

But his words are so deliciously dirty.

They turn me on more than I thought possible.

"Did you imagine that I was fucking you instead?"

My teeth sink into my lower lip in an effort to remain silent. I don't want to tell him the truth. When I say nothing, he pulls his hand away and slowly caresses the outer edges of my lower lips. Eager for more contact, I widen my legs, practically arching off the seat so I can feel his tantalizing fingers coast over my flesh again.

Needing more, a desperate whimper escapes.

His voice turns harsh. *"Did you imagine that I was fucking you instead?"*

His fingers continue to skate over my softness, toying with me. He knows what I want, but refuses to give it to me. Unable to hold it in any longer, I groan. I'm on the verge of splintering apart into a million jagged pieces.

"Yes," I finally whisper.

As soon as the word falls from my lips, he thrusts his fingers back inside me before circling my clit with my own wetness. I nearly scream, it feels so good. Everything inside me tightens as an orgasm builds.

"Do you know how sexy it was to hear you? To know that you were touching yourself while you listened to me fuck?"

It's difficult to imagine that he was even aware of me while screwing another woman.

With masterful fingers, he continues strumming my aching clit. The low murmur of his deep, sensual voice pushes me toward the precipice of release.

"That night, I made two women come."

Those words are what send me careening over the edge. I throw my head back and scream as he pumps his thick fingers in and out of me. He doesn't stop stroking until he's wrung every last drop of pleasure from my body. Until I can do nothing more than lay in an exhausted heap on the seat next to him, breathing hard and ignoring the fact that my dress is hiked up and my lower lips are swollen from his ministrations.

When he removes his hand from between my legs, I slit my eyes partially open and watch as he sticks his fingertips in his mouth before sucking them.

"I knew you would taste just as delicious as you looked."

I didn't believe it possible, but those words instantly make my core throb back to life.

I whimper as a pleased smile spreads across his handsome face.

CHAPTER ELEVEN

The following week flies by in a blur. There isn't much time for me to dwell on how easily I spread my legs for Matteo. Classes at North-western begin as does my volunteering stint at The Art Institute. I tell myself that I have more than enough to keep my mind occupied. I'm nonstop busy during the day and crawl tiredly into bed every night.

I'd be lying through my teeth if I didn't admit that I spent the first couple of days keeping my eyes peeled for my next-door neighbor.

The morning after the limo incident, the ride down to the lobby was nerve-racking. I considered not running. Or going at an alternate time. But then I realized, *I have absolutely nothing to be ashamed of*. I had a sexual encounter with a gorgeous man. I'm certainly not going to skulk around the building as if I did something wrong.

I didn't.

What happened, happened.

No big deal.

End of story.

My palms were a sweaty mess by the time the elevator doors slid open. My knees almost gave out when I realized that he wasn't waiting for me in the lobby. I was so relieved that I ended up running seven miles that morning.

It must have been all the nervous energy thrumming through me.

Every morning for the rest of the week, I held my breath as the elevator doors opened to reveal a smiling George at his post.

I want to ask the doorman what he knows about the resident in Thirty-B, but I don't. Even if George were privy to information, he wouldn't share it with me.

By Thursday, I know our morning runs are a thing of the past. It's just as well. Clearly, Matteo got what he was looking for.

He told me himself that he doesn't date women.

Just fucks them.

The man was blatantly honest about his intentions. I can't claim that he led me on.

And I let him touch me without so much as a peep. I spread my legs wide and allowed him to finger fuck me while talking dirty in his melodic voice.

I want to shake my head as those thoughts crash down upon me.

I'm not sure what's worse- that I let him finger me in the limo or that he brought up the fact that I masturbated while listening to him screw another woman.

It's a toss-up.

It would be in my best interest to avoid my neighbor like the plague until we both forget these two incidents occurred. Until I can look him in the eye and not turn the color of an overripe tomato.

I have a lot going on, so pushing him from my thoughts when he does pop into them isn't a problem. My mind is fully engaged with the art history classes I'm taking this semester. School is challenging, but I wouldn't have it any other way. I'm immersing myself in the program. And I love volunteering at The Art Institute. If I could squeeze a few more hours into my schedule for it, I would.

Each echoing corridor and every beautifully displayed exhibit all bring back nostalgic memories of my family that fill me with comfort. I feel closer to my parents when I'm there. The museum is like a second home to me. I know every collection. I can recite from memory every informational card regarding the displayed work.

I've also made a few new friends, too. Abigail, Zoey, and Clint are in my classes. We've already had lunch on campus. Kim and Jonathan are volunteers at the museum. Jonathan has taken me under his wing and shown me the ins and outs of being a docent.

Every day, life becomes a little fuller. A little less lonely. I'm making a concerted effort to introduce myself to new people, which is something I haven't done in years. What I love most is that no one has any idea about what I've been through recently. Pity doesn't fill their eyes, just interest in getting to know me.

I start each day by running five miles before class. I usually hit the streets around seven, and I'm out for about an hour. It's become habit to stop in the park right by the sparkling blue water to take a moment or two to catch my breath and feel grateful that I'm no longer in the bad place I once was.

I've moved on.

I'm moving forward.

It feels wonderful.

I've already forgotten about the gorgeous guy next door.

Matteo who?

Yep. That's exactly right.

CHAPTER TWELVE

"Dominic Grimaldi is here to see you, Ms. Castile," George says on the other end of the line.

"Thank you. You can send him up."

I grab two small plates and take them out to the sun-filled balcony. I spend more time out here than anywhere else in the condo. I know this will change once the weather turns colder. For now, I just want to soak it all up. Most evenings, I bring my books out to the patio and read or work on homework.

It's so relaxing.

Well, it's relaxing as long as I don't think about Matteo.

My ears are constantly pricked for the slightest noise. So far, there's been nothing but silence. It's like he isn't even there anymore.

Maybe he's on vacation. Or out of town for work. Who knows? I shouldn't even care.

Wait a minute- I *don't* care.

Hopefully, there will come a point in time when I actually believe it.

As soon as I set the appetizers on the table- caprese salad and a buffalo chicken dip I made myself- the doorbell ring. On bare feet, I silently pad across the hardwood floors in the living room to the entryway that leads to the door. This place is too big for just myself, but I love it. I love that there's so much space to move around in.

With a smile, I open the door to find Dominic standing on the other side with a bottle of red wine in his hand. Right away he opens his arms wide, and I immediately step into their comforting strength.

Wrapped in his embrace, I privately acknowledge that Dominic has been my rock through the last couple of years. What would I do without him? When I still felt lost and adrift during senior year of college, he's the one who suggested I get out of Seattle and move back to Chicago.

I untangle myself from him to close the door and link my arm through his.

"I made appetizers for us to munch on."

His eyes light up. "Does a nice cabernet go with what you're serving?"

"As far as I'm concerned, cabernet goes with everything."

He pats my hand as we head to the balcony. For just a moment, he stands at the railing, taking in the view. I do this all the time. The patio is my happy place.

"It certainly is beautiful out here."

I can't resist teasing him. "Well worth the two point nine price tag?"

He rolls his eyes. "I never said that, now did I? I think you might tire of the view. In a few months, you'll be trying to unload this dump."

I sputter out a laugh before waving a hand toward the picturesque sight. "Do you really see me tiring of this anytime soon?" Not in a million years.

He pauses as if giving my question serious consideration. "I suppose it could happen."

I shake my head as we settle in at the small round glass and iron table. It reminds me of the charming café tables lining the streets of Paris.

"You know," he says, "I have even better views at my place. Right on the water with a nice strip of beach all to ourselves. We could sail and swim every day. The heated pool feels amazing this time of year."

I slant a look his way. "There's a heated pool here."

"It's not private," he points out.

"It's private enough," I fire back in a singsong voice.

I've lived at Lexington Place for over a month. Not once have I given Dominic any reason to suspect that I'm unhappy or have experienced buyer's remorse regarding the condo. Yet he keeps tossing out comments about me moving into his house. I think he'd be thrilled if I decided I'd had enough of living in the city and stayed with him for a while.

I guess he's lonely rattling around in that big house all by himself. He has Maria. She runs the household and cooks, but still, it's not the same as having a family. I've also noticed that he doesn't seem quite as busy as he once was with his law firm. As the practice flourished over the last fifteen years, he's hired a number of associates. I think he's starting to slow down. Not long ago, Dominic often put in eighty-hour work weeks. There were times when we wouldn't see him for months because he was slammed with clients.

Our verbal skirmish has the corners of his lips tipping up impishly.

He really is handsome. And he only seems to grow more so as the years go by. I have no idea why he isn't seriously involved with someone. Now seems like the perfect time.

"Fine, fine, fine. Just know that my door is always open anytime you want to come home."

"Thank you. That means a lot to me." More than he could possibly understand. With my parents gone, it's nice to know that someone cares about me. That I'm not alone. I have Dominic.

He glances around again before taking a sip of his red wine.

"You're happy here?" I think he needs reassurance that I love my new home. That I'm not trying to put on a brave face for his benefit.

For a moment, I take in the view as a light breeze slides over my cheeks. "I am. I love it."

It may not be the answer he wants to hear, but he looks satisfied. "Good. In the end, your happiness is all that matters."

We munch on the appetizers, and I tell him all about The Art Institute and how my classes are progressing. We talk about Chloe and how she and I have fallen right back into our friendship. He asks a few questions, but mostly allows me to talk about everything that's been going on.

"I'm proud of you, Gracie. You're settling in and making this place your home. Obviously, moving here and starting school have been good for you." After a pause, he adds softly, "I haven't seen you this happy in a long time."

I allow his words to wash over me, realizing that he's right. I *am* happy here. My life feels as though it's on track again. As if I'm moving forward with purpose and not just trying to slog through each day. Thinking about my parents doesn't crush my soul the way it used to. I can remember the good times we shared, how wonderful they were, and how much I loved them without spiraling into a depression.

Needing the physical contact, I reach across the table and wrap my hand around his. "I can't begin to imagine where I would be or what I would be doing if I didn't have you in my life." It's a frightening thought. "I appreciate everything you've done for me."

His eyes soften. "Your parents meant everything to me. And so do you. I love you, Gracie. You and I are family. Nothing will ever change that."

I nod in agreement. My heart feels full, almost as if it's bursting at the seams. "I love you, too."

Breaking the thick undercurrents of emotion coursing between us, he gives me a little wink before saying, "It's just you and me, kid. Against the world."

I laugh. For as long as I can remember, he's said that to me. When I was little, he would sneak me a treat or a small present. Then he'd give me a wink and say that phrase. Dominic has always been the one man in my life I could trust implicitly.

I hope that never changes.

Glancing down at my fingers, I force myself to ask a question that's been eating away at me. "Am I the reason you don't have someone special in your life?"

The last thing I want is for him to put his life on hold for me. He's been doing that for too long. It's time for both of us to start living again.

"What?"

My eyes lift to meet his curious blue ones. "It just seems like you've been spending so much time with me lately. I don't want to get in the way of your social life."

He chuckles before relaxing in his chair. "Is that what you think?"

I shrug. I'm not sure what to think about the situation. I know that Dominic used to have a pretty active dating life and now... not so much. "You don't have to babysit me. I'm okay on my own."

"I don't consider us spending time together to be babysitting. I love that you now live here, that we can get together whenever we want." He gives me a look. "You have to know that."

Sucking in my lower lip, I nod. "It's just that you haven't mentioned seeing anyone lately. I don't want to be the reason for it, that's all."

One of his brows rises as he continues watching me from across the table. "I've been out a couple times, but it's nothing worth mentioning. I'm actually tired of all this dating nonsense."

A chuckle bursts free. His words are almost shocking. "*What? You? Tired of dating?* I don't believe it! You used to have a different woman on your arm every time we saw you."

Unapologetic about his past, he merely grins.

It's easy to see why woman are so attracted to him. With thick blond hair, bright blue eyes that are always laughing, an athletic build from when he played college football, and now a successful law practice, Dominic Grimaldi is a catch. He was listed a few years in a row as one of Chicago's most eligible bachelors. The two-page spread of him in the magazine was hilarious. My parents teased him mercilessly about it.

"That was a while ago. Apparently the unthinkable has happened and I've matured."

I grab at my heart. "No! Say it ain't so!"

"I'm afraid it be so, sweetheart. All good things must eventually come to an end."

I lean forward. "Does this actually mean that you're ready to settle down with one woman?"

His gaze becomes hooded as he continues to sip his wine. "I think it might be time."

I can't believe we're having this conversation. Dominic has always enjoyed a steady stream of women that were readily available at his fingertips. "Any serious contenders on the horizon? Anyone I should meet?" I can't resist teasing him. "Just remember, they'll need my stamp of approval before things get too serious."

He shrugs. "Oh, there might be one or two worth taking a closer look at." Since he just came from the office, he's still wearing a dark gray suit. His tie has been loosened, and the top button of his white shirt is open. He looks more casual, more approachable than when he's at the office.

Even though I want him to find someone to share his life with, I love that we're able to spend so much time together. I have a hard time imagining what it would be like if someone else shared all these moments between us.

A quietness settles over us as we get tangled up in our own private thoughts. The lull isn't uncomfortable. We know one another so well, that we can just sit silently.

We can just... *be*.

After a while, he clears his throat. "There's no easy way to bring this up, but I think it's something we need to talk about."

Glancing up, I know that whatever he's about to say is serious. I can tell by the somber tone now filling his voice. Which can only mean that it must have something to do with my parents. I brace myself for whatever he's going to say next.

"The house in Seattle..." He leaves those words hanging in the air before continuing. "Have you given any consideration as to what you want to do with it?"

The air slowly dissipates from my lungs until there's nothing left. For a second, I feel panicked. It's as if I can't breathe.

Feeling trepidacious, I admit, "I haven't given it much thought." I'm almost afraid to ask. "Why?"

"I hate to see it sitting empty. It's been two years now. And with you seeming so settled here in Chicago, I just assumed you wouldn't want to return."

"I... I don't know." We moved to Seattle when I was in seventh grade. I spent six years in that house until I left for college. When

Mom and Dad died, I stayed there with Dominic for three months, but after that...

I couldn't bring myself to go back. Even for a weekend or spring break, it was just too heart-wrenching.

Dominic eventually closed up the house and found a company to take care of the maintenance. A couple months ago, before the move, I contacted them about which pieces of furniture I wanted shipped to Chicago. Even then, I shied away from stepping foot inside that house.

"Gracie?"

His sympathetic gaze meets mine when I glance at him. I don't even realize that tears have gathered in my eyes until one slowly slides down my cheek. Dominic's chair scrapes against the patio's cement floor as he comes around the table and squats in front of me. He places his palms on my cheeks. Using the pads of his thumbs, he wipes the tears from my face.

"I'm sorry, sweetheart. I'm a jackass for bringing it up. It's way too soon to think about selling the house."

I ask in a small voice, "Is that what you think I should do?"

I haven't given it much thought. Mainly because the idea of letting the house go feels like losing another piece of my parents. One of the last pieces. Their cars are still parked in the garage as though they'll be back from vacation any day now.

But they aren't coming back.

They'll never live in that house again or back their cars out of the driveway to head to work in the morning.

Selling the house they painstakingly restored is like permanently letting go of them, and I'm not ready for that. Not yet. I find it oddly comforting that the house still stands, left precisely as it was the day they died. Mom and Dad's clothing hangs in the closets and lay neatly folded in their dresser drawers. Paperwork is still strewn about my dad's desk.

God... that sounds sick.

Dominic's eyes are both tender and sad. They're filled with remorse for the emotion he's unwittingly stirred within me. "At some point, you'll have to think about what you want to do. But it doesn't have to be right now." He adds, "Hell, nothing ever has to be done, I guess. But..." He trails off.

Curious about what he has to say, I ask, "But?"

"It seems like a shame to leave it sitting empty like that. It's such a beautiful house. Your parents worked so hard on it. Do you think that maybe you'll go back someday?"

"No." The word pops out of my mouth. I can't imagine being there without them. Plus, I was only there for six years. The place doesn't feel like home the way Chicago does. And it's not like I have any family there. Or even friends. I've drifted from the people I met in middle and high school. They were my friends at the time, but we never shared the kind of deep history that binds you to one another.

It could never compare to the history I have with Dominic or Chloe. Ones like that takes time to evolve. It doesn't happen overnight. After moving, I wasn't interested in putting forth that kind of effort. I didn't want to invest myself. Home was Chicago. Not Seattle.

Never Seattle.

Biting my lower lip, I ask, "Is it too costly to maintain? Is that the problem?"

Maybe there are financial concerns Dominic hasn't shared with me. At this point, the house has more sentimental value than anything else. I have no intention of holding on to the property forever. I'm just not ready to relinquish it yet. But if I can't afford to keep it, there isn't much choice in the matter. Which isn't something I had considered before.

Dominic hesitates before shaking his head. "Financially, you're fine. I just hate to see you spending money on maintenance, taxes, and insurance if you have no plans to return. It seems like a waste of money. I'd rather see you unload the property for a profit while the market is hot and invest the proceeds wisely."

His explanation makes sense. I would expect no less from Dominic. He's good at separating the emotion from the financial decisions that need to be made.

But still... I don't feel ready to part with it.

"Could we revisit the issue in six months? Maybe I'll feel differently when I'm more settled in my new life here."

He continues stroking my cheeks with his thumbs. "I think that's a good plan. The house isn't a pressing issue." His eyes continue holding mine. So much love shines in them. "I never meant to upset you, Gracie." His voice takes on a husky quality. "I hate seeing you cry. It rips me apart inside."

I force my lips into a watery smile. As our gazes hold, he closes the distance between us and presses a kiss against my mouth. Before surprise can even register, he stands, pulling me up with him.

"What do you say to getting out of here for a while? It's a beautiful night. Let's go to Navy Pier." I feel relieved that he's dropping the subject of the house. "Remember how much you used to love the Ferris wheel?"

Tamping down all the riotous emotion brewing inside me, I teasingly ask, "What do you mean- *used to*? I still love it."

"Of course you do." Dominic pulls me against him and wraps his arm around my shoulders. "All right then, come on. The Ferris wheel awaits."

CHAPTER THIRTEEN

On Monday, Wednesday, and Friday, I work from one in the afternoon until five in the evening at The Art Institute. The first week, I spent most of my time shadowing Jonathan as he gave guided tours through different collections at the museum.

By the end of the week, I led private tours by myself. If anything, I have to scale back what I talk about because there's just so much history regarding the museum, as well as the exhibits currently on display. I love art so much, I just want to open people's eyes to the amazing works housed right here in this city. Chicago's Institute of Art is one of the finest art museums in the world. It's on par with The Louvre and Smithsonian.

Seriously, how remarkable is that?

Jonathan joins me as my last group of the day splinters apart. There are a few people who linger with additional questions which I am all too eager to answer.

"You're a natural at this," he comments, nodding toward a group of three college aged guys who continue to straggle. "Although this group seemed more interested in you than what you were talking about."

With a slight heat suffusing my cheeks, I roll my eyes. "Please."

Not that I'll admit it to him, but I noticed it, too. They were cute enough. In a young, unpolished way.

Instead of commenting, I merely smile before deftly changing the topic. "You know what's funny? I really hate public speaking."

Jonathan folds his arms across his chest. "You would never know it. You're confident and poised in front of your groups."

I grin at the compliment. "Thank you. I think it's only because once I start looking at the art, I can find so much to talk about." I shrug. "And these people are a captive audience."

"Well, you're doing a fantastic job, keep it up. I know Marilyn is impressed, and that's no easy feat." He gives me a wry look before muttering, "Trust me on that." With the next breath, he asks, "So, got any big plans after work? Maybe with a boyfriend you haven't mentioned?" He wiggles his brows. We've managed to keep all our conversations professional so far, without delving into our private lives.

Or maybe I should say that *I* haven't delved into *my* personal life. I'm trying to keep everything superficial right now. But I'm beginning to realize that keeping things casual around Jonathan is difficult. He asks a lot of questions.

My guess is that Jonathan is somewhere in his mid-thirties. We bonded over our shared appreciation of art right from the start. I think he loves this place as much as I do. He and his partner enjoy exploring all of Chicago's museums. One of the perks to volunteering is that you receive free admission to the other museums in the area, as well as Shedd Aquarium.

"I already told you that I don't have a boyfriend." For some reason, Jonathan thinks I'm lying. "I have some homework to finish up tonight. That's about it." He's determined to sniff out any dirt I might have.

He rolls his large, hazel eyes. "Sounds incredibly dull. I'm starting to suspect that you don't have much of a social life. We need to change that."

I laugh and shrug. "I would have to say that your assessment of the situation is correct. There hasn't been time for fun since school started." Once I have a handle on the amount of homework I've been receiving, I'll be able to go out a little more. Chloe has called several times asking if I want to meet up at Covet, but I've had to decline.

"Are you sure there's no hot man on the backburner somewhere? You're way too cute to be single."

"Nope, none." The last thing I need right now is entanglements. I have more than enough on my plate with school and volunteering.

He strokes his fingers against his stubble-covered chin, pretending to contemplate me. I hope he's pretending. I don't want a well-intentioned set-up. The thought of one makes me shudder.

"You know," he drawls slowly, "Jamie has a younger brother who works at the Chicago Stock Exchange. He kind of has a stick up his ass, but you seem exactly his type."

I'm not sure how to respond to that.

Ummm, thank you?

His words make me laugh. "A stick up his ass is his biggest selling point?" I shake my head. "Sorry, I'll be taking a hard pass on that one." I can't help but ask, "Exactly how is that my type?"

Jonathon grins. "Well, he's really hot. Does that help at all?"

I let the idea roll around in my head for a moment. "It might," I tease. Although I don't think so. If I want a man, I'll find one on my own.

He makes a *don't worry* gesture by flicking a hand at me. "I'll text you a picture. You'll change your mind. The man is obsessed with working out."

I groan and stare up at the gorgeous glass ceiling that allows light to pour inside the corridor we're standing in. "I'll find my own men, thank you very much."

He snorts, which is hilarious. "Exactly who are these men you speak of? I haven't seen or heard anything that could be misconstrued as juicy or interesting regarding the male species. You're like a little nun."

"We barely know each other. I could be totally wild and crazy." Running my hand along my body, I say, "Maybe this is all a big charade."

He arches a brow. "Please. I had you pegged from the moment you walked through the door in your knee-length skirt and sensible flats." He waits a beat. "And you've *yet* to prove me wrong."

Sensible flats? "These aren't flats."

Looking unimpressed, he glances down at my footwear. "They might as well be."

By the way we banter back and forth, you'd assume that we've known each other for years instead of weeks. There's something about Jonathan. He's easy to get along with, and it kind of feels like we're kindred spirits. I think he recognizes it as well because right from the start, he took me under his wing.

"So, what type of guy do you usually go for?"

When I remain silent, he pretends to whine. "How can I find you the perfect man when you won't help?"

"Tall. Dark. Handsome." As soon as those these descriptive words roll off my tongue, I almost cringe, knowing exactly who I just described. I'm tempted add *dangerous. Sexy. Incredibly good with his hands. Wide palms...*

I really need to stop thinking about Matteo.

And that unfortunate limo ride back to Lexington Place.

"Hmmm... kind of like him?"

Jonathan jerks his head toward a man standing across the gallery. Following his stare, everything inside me stills as my eyes immediately collide with Matteo's. He returns my gaze with a dark, brooding one of his own.

I gulp, my throat having gone bone dry. All I can do is stand rooted in place as our eyes continue to hold. People wander across our line of vision, but our stare never falters.

"Don't tell Jamie that I'm drooling right now." He sighs. "I'm pretty sure he would be, too. I just love dark, swarthy men. He looks... *Mediterranean.*"

"Italian."

Jonathan manages to rip his eyes away from Matteo only to pin me with an incredulous stare. *"You know him?"*

Heart pounding, I shake my head. "Not really. He lives in my building."

His expression turns speculative, and I know I'm in trouble. "Hmmm, I think you've been holding out on me."

"He's a neighbor," I say firmly, as if that will make it true, "nothing more."

"That's a shame. Please, please, please, tell me he's not married."

"He's not married," I mutter. Sucking in a breath, I repeat Matteo's own words, hoping they'll feel like a glass of cold water in my face. My libido needs immediate dousing. "He doesn't date, if you catch my drift."

"Oh, I catch it, all right. And to that, I say *who the hell cares?*"

I've yet to pull my eyes from Matteo. I don't think I can. When he starts moving toward me through the crowd, nerves gather in the pit of my belly.

"I should give you two some privacy," Jonathan murmurs out of the side of his mouth, "but I'm not going to."

"Don't you dare leave me," I whisper harshly under my breath. "I will literally kill you."

He chuckles gleefully. "Trust me, I wouldn't miss this for the world."

I don't want an audience to whatever is about to unfold, but I can't be alone with Matteo.

"God, the closer he gets, the hotter he gets! I want to rub my eyes just to make sure he's real." Jonathan mutters those words just seconds before Matteo joins us.

"Grace."

He looks gorgeous in an expensive suit that fits his body as if it had been tailored specifically for him. Which probably isn't too far from the truth.

When I stand there staring, Jonathan jabs me in the ribs with his elbow.

"Hello!" Feeling awkward, I clear my throat before introducing my new friend and colleague. "Matteo, this is Jonathan. He's a volunteer at the Institute as well."

Jonathan straightens to his full height, which is still a good five inches shorter than Matteo and thrusts out his hand. "Nice to meet you. I've heard absolutely nothing about you."

"Jonathan!"

I really am going to murder him. This is already an uncomfortable situation, he's only making it worse.

Matteo's lips lift as his eyes land on mine. "Is that so? Nothing at all, hmm? Well, that is strange. Grace and I have been spending quite a bit of time together." His voice is smooth and dark, like the finest chocolate.

I may have to murder him as well.

Double homicide.

Jonathan's eyes grow wide as saucers and bounce like a ping pong ball between us.

Before I can say anything, Matteo continues silkily, his accent barely perceptible. "We were running together by the lakefront just last week." He arches a brow. "Isn't that so?"

Everything in me that had become whipcord tight releases. "Yes," I breathe with a sigh of relief, "you're right. We did run together a few mornings."

He smiles, and I know that he's not thinking about the time we spent outdoors. By the hungry look in his eyes, my guess is that he's conjuring up images of us in the limo. I swear to God that I'll kill him without a second thought if he alludes to it.

Jonathan continues to eye us curiously as if trying to decipher what's really going on. Good luck to him, because not even I know. Since Matteo has been MIA this week, I'd thought it was nothing at all.

"I guess I won't try to hook you up with Jamie's brother, after all," he mutters to no one in particular.

Matteo's dark espresso-colored eyes instantly shift to Jonathan's. "I think not."

Mine widen at his audacity. "Who I see is none of-"

Not allowing me to finish the sentence, he turns back to Jonathan. "Would you mind if I speak to Grace in private?"

The words may be posed like a question, but they're not. And Jonathan is smart enough to realize it. I asked him not to leave me alone with Matteo, but I can tell that he's moments away from fleeing.

His eyes shift to my wide ones as if already apologizing for abandoning me. I try giving him a subliminal message. One that goes unreceived. Or he just chooses to ignore it. "Of course. No problem."

"Would you happen to know when Grace is finished for the day?"

Jonathan's gaze flickers to mine for a moment. I'm pretty sure smoke is pouring out of my ears. Glancing at his wristwatch, he throws me to the wolves. "Um... right now. She's officially off the clock."

Matteo's lips slide up at the corners, rendering him even more striking. It's not a full-blown smile, but for all intents and purposes, Jonathan is blown away by it. "Thank you."

Just like that, my friend abandons me like a rat fleeing a sinking ship. Irritated, I turn my wrath upon Matteo. It's a relief to feel anger pumping through my blood. It's much safer than the attraction that liquefies all my brain cells until I'm reduced to nothing more than a mass of needy, quivering flesh.

"I was hoping to take you out for dinner."

I'm so tempted to screech and stomp my foot, but this place is like a church to me. And I would never behave that way in a place of worship. I do, however, grind my molars until I have control over my temper.

"I'm sorry, that doesn't work for me."

He lifts an elegant brow. "No?"

"Nope."

As he steps closer, his delicious scent wraps around me, cocooning me in sensory overload. "I thought you would be a bit more amenable to spending time together after what happened in the limo."

I grind my teeth again. "What are you doing here?"

His eyes never leave mine. I feel as if I'm being impaled by them, as if there's nowhere for me to hide. "Admiring the art," he responds softly. "There is so much beauty here. Don't you think?"

I'm weakening.

Starting to waver.

I feel it happening as we speak.

His proximity is my kryptonite.

"How did you know I was here?"

He closes the little bit of distance left between us. I become lost in the vastness of his dark eyes. They're mesmerizing. Powerfully seductive. "I make it a habit to learn about the things that interest me."

I'm not quite sure how to take that. And it certainly doesn't help that something inside me-a part I'd rather not acknowledge-feels thrilled by that innocuous statement.

"I really shouldn't," I mutter. The words are more for me than him. "I don't make good decisions when I'm around you."

He grins. It's so devilish in nature that a bolt of lust arrows to my lady parts. "If it makes you feel better, I find no fault with your decision-making skills."

"It doesn't."

"Have dinner with me, Grace."

In a last-ditch attempt to derail what I now realize is inevitable, I throw his own words back in his face. "I thought you didn't date women." Shooting a quick glance around me, I whisper, "You just fuck them."

His eyes continue searing into mine. "By the end of the evening, you will beg me to fuck you."

Eyes narrowing, I gasp. "You're rather conceited, aren't you?"

He smiles smugly and extends an elbow toward me. "I have good reason to be, bella. Wouldn't you agree?"

CHAPTER FOURTEEN

Matteo ushers me through the glass doors of Osprey, one of Chicago's most exclusive restaurants. It normally takes six months to get a reservation. I'm a little stunned when we walk right in, and the maître de practically throws himself at Matteo, gushing about how delighted he is to see him. We're immediately escorted to a table right in the middle of the dining room.

Feeling conspicuous, I glance around from beneath my lashes. All eyes are trained on the man I'm sitting with. A few female ones size me up as well. I feel woefully underdressed. I'm in a white blouse and navy-blue dress pants and a pair of low heels. I'm on my feet all day, giving tours of the museum, so comfortable shoes are a must contrary to what Jonathan thinks. This is the kind of place where women are draped in elegant cocktail dresses, and men are decked out in expensive suits.

Matteo fits right in.

Me? Not so much.

I wish he'd told me where we were going so I could have stopped at home and changed. But if I had, I probably would have latched on to the first excuse I could find to bail. I'm sure he suspected that was a distinct possibility. Looking anywhere but at him, I realize I don't have a clue as to what I'm doing here.

We don't fit.

My fingers bite into the thick menu as my nerves flare. Blinking back to the moment, my eyes coast over the neatly scripted words.

Italian.

Without English translations.

A waiter stops by our table with a bottle of wine and fills our glasses. Needing liquid courage, I take a small sip as Matteo converses with the waiter in fluent Italian.

That shouldn't be so sexy since I have absolutely no idea what they're saying. But it is. Ridiculously so.

As the other man retreats, Matteo's dark gaze fixes on me.

"I took the liberty of ordering for us. I hope you don't mind."

I raise a brow.

"Have you ever tried *Bistecca alla Zorich*?"

I shake my head. I have no idea what he just said.

"It's a peppercorn filet mignon. I also ordered a pasta dish- *Capellini Fra Diavolo*. It's shrimp and arugula in a spicy red sauce." Eyes dropping to my lips, he murmurs, "Delicious."

A shaft of desire bolts through me, leaving ripples of desire in its wake. How does he do that? The man utters one word about something unrelated, and my mind immediately diverts to sex. It tumbles right back to what it felt like when his fingers glided over my skin, pumping deep inside me. I shift on the plush seat before taking another sip of wine, hoping it will alleviate the need curling in the pit of my belly.

Okay, okay... curling much lower than that.

The wine is amazing. It's one of the best I've ever tasted. Sitting here, dining with this man, I feel way out of my league.

Trying to tamp down my nerves, I run a finger over the rim of my wine glass. I hear myself ask, "How did you find me?"

In all honesty, I'm more interested in *why* he sought me out in the first place. But I'll save that question for later.

Sitting back, Matteo takes a taste of his wine. His eyes never deviate from mine. "It's amazing what you can discover when you dig deep enough."

That doesn't answer my question. But it does send a shiver of excitement skittering down my spine.

Before I can ask anything else, he says, "Tell me something I don't know about you."

Snorting, I quickly retort, "You don't know *anything* about me." Or does he? Is that the implication of his words? That he's looked into me?

His mouth tilts upwards. My belly plunges as if I'm sitting at the top of a roller coaster. "Don't I?"

Fighting to remain calm, I narrow my gaze. I have no idea what kind of game this man is intent on drawing me into. Worse, I don't know the rules. I'm at a disadvantage, and I know it. He must realize it as well. I'm nothing like the women he normally sees.

"I'll give you three truths and a lie. You have to figure out which one is the lie."

Looking intrigued, his face sharpens, his expression growing more predatory. "What do I get if I guess correctly?"

I bite my lower lip. Suddenly this game seems more dangerous than I intended. "What is it that you want?"

His dark eyes glimmer with hunger as he leans closer. "A kiss."

A relieved breath rushes from my lungs as I scoff. "A kiss? That's it?" I thought he would want something far more valuable. Far more inappropriate.

"Well, I never said where the kiss would be, now did I?"

I suppose not.

Feeling restless, I finger the thick, white linen napkin lying under the polished silverware. I pick it up and set it gently on my lap.

He cocks a dark brow in my direction, his face painted with impatience.

"I was born in Chicago."

He picks up his wine and swirls it around his glass. "Truth," he says in a bored tone.

The easy, effortless way the word slips from his tongue rattles me. I should have gone with something more challenging. Something he wouldn't be able to figure out. "Are you not going to wait to hear all of them before deciding which is the lie?"

"No."

Locking my jaw, I rack my brain. I want to throw him off. But I'm not sure how to do it without revealing too much of myself. It feels as though this man sees way too much. I don't like it.

"I'm an only child."

He's silent for a moment. "True."

My hand trembles as I pick up the wine glass and take another sip. Drinking too much would be a mistake. I can feel the red liquid rushing to my head.

"My parents live in Seattle," I say quietly. My heart aches under my breast. I didn't realize how painful the lie would feel slipping free from my lips.

His eyes meet mine and everyone else in the restaurant fades away. It's just the two of us. "False."

The way he says that one word nearly bursts the dam. The wine, so fruity and delicious only moments ago, turns to vinegar on my tongue.

When I remain quiet, he murmurs, "I believe you owe me one more truth."

Unwilling to continue this game, I shrug. "What's the point? You already guessed the lie."

"The point was to get to know you. I'm still working on that."

"I attend Northwestern University." I don't wait for him to say *truth*. I have a feeling he already knows. I pick up the glass to occupy my fingers, swirling the remaining liquid. My eyes drop as I continue watching the wine. "Did you find out anything you didn't already know?"

"No."

I'm curious as to where he got all this information. I doubt George would have told him anything, but who knows. I have an unsettling feeling that Matteo plays by his own set of rules. And that scares me. It would frighten anyone with half a brain.

Our food arrives, thankfully dispelling the ramped-up tension churning between us. It's delicious. We share the steak and the pasta dish which, feels too intimate for a first date.

Wait a minute… is that what this is?

A date?

No. This man doesn't date. He said so himself.

Which is precisely why I feel confused as to what's going on between us. I need to get through this dinner with my wits intact, not to mention my legs closed, and then do whatever is necessary to keep my distance from him. Matteo is not a man to be toyed with. None of my previous experiences have prepared me for someone like him. I won't fool myself into believing that I can tangle with a guy like him and then waltz away unscathed when we're finished. I'm not equipped to deal with that kind of heartache after recently enduring so much.

I'm just starting to get back on my feet and I don't need someone knocking them out from under me.

By the time dessert rolls around, I'm on my second glass of wine. No matter how much I consume, my nerves refuse to settle. They're practically vibrating. Skittering and careening beneath my over sensitized flesh. I wish I could look across the table and feel nothing, but that's impossible. Everything about this man affects me.

Everything.

His sultry, espresso-colored eyes that see right through me.

The thick sweep of his eyelashes, especially when he lowers his lids until they sit at half-mast.

Those full, gorgeous lips I find myself tempted to nip.

Those wide hands which only have to trail across my flesh to ignite a firestorm of lust within me.

By the time Matteo orders cannoli for dessert, I feel as if I might spontaneously combust. My panties are drenched, and we haven't done anything except eat dinner. There haven't been any innuendos or anything untoward. Whatever's happening in my body is completely my own doing.

Matteo has done nothing to stoke my desire and yet here I sit across from him in one of the poshest restaurants in Chicago, and I've never been more turned on in my life. It's crazy. The insides of my thighs rub together, sending more sparks of need shooting right to my clit.

When the cannoli is served, it's placed in the middle of the white-clothed table with two forks. Matteo slides it towards him, which is fine. I'm not very hungry.

For food anyway.

Using the side of his fork, he cuts into the decadent dessert and holds it out to me. I automatically lean toward him, closing the distance before wrapping my lips around the tines. His glittering eyes fall to my lips.

Savoring the Italian pastry, my eyes close as all the flavors meld together in my mouth. By the time I swallow and reopen my eyes, everything stills as I glimpse the lust filling his gaze.

His voice is nothing more than a growl. "Good?"

"Completely decadent," I whisper.

His hungry gaze drops to my mouth as he forks off another piece and holds out the utensil. This continues until the cannoli finally disappears. I try to remember if we shared it at all.

I don't think so.

Heat suffuses my cheeks. I didn't realize that I'd eaten the entire thing by myself.

"Did you have a bite?"

"No."

"Why not?"

I can't deny that this has been the best meal I've ever eaten. No wonder this place has a six-month wait for reservations.

"Because I only wanted a taste."

My brows furrow. "Did you get it?"

"Not yet."

I glance at the empty plate. "There's nothing left."

His look grows more heated. "I'll still have a taste."

My eyes widen. "Oh."

That's all I can say. My brain is empty.

"Are you ready to leave?"

"Yes."

A tidal wave of relief washes over me. I'm more than ready to head home. I need distance from this man. My legs wobble as I stand. Liquid heat gathers in my core. I'm painfully aware of the desire pooled there. I'm vibrating with the need to be touched.

With his hand searing into the small of my back, we make our way out the front door. His driver waits at the curb. Seeing us, he opens the back door of the limo. Matteo helps me inside first and climbs in after me. As we enter traffic and move through the city, I want to relax on the rich leather and close my eyes.

But I don't.

Doing so would be a mistake. It would be dangerous to let my guard down with this man. He's much too handsome. Much too masculine. Much too forceful. Much too used to getting his own way.

I may not know much about him, but I recognize these characteristics within him. They are a potent, intoxicating combination.

Turning my head, I meet his gaze. His dark eyes pierce mine. A jolt of electricity slides through me, igniting a spark of need. No matter how many times I'm around him, my reaction is always the same. Intense and powerful. It hasn't lessened the way I'd hoped it might.

"Did you enjoy dinner?"

"Yes. Everything was delicious."

"Good. I'll let the staff know."

The ever-so-slight accent makes his voice sound almost melodic. Soothing. Like warm honey flowing over my body. The effect he has on me is crazy.

"You enjoyed the cannoli?"

"Very much." I remember the rich, creamy taste and lick my lips. His eyes fall to my mouth. Need spikes between us as if it is a living, breathing entity.

"You still owe me a taste."

Before I can absorb the words, his hand slides to the back of my neck and tangles in my hair, pulling me toward him until his lips sweep across mine. The feel of his mouth coaxing mine open makes me whimper. His tongue slips inside to tangle with mine, stroking and playing. Taking me under. Other than his hand in my hair, he doesn't touch me anyplace else.

It's demoralizing how much I want his hands on me. My body is on fire. If he grazes me with a finger, I'll explode like a firework.

I've never been so responsive, so attuned to another human being's touch.

I never realized I could be like this.

Needy.

Reactive.

Explosive.

I don't know how long we stay locked together with our tongues dueling, tasting, and mating. All too soon, the limousine is pulling up in front of Lexington Place. Matteo is more cognizant than I am because he pulls away seconds before the driver opens the door. I feel dazed by what just happened. He, on the other hand, looks perfectly composed. Completely unaffected. Matteo slips out and offers me a hand. Once my fingers are ensconced within his, he doesn't let go.

At this point, I don't want him to.

"Good evening Ms. Castile, Mr. V."

George tips his hat to us. If he's surprised to see us walking in together, or Matteo holding my hand in such an intimate manner, it doesn't register on his face. George is a consummate professional, though. I could waltz through the lobby completely naked, singing at the top of my lungs, and he wouldn't bat an eye.

I wonder how many women George has seen Matteo usher through the lobby. Ten? Twenty? A hundred? Even more?

That thought is swiftly followed by the ugly realization that I've done precisely what I said I wouldn't do. All he did was lay his lips on me, and I was more than willing to do whatever he asked in response. Sure, it was just a kiss. But had he wanted more, I doubt I would have put a stop to it.

What the hell is wrong with me?

I have no self-control where this man is concerned.

Those thoughts are enough to extinguish the fire burning out of control inside me. Something painful twists in my chest.

A heavy silence falls over us as we ride up to the thirtieth floor. I'm lost in the chatter that grows in volume inside my head. What's going on between us? Is this anything more than him trying to hustle me into bed?

Disembarking from the elevator, we head down the lavish marble-tiled hallway. I'm keenly aware of him at my side. Every move he makes echoes and resonates deep within my being. Matteo has an overpoweringly masculine presence that is impossible to ignore. I never thought I'd find myself attracted to someone like him.

But I am.

Undeniably.

When we stop in front of my door, I finally lift my eyes to his. A shiver of pleasure slides through me as our gazes connect. "Thank you for dinner."

His hand comes up and strokes the side of my face. The urge to close my eyes as I turn into his warm palm floods through me. I manage to restrain myself. Barely. "You're welcome."

My breath gets clogged in my throat as his eyes continue drilling into mine. I know I should pull away before anything else happens, but I don't move a muscle.

Biting my lower lip, I wait for him to take what he wants. What I want, too. The moment continues to stretch and lengthen between us. My insides coil tightly in anticipation. I want to feel the slow slide of his mouth on mine again.

I need it.

Instead of kissing me, his hand falls away, back to his side before he steps away from me. His gaze is hooded. A spark of amusement dances in his eyes.

"Sweet dreams, bella."

Before I can blink, he's gone, disappearing down the corridor with long-legged strides. I stand there, staring in shock as confusion rushes through me.

Did he seriously just leave me standing here full of anticipation and need that he caused?

Yeah. That's *exactly* what he did.

The door to his condo opens and closes with a thud. The sound echoes through my brain like a gunshot. It wakes me from the sexual haze I'm trapped in. Spinning on my heel, I open my door before quietly shutting it. Not once did I hear laughter, but for some reason, the dark remnants of it reverberate throughout my head.

CHAPTER FIFTEEN

Lying in my bed, I toss and turn in an effort to get comfortable.

But it's impossible.

In the back of my mind, I know sleep won't claim me anytime soon. The cold shower I forced myself to take did nothing to extinguish the lust Matteo created inside me.

Thoughts of him have been rolling through my head for the past hour. I've never had a man crawl under my skin the way he's managed to. No one has ever made my insides burn to such a fever pitch.

Feeling frustrated, I throw off the light blanket and pace the wood floor. A low ache throbs in my core despite the frigid shower.

I need to do *something* or I won't find any relief tonight.

Was this his master plan?

To drive me insane with lust so that I come crawling to him?

That thought makes me grit my teeth.

Sure, I could use my own hand, but the idea holds very little appeal. The last thing I want to do is fantasize about him. It'll only make matters worse. Imagining what Matteo would feel like inside my body is much too dangerous.

There has to be a better way to diffuse the intensity building inside me.

I need to burn off this excess energy humming under my skin, and the only way I can do that is by going for a swim. The pool on the rooftop is heated, so it should feel refreshing and not too cold.

It's open twenty-four hours a day. I'm sure it will be deserted. I can't imagine anyone else will be there at this late hour. It's close to midnight. Unless there are other women in the building also fantasizing about Matteo. I almost snort at the thought. Perhaps we can start a club.

Or, better yet, a support group.

Going over to my dresser, I strip out of my underwear and tank, throwing on the first bathing suit my fingertips come in contact with. It's a little black string bikini. I bought it a few years ago when I was dating Eric. I don't wear it often because it always feels like my breasts are on the verge of busting out of the tiny triangles. But right now, I don't care. I need to immerse myself in the cool, calming water.

Grabbing a towel from the bathroom, I slip my feet into a pair of black flip-flops before heading out the door. It's late, and I'm on the top floor, so I'm not worried about running into other residents.

The short ride up to the rooftop is uneventful. Just as I assumed, the place is deserted. Chairs and tables are scattered around a rectangular pool with a small area for grilling off to one side. The other half is a lush garden oasis filled with small, ornately sculpted shrubs, a walking path, and tons of brightly blooming flowers.

It's all stunningly manicured.

Kicking off the sandals, I throw my towel onto a chaise lounger and walk toward the edge of the pool. Using my arms for balance, I dip a toe in the water, hoping it won't be too cold.

A low groan escapes me.

It's a tad cooler than bath water, but not by much.

Diving in, I'm immersed in warmth while gliding through the clear liquid. I'm about fifteen feet away from the other side of the pool when I finally surface. It's larger than I realized. Certainly not Olympic in size, but big enough to swim laps and get in a good workout. Ducking under, I do a few breast strokes before changing over to freestyle. Then I turn over, slicing my arms through the water as I begin backstroking. Gazing up at the velvety night sky, I feel the tension inside me wane.

The dull ache I seem to get every time I'm around Matteo dissipates.

This swim is precisely what I needed.

I'm glad I decided to come up here. Between running along the lake and swimming in this gorgeous retreat, who needs therapy?

A good forty minutes pass by before I make my way to the side of the pool. I don't think I'm ready to leave yet, though. I want to wrap up in my towel and sit under the starry night sky, enjoying the quietness of the city for a while.

A noise punctuates the air, drawing my attention to one of the loungers off to the side. My breath stalls in my lungs as my gaze collides with Matteo's.

He no longer wears the suit jacket he had on earlier, but the black pants and white shirt remain. His tie is gone, and the first two buttons of his dress shirt are unfastened. His long, muscular legs are spread out in front of him. His elbows rest casually on his knees. His eyes never relinquish mine. He picks up the towel I carelessly threw on the chaise before diving into the pool.

Unfolding it, he says huskily, "Out of the water, Grace."

Goosebumps break out across my flesh at the way he says my name.

He's not asking.

He's telling.

I know it's safer to hide out in the water, yet I lift myself out in one fluid movement. I wouldn't put it past him to wade in after me. With one leg, I kneel on the blue tile before straightening to my full height.

He doesn't say a word about my revealing suit. The only telltale sign that he's affected is the heat that sparks in his eyes as they roam over my body. Although the night air is cool, his gaze makes me feel flushed from head to toe.

Wordlessly, he holds out the towel. I tentatively reach for the terrycloth, hoping he'll hand it over.

He doesn't.

"Turn around."

The command shoots straight through me. In the blink of an eye, the forty minutes spent in the water evaporates, and I'm just as achy as when I was tossing and turning in bed while thinking about him.

He stands and moves behind me. The heat of his body radiates outward. I'm painfully aware of him. My body tenses as I await his touch. My breath hisses out as he gathers up the long strands of my hair in his hands and closes the thick towel around them before gently squeezing. He repeats the motion a few more times until my hair is no longer dripping.

It's so relaxing that my eyelids drift shut as I enjoy the sensation of being taken care of. He moves down to my shoulders and arms, thoroughly rubbing each section of wet flesh until it's dry. He lowers the towel to the center of my back and rubs in soothing circles. I want to moan at the feel of his hands on my body but don't. My lips stay firmly pressed together.

He makes his way to my barely covered cheeks, where he spends a lot of time massaging the firm globes with the towel. I'm so relaxed that I could melt into the ground.

"Turn."

A shiver courses through me. His voice sounds rough as sandpaper. Barely harnessed power vibrates from his chest.

He strokes the towel over and around my breasts, lifting them so that not a drop of moisture remains. As he continues drying my chest, my nipples stiffen into peaks that beg for more attention. His eyes stay fastened to them. I see desire and longing swimming in their heavy-lidded depths.

When I can't stand another moment of his torture, he drops his hands to my ribs and exposed belly. He takes his time sweeping the fabric around my waist and hips before dipping lower. He sits back down on the lounger.

"Spread your legs."

As soon as I part them, he resumes patting me dry. His hand goes right to my core, pressing the cottony material against my clit before rubbing in a slow, circular motion with the perfect amount of pressure to make me feel as though I might explode at any given moment. I try to stifle it, but the deep, guttural sound still manages to find its way into the night air.

Watching his expression, I try to get a read on his thoughts, but can't. His feelings are shielded by shuttered eyes.

He smooths over my inner thighs with care before skimming down my calves. Sweeping back up again, his hand arrows to my aching lower lips.

His hungry eyes flick to mine. "You still owe me a kiss."

"You got your kiss in the limo," I remind him breathlessly.

His gaze turns flinty, his lips bowing into a wicked grin. He reaches out and fingers the strings of my bikini bottoms. Within a heartbeat, the ties are plucked, and the tiny black bottoms float to the ground.

"It wasn't those lips I wanted to kiss."

My belly hollows out.

His eyes dart to my freshly waxed pussy. His face is perfectly level with my lower lips. I want to feel his mouth against me more than anything.

He reaches over and slowly strokes one thick finger over my slit.

Another low moan of desire slides from my mouth. I couldn't stop it if I tried.

Matteo leans forward and traces the same path his finger traveled seconds ago with his tongue. I want to die. Or maybe I want to sink to the ground and spread my thighs so I can feel the velvety flatness of his tongue stroking over me. Darting inside.

He grazes the top of my slit rather than probe deeper with his tongue. Of their own volition, my fingers thread through his inky black hair as he continues laying butterfly-like kisses against me. I want him to bury his face between my legs and ravage me instead of giving me chaste kisses. It's pure torment, and he knows it.

"Please," I whine. "I need more."

But he doesn't give it to me.

He instead pulls away, leaving me to shake and gasp before reaching down and picking up my bottoms. He holds the material against my trembling hips, tying both sides together so that I'm once again covered.

It feels like my entire body is being scorched by flames.

Gaining his feet, he wraps the towel around my shoulders and picks me up, cradling me in his arms.

"Are you ready?"

Ready to leave?

Ready to be fucked?

I have no idea what he's asking. But the answer to both questions is the same.

"Yes." My throat is dry and raspy. My body feverish. I've never wanted a man more than I want this one.

CHAPTER SIXTEEN

When we reach my door, he doesn't release me. I'm so agitated. The feel of those wide hands holding me against his muscular body, singes my flesh. I'm barely coherent at this point. All I know is that I need to feel this man buried deep inside me. I have no idea what's happening between us, if this is nothing more than a one-night stand. Maybe we're just finishing what was started in the limo a week and a half ago.

I don't know.

And furthermore, I don't care.

This is what he does to me.

I don't think rationally when I'm anywhere near him. And when he touches me, I'm lost.

All the reasons this shouldn't happen flee from my mind.

After I open the door, he strolls into my condo with me cradled in his arms. He moves stealthily through the front entryway, into the living room, to where the wide sweeping windows showcase the city below.

As soon as my bare feet hit the hardwood, his fingers pull at the ties of my suit until both the top and bottom fall to the floor and I'm standing naked in front of him. My natural impulse has always been to shield myself or quickly duck under the covers. Like any woman, I have flaws and body image issues. I like my breasts and the curve of my ass, especially now that I've gotten back into running. But my legs are short, not long and lean the way I wish. And my waist isn't as whittled as it once was.

I resist the urge to hide. Instead, I draw in a deep breath to calm everything racing around inside me. I'm backlit by the lights blazing from downtown. Matteo's eyes roam over every part of me just as they did out by the pool. The condo is plunged in darkness, but I'm able to see the appreciative glow in his eyes.

"You are stunning, bella. Completely stunning."

Needing to make the first move, I walk toward him, unfastening each shirt button one at a time. Excitement I've never experienced before rises up within me. It's crazy just how much I want this. How much I'm savoring the process of stripping Matteo bare.

Once I've removed the white shirt, I start on the trousers. I unbuckle his belt, pop the button, and slowly lower the zipper. The soft sound sends shivers racing down my spine. The gabardine loosens, settling around his narrow hips before I push it down his thighs.

Matteo steps out of the pants, left in an impressively tented pair of black boxer briefs. I skim my palm over his long, hot length. He's more than a handful. My mouth waters because I desperately want to see all of him.

My fingers hook into the elastic band and push them down. His thick erection springs free. I shove the boxers down and wrap my hand around him, stroking his shaft from root to tip.

"Mmmm, that feels so good," he murmurs.

Yes, it does.

Standing on my tiptoe, I brush my lips against his. He opens, and I slip my tongue inside his mouth. I may have been the one to start this, but he quickly takes control. In an instant, the kiss turns more demanding.

He's the one in charge, and I love it.

"Do you want to be fucked?"

"Yes." I breathe the word out on a lusty sigh.

"Hard? You want me to fuck you hard so that you can no longer think?"

"Yes," I whimper at the stark image he paints, "that's exactly what I want."

"Good. Because I need to fuck you nice and hard until all you can think about is my cock pummeling your pussy."

Wanting more contact, I try to kiss him again. He evades me and captures my hands, backing me up until I'm pinned against the window. I gasp at the feeling of the cool glass against my heated skin, and the erection pressing into my belly. I'm so drenched that wetness smudges my inner thighs.

I'm so ready for him.

I've never felt this kind of hunger before. I'm so close to splintering apart that one deep stroke will push me over the edge.

Matteo fists the base of his cock and brings the head to my opening. He caresses the tip against my aching pussy lips but doesn't dip it inside me. He simply continues to stroke the hard length against my quivering flesh.

"So very wet. Your pussy is crying for me, isn't it?"

"Yes," I groan. I feel flooded with wetness.

Taking his time, he continues rubbing his cock against me with measured strokes, giving me just enough to tease. When I can't stand a moment more, he positions himself at my entrance. I want to impale myself on his thick shaft and be done with it already. I crave the satisfaction I'll find once he's buried in me. But he doesn't slide in any further. My insides stretch to accommodate his girth, the muscles contracting, wrapping around him, trying to draw him deeper.

He groans.

Flexing his hips with tiny movements, he thrusts. With each quick piston-like action, I tighten my muscles around him until his jaw clenches. Until sweat breaks out across his dark brow. Until his entire body is whipcord tight. Just when I think he'll bury his cock inside me and give us what we both want, he pulls out.

"What-"

I don't get another word out before he twists me around so that my naked front is forced against the window overlooking the city. Turning my head, I lay my flushed cheek against the glass and close my eyes. The heat of his body disappears, and I shiver. I hear the ripping of a package, and then he's back in place. His body completely covers mine from behind. Heat once again floods through me.

"Open your legs."

I don't need to be told twice.

My back arches as I widen my stance. He spreads my cheeks and thrusts inside me with one smooth movement, driving his thick cock all the way home.

A scream tears from my mouth at the fullness now seated deep inside me.

I can't believe how perfect this man feels. He gives me a moment to adjust, to breathe, before flexing his hips. His pelvis grinds against my ass. He slips almost all the way out before quickly propelling back inside again. Each time he slides home, I moan in ecstasy.

My eyes open as he continues fucking me against the window. There's something erotic about being sandwiched between cool glass and his warm body. My breasts are smashed against the pane, my nipples flattened. It feels exquisite. The animalistic way he continues pounding into my hot sheath sends me climbing until there's nowhere left to go but down.

"Fuck, bella, fuck!"

Exactly.

The feel of him pummeling me is sheer poetry in motion.

Utter bliss.

It doesn't take long for an orgasm to streak through me. Cries of pleasure fall from my lips. He grunts, quickly following me, muttering words in Italian that I don't understand, but love hearing nevertheless.

Once I've been wrung completely dry, my entire body goes limp as a noodle. I'm exhausted. But completely sated.

What just took place between us feels addictive.

The sex I've had in the past has been *nothing* like this.

Matteo pulls out and gathers me in his arms before I sink to the floor. He carries me to my bedroom, heading straight to the bed I'd left almost two hours ago in search of relief.

Pulling back the covers, he gently sets me down before slipping in beside me.

A contented smile stretches across my lips. "You're staying?"

Surprise laces my weary voice. I figured he would gather up his strewn-about clothing and get the hell out of Dodge.

"For a little bit." His mouth curves into a devilish grin. "I'm not finished with you yet."

One thought floats through my head as I curl up next to him.

Thank God.

CHAPTER SEVENTEEN

I open the door as Chloe raps her knuckles against it. Her eyes skim down me and fill with concern.

"You not feeling well?"

Her question throws me off. "I feel great." My brows pinch together in confusion. "Why?"

Truth be told, I feel *marvelous*.

I think Matteo pounded the last six months of stress right out of my now limp-as-a-noodle body. Maybe even a year. I feel lighter and brighter than I have in a long time.

She gives me another hard look and says, "Because it's one o'clock on a beautiful Saturday afternoon, and you're sitting around wearing sweat-pants and a T-shirt. That's why."

I glance down at my outfit before correcting her. "Actually, they're yoga pants. Completely acceptable attire."

One perfectly manicured brow gets cocked. "That doesn't make it any better."

I shrug. "It's a lazy weekend."

"Hmmm. I don't think so."

"Excuse me?"

Her eyes narrow and fill with suspicion. "No. It's more than that.

You look...." She trails off as she searches for a word, "*different*."

"Excuse me?" A gurgle of surprised laughter escapes. "What are you talking about?"

"I think," she declares triumphantly, "that you got laid last night. Which means that you've been holding out on me."

My mouth tumbles open.

How can she tell? Is it written across my face?

When I say nothing, she continues. "Yeah, you're definitely glowing! And you seem a whole hell of a lot looser than before. Like someone gave you a much-needed tune-up. Maybe a few of them."

I wave a hand dismissively. I don't want to discuss Matteo. There's nothing more to say other than, *Yes, we had sex last night. And it was incredible.* "You're crazy."

"That goes without saying," she replies easily.

I lead her through the living room and head out to the sun-filled terrace.

"So, am I right? Did you get lucky last night?" Before I can formulate an answer, she says, "I didn't even know you went out. Where'd you go and why wasn't I invited?"

As we sit down across from one another, she gives me another searching look. One that tells me she won't be dropping the subject easily. Chloe can be as tenacious as a terrier when she sinks her teeth into something juicy.

Her hand flies to her mouth. "Don't tell me that Sasha finally wore you down."

I burst out laughing. "No, it wasn't Sasha!"

"But it was, in fact, *someone*." She looks moments away from leaping over the table. "Who? I want a name!"

"No one you know," I admit begrudgingly. What made me think that I could hide this from her?

She considers me thoughtfully. "Are you sure about that?"

"Positive." There's no way Chloe knows Matteo. Why would she?

"Come on, put me out of my misery and tell me who it was."

For my own sanity, I need to downplay the situation. Matteo and I aren't together. Last night changes nothing between us. We screwed each other's brains out. That's it. End of story. If he holds true to his normal pattern, he'll disappear for a while before turning up in a week or so. My heart twists at that harsh slap of reality, and I push the pang of sadness aside, ignoring it.

"It was a one-time thing. There's no point in discussing a guy who isn't in the picture. But you're right, okay? I did spend the night with someone."

Chloe settles back in her chair with a pleased expression. "Good for you, girl. I'm glad to hear it. Sounds like Little Miss Grace finally got her groove back. Lord knows you were wound tighter than an eight-day clock." Her eyes skim over me again. "You seem way more mellow."

As I pick up my glass of ice water and take a sip, she asks, "So it wasn't that hot-ass uncle of yours?"

I fight not to spray the water from my mouth like a fountain. Instead, it goes down the wrong pipe, and I end up coughing and sputtering. Chloe grins as if she's enjoying the entertainment I'm providing.

I barely force out the words without pounding on my chest and sucking in a few deep breaths. "Of course it wasn't Dominic!" My eyes water as I continue coughing.

Regarding me with a cagy look, she shrugs. "Maybe you should give it some thought. You two would look awfully cute together."

I shake my head in exasperation. "Oh my God, I think you've completely lost your mind!"

"What's wrong with what I just said? I've crushed on that man for the better part of my life. If he wanted to give it a whirl, I'd be on board with the idea. Older men are *definitely* hot. More than anything, they appreciate a young, nubile body. Trust me on this." She gives me a sassy wink which makes me wonder what she's been up to these last two years.

Sasha?

Older dudes?

What's next?

Never mind... I don't want to know.

She interrupts my thoughts with another comment. "He would treat you like a total princess."

It feels like my eyes are going to pop right out of my skull. Yes, we used to get all ooey-gooey thinking about Dominic when we were fourteen years old. But as adults? Come on... I can't even imagine it. Chloe's banter may sound casual, but she's not joking around.

"You would really go out with him?"

She doesn't bat an eyelash. "In a heartbeat." Her green gaze sears mine. "You wouldn't?"

"I don't know," I reply slowly. "I've never thought about him like that. Dominic is my godfather." When I was younger, I used to call him Uncle Dominic because it was appropriate. When I left for college, he told me that the uncle part made him feel old and asked me to stop using it. It was weird at first and took some getting used to.

"I think about him like that *all* the time."

Sometimes I think Chloe just likes to be provocative, and stir up trouble.

"Well, I don't," I say.

I haven't.

Not really.

Chloe doesn't look convinced. "Hmmm. Okay." Shrugging, she adds, "I could have sworn that I sensed some vibes between the two of you at the party last month."

I shake my head. "No. It's never been like that between us. I'm his godchild." As I say the words, I remember the way he pressed a kiss to my lips the last time he was over for a visit. My belly drops as the incident plays out in my head. I'm pretty sure he did that to comfort me because I'd been upset about selling the house. It was nothing more than that. Easily dismissible.

Mentioning it to Chloe will only spur on the crazy notions she has in her head. That's the last thing I want to do.

"I'm sure he's involved with someone. Or, knowing him, a whole bunch of someones." Smiling, she sips her drink and muses, "Remember how he was with a different woman every time we saw him when we were younger? We would hang out on the balcony overlooking the family room and moon over how lucky she was to be with him."

I smile thinking about all the times we spied on him. We spent a lot of time crouched on the catwalk, sighing our fourteen-year-old hearts out. We were so silly. But it was fun. Just harmless little crushes on both our parts.

"That was a long time ago," I remind her.

"Yes, it was."

So much has changed.

Too much.

It's still difficult to grasp just how different my life is now.

"Not to change the subject from your yummy uncle-"

I breathe a heavy sigh of relief.

"-but a few of us are thinking about taking a trip to the Virgin Islands in the spring and maybe renting a kickass house on St. Thomas. You interested?"

The tension filling my shoulders from talking about Dominic fades. "Yeah, that sounds amazing! But it would have to be during my spring break. Otherwise I can't go."

"That's why I'm bringing it up now. I really want you to come with us. Let me know what week works best, and we'll see if we can coordinate everyone's schedule."

I'll have to discuss it with Dominic.

I know we talked about waiting until I'm settled, but I want more control over my finances. I don't want to go to him every time something like this comes up. I'm twenty-three years old. More than old enough to be responsible and make good decisions.

Reaching across the table, I grab Chloe's hand and squeeze it. "Thank you for thinking of me."

Her eyes soften. "Hey, no matter what happened, you're still my best friend. As far as I'm concerned, you were *always* my best friend." Alluding to our past, she says, "Look, I knew you were going through a shit time. I'm sorry for not sticking by your side regardless. I should have kept calling and texting." She shrugs. "I didn't know how to help or make anything better."

Her words strike a chord in me. We may not have been communicating, but deep down I knew that if I reached out, if I had needed her, Chloe would have dropped everything to be there for me. And vice versa. "I shouldn't have pushed you away. I didn't know how to deal with all the grief and depression I was going through."

"I'm so sorry, sweetie."

"I know you did what you could. We were both in school, just trying to keep our heads above water. It wasn't like we were at the same college or even a few hours away from one another."

"No," she agrees somberly, "we were practically across the country."

Inhaling deeply, I remind her, "It's all good. We got through it."

Her lips quirk. "I'm glad you're back in Chicago. And that we can spend as much time together as we want."

"Me, too."

Unclasping her fingers, I sit back as another layer of the past falls away.

"Don't think for a minute that we're done talking about this mystery man of yours."

I roll my eyes.

She grins in response. "Or Dominic."

Please. I know Chloe way better than that.

She's merely warming to both subjects.

CHAPTER EIGHTEEN

Sunglasses cover my eyes as the wind whips against my cheeks. Tilting my face toward the sun, I enjoy the heat as it warms my skin. It's a lazy Sunday afternoon. Dominic sent his car for me three hours ago, and we've been out on his sailboat ever since. On a beautiful September afternoon, when the sun is high and bright, and there's nary a cloud in the sky, there's no better place to be than floating on Lake Michigan.

Dominic bought the house fifteen years ago, so this place has always felt like home. There are many happy, cherished memories here. Childhood memories. Memories of my parents. Of the four of us together. Mom and Dad may be gone, but I believe they'd be happy about how much time Dominic and I spend together. That we're still a family and tighter now than we were before.

That thought brings me a lot of comfort. Everything I do is with my parents in mind. I still want them to be proud of me.

Eyes settling on Dominic, I watch as he stands at the controls from my sprawled-out position on the padded bench up front. Aviators cover his bright blue eyes. His blond hair is shot through with silver. The way it blends makes him look even more handsome.

Chloe's words from yesterday ring unwantedly through my head.

"You about ready to head in?"

I shrug. "Sure." Honestly, I could stay out here all day. I enjoy spending time on the water. Living so close to the ocean was one of the things I loved best about Seattle. The Pacific Coast, especially in that area, is gorgeous.

Wooded, rocky, and wild.

Breathtaking and powerful.

"I thought we could have an early dinner out on the patio. Maria is preparing fresh salmon. I know it's one of your favorites."

"Mmmm, that sounds delicious." A home-cooked dinner with restaurant quality cuisine sounds heavenly right now. My mouth is already watering in anticipation.

I enjoy cooking, but don't have much skill in the culinary department yet. Living in the dorms didn't afford many opportunities. I'm learning, though. I've tuned into a few cooking shows but it's hard to find the time to experiment with recipes. With school and volunteering at the museum keeping me busy, I live on things like macaroni and cheese or frozen pizzas. Sometimes Maria sends leftovers home with me. I'm hoping that once everything slows down, I can try cooking a few meals that my mom used to make.

We stay out on the water to enjoy the sunshine for another thirty minutes, before heading back to shore. The marina where Dominic rents a slip is about ten minutes from his house. As we make our way through the parking lot, he surprises me by tossing his car keys in my direction.

When I stare at him in question, he says with an easy grin, "I thought that maybe you'd like to drive home."

My jaw drops. "Are you kidding?"

He laughs at the look of disbelief on my face. A few years ago, Dominic bought a Ferrari. It's a gorgeous, sleek machine. I've drooled over it many times. It's red with a black leather interior. I've begged to take it out for a spin. The answer has always been a resounding *no*.

I couldn't be more stunned that he's now giving me the green light. This car cost him a small fortune. Even though my parents had money, they never drove anything extravagant. They were much too practical for that. My mom drove a Subaru Outback, and my dad had a Buick Enclave.

I clutch the keys tightly. "Are you serious?"

He shrugs as if it's no big deal. "Sure, why not?"

My breath stalls as I stare at the metal in my hand. Voice dropping to a whisper, I ask, "What if I crash?" I think he'd strangle me if something happened to his baby. Unwilling to contemplate the idea, I thrust the keys back out for him. "Maybe another time."

Wrapping an arm around my waist, he holds me close as we continue walking towards the Ferrari. "It'll be fine. I trust you, Gracie."

I gnaw my bottom lip in silent contemplation. I've always wanted to take his car for a spin, and after three years, he's letting me do it. I should be jumping up and down with unbridled excitement. Instead, I continue to hedge. "Are you sure?"

Pulling me along, he chuckles. "Positive. Now, come on. Let's go. I really thought you would be more excited about this."

Yeah... me too.

Now I'm an anxious ball of nerves.

He opens the door for me, and I climb inside. Inserting the key into the ignition, I turn it. The car purrs to life. Still nervous, I wrap my fingers around the steering wheel, throwing a glance at Dominic, who is now seated next to me.

"You still want me to do this?"

He's wearing his aviators, and I can feel him roll his eyes at me. "Drive. You know you want to. You've been begging me for years," he reminds. "So just do it."

He's right. I *have* been dying to get behind the wheel. "Okay," I sing song, "You had a chance to put an end to this madness."

He chuckles. "Enough talk, put the pedal to the metal."

I step on the gas, revving the engine a few times while giving him a bit of side-eye, daring him to change his mind. He sits beside me with a bored expression.

"How about you stop being a cheeky bastard and we actually get out of this parking lot?"

Nerves melting away, I laugh and hit the clutch, shifting into first and stepping on the gas. Then, smooth as can be, we're pulling out of the marina and onto the road. Since both of my parents' cars were automatic, Dominic taught me how to drive stick when I was seventeen years old. Normally I prefer automatic since it's easier. But when you have a sports car like this, stick makes driving it more fun.

We cruise along at about forty-five miles per hour. I'd love to take this out to the country and open it up. Hit a hundred and twenty miles per hour on an open stretch of empty road. In a car like this, it feels like a necessity.

Sooner than I'd like, I steer into Dominic's circular driveway. By the time I turn off the engine, I'm grinning from ear to ear. That was so much fun! I hope he realizes that he just opened a huge can of worms by finally allowing me to get behind the wheel. Once will never be enough now that I've had a taste.

Removing his sunglasses, he smiles knowingly. "Pretty amazing, isn't it?"

"So amazing," I agree in a rush.

"And my car made it home in one piece. See? It's a win-win for everyone."

"Guess that means you'll let me drive it more often." I wiggle my brows. "Maybe even take it back to the condo."

He laughs as we exit the car. "Let's not talk crazy, okay?"

Slipping his arm around me again, we head toward the house. Right now, everything feels right. Light and happy. I'm content with how my life is unfolding. I love spending time with Dominic. It's nice being with someone who knows me so well. Someone I have a history with. Someone I trust.

I never have to explain myself because he already knows what I'm thinking or feeling. He gets it. He gets *me*.

Making our way inside the two-story, front entryway, I head for the curving staircase. I feel windswept from being out on the boat for the past couple of hours. My hair must look like a rat's nest.

"I'm going to shower and change before dinner."

"Take your time, sweetheart. Everything will be ready and waiting when you're finished."

One look at the enormous soaking tub in the bathroom, and I quickly change my mind, deciding on a bath instead. Once it's filled, I settle inside. There are a ton of bubbles. My eyes drift shut as I enjoy the warmth of the soothing water. I barely lift my eyelids when there's a knock on the bathroom door.

"Are you decent?"

I'm submerged up to my neck in hot, sudsy water. "Yup."

Dominic comes in bearing a glass of white wine. "I thought you might want a drink after your shower, but this is perfect. You can enjoy it in the bath."

I reach for the stem and settle into the water again. A contented smile tugs lazily at the corners of my lips. Today has been great. I love being at Dominic's house. It feels like home. Sometimes with his work schedule and everything I have going on lately, it can be challenging to find the time to get together.

"Thank you."

"No problem. Dinner will be ready in about forty-five minutes. Take your time. Don't rush."

I sigh with pleasure, feeling drowsy and relaxed. "Perfect."

Heading toward the door, he asks, "Need anything else?"

"Nope. Nothing at all."

"All right then, I'll see you downstairs in a bit."

Forty-five minutes later, I'm dressed in a cozy sweater and jeans. The evening air is a shade cooler than it was this afternoon. The temperature will only continue to drop as the sun sinks further in the sky.

I love summer, but I'm looking forward to the change in seasons. Believe it or not, I can't wait for winter. I love when freshly fallen snow clings to bare tree branches throughout the city. But I know that as beautiful as it can be, it quickly turns into a slushy, gray mess from traffic.

When I enter the kitchen, I find Dominic already sitting at the table on the patio. Joining him after an afternoon of sailing and then a nice, relaxing bath feels like the perfect way to end the weekend.

Pulling out a chair, I take a seat beside him. My eyes settle on the horizon. The pinks and purples painted across the sky are stunning. As I take in the view of the lake and sunset, a sense of rightness blankets me.

Maria serves us fresh pesto salmon that has been grilled on a plank but is now nestled on a bed of wild rice. It's paired with an arugula salad topped with shaved almonds.

Mouthwateringly delicious.

There's just no other way to describe it.

We chat about Dominic's work, my school, and what the next couple of weeks look like schedule-wise. I tell him about the spring break trip I'm hoping to take with Chloe, and he's quick to say that it won't be a problem. Dessert is a sliver of cheesecake served with fresh berries. By the time we're finished, I'm completely stuffed.

Night has fallen, and Dominic turns on the long, rectangular-shaped gas fire pit. The clear glass crystals lining the bottom give it an elegant look, and the heat is nice and toasty. Feeling content, we sit together on a large outdoor couch.

I don't want to leave, but I tell him, "I should probably head home soon. I have an early class tomorrow morning."

"Why don't you stay at the house tonight, and I'll make sure you're home by seven o'clock. It's been such a lovely day. I hate to see it end."

I feel the same way. Boating. Dinner. Hanging out and enjoying each other's company.

When I remain silent, Dominic slides an arm around my shoulders and pulls me closer. "Want to stay over?"

The thought of heading back to my empty condo doesn't hold much appeal. We'll need to head in soon, but I want to make this moment last a bit longer. "Yeah, I think so."

He seems pleased by my answer. "Good."

We're both quiet. Almost contemplative as we watch the dancing, twisting flames.

"I hope you know that your parents would be proud of you, Gracie. They would have loved how you're making your dreams come true."

Ripping my eyes from the orange blaze, the edges of my lips lift a fraction. "I really hope so." His words mean everything to me. Not a day passes when I don't think about Mom and Dad. When I don't miss them. Their absence has left a huge, gaping void in my life. One that can never be filled. I know Dominic is trying to be there for me, to offer guidance when needed, but it isn't the same.

"There's no question about it," he says firmly. His words offer the reassurance I so desperately need right now. "They would love that you've come back to Chicago and that you're pursuing a career in something you're so passionate about." His next words cause a thick lump of emotion to form in the middle of my throat. "And they would be relieved to see that you're moving on, that you're finally putting the accident behind you and living your life again. They would be proud of you for not allowing your grief to consume you the way it did in the beginning." He pauses before adding softly, "It was difficult to watch, Gracie. There were times when I didn't know how to make anything better for you."

I blink back the tears his words bring to my eyes.

The months following the accident were the hardest. The scariest. It felt impossible to climb out of the deep, dark hole I had fallen into. Sometimes I'm amazed that I was able to claw my way out of it. Where I am today, two years later, is because of the man sitting beside me. Without him, who knows how I'd be doing. Who knows if I would be here, working toward turning my dreams into reality.

I owe Dominic a debt of gratitude that can never fully be repaid.

"I have you to thank for where I am," I admit. "You were always there for me, no matter what. Your support has been unwavering. Without you, I don't know where I would be." Tears burn the back of my eyelids.

In the blink of an eye, the layers of armor I wear for the world, get stripped away. All that's left in its place is bone crushing honesty.

His eyes pin mine in place. "Your father was my best friend. I loved him like a brother. Your mother like a sister. She was the sweetest, kindest woman. She was a good wife and a fantastic mother." He pauses, and I feel the emotion rolling off him in thick, heavy waves. As difficult as it is to bring them up, it's also like a balm for my soul. I cannot *not* talk about them. "And you... *you* mean everything to me. Don't ever question that. There will never be a time when I'm *not* here for you. It's just you and me, kiddo. Against the world."

Those words make a small sob rise within me. Closing the space between us, I throw my arms around him, squeezing as if I'll never let go. There are times when I want to tether myself to Dominic so that I don't float away on the breeze. Because that's the way it feels sometimes. As if I'm aimlessly floating. Without my parents, there is nothing, no one, to ground me. It's the loneliest feeling in the world.

Dominic's words cocoon me in comfort. As long as I have him, I'm not alone. I have someone who loves me. Someone who cares about what happens to me.

"You're stuck with me." I sniff.

His lips curve. "We're stuck with each other."

CHAPTER NINETEEN

"You about ready to go?"

I look at *Sue the T-Rex* one last time and shoot Dominic a smile. We've spent the last four hours meandering around The Field Museum. Taking our time, we read the informational placards regarding the displayed artifacts on each of the three exhibit floors. I could easily spend another few hours wandering through these hallowed halls. I love this place, especially the main hall with its gorgeous columns and arched gallery entrances that rise above our heads. We stopped in the gift shop on the second floor, and Dominic bought me a *Sue* magnet for my refrigerator.

Exiting through the heavy front doors, we walk down the wide stone steps and stroll along the sidewalk by the lakefront which leads to Adler Planetarium.

We're about midway there, when Dominic says, "Would you mind if we sit for a few minutes?"

The day is gorgeous with the slightest nip in the air. Slowly the weather is turning cooler. I have a thick sweater wrapped around me. The sun is so bright and shiny that it cuts through most of the chill. The heat feels lovely on my face. I never turn down an opportunity to admire the churning blue water.

We sit on a bench as a couple of small children chase each other on the grassy embankment separating the lake from the sidewalk. I immediately get sucked into their antics. The girl looks to be about five and her brother, I assume, is around seven. I glance at their parents, who keep a close eye on them since there's a steep drop to the water.

After a few minutes, the family moves toward Shedd Aquarium which is a couple hundred yards away. Shedd, just like The Field Museum and Art Institute, is a stately old building with echoing corridors in the older sections. There are stunning marble floors and soaring ceilings with windows that allow sunlight to pour in since it was constructed before electricity was widespread. There are gorgeous columns and intricate aquatic carvings on the walls.

"Cute family."

My eyes slice back to Dominic, and I chortle at the offhanded comment.

"What?" I can't contain my laughter. I don't think I could even if I wanted to. "You're commenting that a family is," I pause to add more emphasis, *"cute?"* My palm lands on his forehead. "Do you feel okay? You must be coming down with something."

His lips bow upward in response to my teasing. "Hardly."

"Other than me, I've never seen you around children. In fact," I add, gently elbowing him in the ribs, "if I recall correctly, you wouldn't even go out with a woman if she had kids." At this point, I'm daring him to disagree with me.

He doesn't.

Instead, he rolls his eyes at the reminder. "Well, I'm in my mid-forties now. Perhaps the unthinkable has finally happened, and I've matured."

That statement makes me laugh harder. "Please," I practically shriek, "you're a confirmed bachelor through and through. I'm beginning to suspect that you always will be."

He acknowledges my words with a dip of his chin. There's no way he can deny twenty plus years of acting like a playboy. To my surprise, he grows pensive and his voice takes on a serious tone. "You're right. That's exactly how I've lived my life. But it gets old." Pausing, he adds, "Everything feels different now."

My laughter and good-natured ribbing die on my lips. I'd thought he was joking around, but obviously, he's not. A thoughtful light fills his eyes as he silently stares out across the water at Navy Pier, with its huge Ferris wheel, in the distance.

My attitude sobers. The air between us shifts. "Different how?"

For a long moment, his gaze stays firmly trained on the water as whitecapped waves roll toward the shoreline.

"Over the last two years, I've gained a greater appreciation for how precious life can be." His lips flatten into a grimace. "The truth of the matter is that nothing lasts forever."

He looks away from the water and meets my gaze. There's no guard or shield in place. Everything in him is laid bare. "Your parents' deaths made me realize how fleeting life can be. I don't want to end up alone. I've spent my entire life chasing after professional success." He sighs. "Once you get a taste, you become greedy for more. The accolades. The power. The success. The money. And all the trappings that come with them." His eyes stay locked on mine. "It's taken me a long time to understand that those aren't the things that matter in life. When I die, all of that dies with me. No one will give a damn about what I've achieved over the last twenty years. I don't have a wife or children who love me. There's no one."

I slip my hand into his and whisper, "That's not true, Dominic. *I* care. You know I do." Hearing him talk about his own mortality makes me feel like I've been shot through the heart with an arrow. I'm almost breathless with the pain blooming in my chest.

He gives my fingers a gentle squeeze in return. The tense muscles in his face relax marginally. "Of course, I know that. But I want someone to share my life with. I'm tired of living alone. Tired of not having someone to come home to at the end of the day. That's what has been missing. It's taken me a long time to figure it out."

After all these years of playing the field, of dating one woman after another after yet another, has Dominic finally found someone special to settle down with?

The thought seems inconceivable.

I rack my brain, trying to recall the conversations we've had recently. Were there any hints or subtle remarks I missed? Every time I sift through my memories, I come up empty-handed. I don't remember him mentioning a woman at all. Or that he felt ready to settle down. At the welcome home party he threw for me a month ago, there was no special woman in attendance. I can't recall him paying attention to anyone specific.

Am I missing something?

Clearing my throat, I tentatively ask, "Do you have someone in mind?"

"Actually, I do."

It feels as though the wind has been knocked from my lungs. "Who?" As selfish as it sounds-and it does sound selfish-Dominic is all I have left. The idea of sharing him with another woman doesn't sit well with me.

What if she doesn't like me?

Or isn't comfortable with the relationship he and I have?

Pulling away from him at this point would kill me. We've been through so much together. He's the one who picked me up when I couldn't take care of myself. He kept me going. And now, after all this time, I feel like I'm finally getting back on my feet. Finally living my life after being shut down for two years.

Life is just beginning to feel good again.

Is it possible that he's been waiting for me to reach this point before springing the news on me? Has someone been waiting in the wings for a while now?

It's not that I don't want Dominic to find happiness. He needs a woman to share his life with. It feels selfish to keep him all to myself, especially when he feels as though something is missing.

Sucking in a shaky breath, I scramble to get my feelings under control. It will take time for me to adjust to whomever he's chosen to move on with. To adjust to the fact that it's no longer only the two of us. To accept that someone more important than me will be the center of Dominic's attention.

That's the way it should be, right?

Angling toward me, he inhales deeply as if steeling himself to tell me something unpleasant. It sets my nerves on edge to see him this anxious. It's so uncharacteristic of him. He's usually confident and self-assured.

I don't think I've ever seen Dominic nervous before. Not even when he tried cases for multimillion-dollar settlements. My heart clenches under my breast. Whatever he's about to say is important. I'm practically sitting on the edge of my seat, waiting for him to drop a major bomb. I'm no longer aware of other people on the sidewalk. I'm solely focused on Dominic.

"I need you to hear me out on this. Okay?"

Oh God...

I wish he would spit it out already. The wait is killing me.

Glancing down, I realize that he's still holding my hand.

"You've always held a special place in my heart, Gracie. I've watched you grow from a little girl with a curious mind into a beautiful, smart, engaging young woman. What happened to your parents was a tragedy. I've never dealt with such grief and to watch you go through it alone nearly broke my heart. I think the only reason we survived was because we had each other. I think our relationship is stronger, closer, deeper because we made it through hell together."

His words resonate in my head. Feeling jittery, I jerk my head in agreement. My mouth is so dry that I couldn't speak if I tried.

"But it feels as though our relationship has shifted. It doesn't feel like we're uncle and niece anymore. I think we have more of an adult relationship now." He pauses before adding, "A friendship."

I stare, waiting for him to tell me about the woman he's fallen in love with and how I don't need him the way I once did. I want to tell him that he's wrong. That I still need him. That I will *always* need him no matter how old I am.

"Christ..." He plows his free hand through his hair in agitation before continuing. "I'm not saying this right." He blurts, "I think our relationship has developed into something more serious. When I think about my future, you're the one I want by my side."

Silence engulfs us as his eyes cautiously search mine. I blink as those huskily spoken words sink in. The wheels in my brain are spinning, but I can't grasp their meaning.

Dominic continues almost urgently. "We know each other so well

and have so much in common. These feelings I have for you just feel...
right." Again, he falls silent, his concerned blue eyes watching mine for
a response.

"Gracie?" Wrapping his fingers around my other hand, he gives
them both a gentle squeeze. "Did you hear what I said, sweetheart?"

"I..." I shake my head to clear it.

Did he just admit that the woman he's interested in, the one he
wants to make a life with... is *me*?

"I know, I know... I'm sorry. Maybe I shouldn't have sprung this on
you out of the blue. We have this connection, this unbreakable bond.
I've never experienced that with someone before, and I don't want to
lose it."

I can only stare.

"Gracie," he whispers, "please say something."

"I'm a little stunned," I admit. "I didn't expect you to say any of
that. I thought you'd been keeping someone from me."

He laughs, but the sound is strained around the edges.

"I'm sure you need some time to digest this. I don't want you to
feel pressured, okay? I just..." he glances away for a moment before his
gaze slides back to mine. "I just needed to finally say the words. It was
starting to eat me up inside. If you don't feel the same or aren't interested, then nothing will change between us." His eyes brim with
sincerity. "Not ever."

Biting my lower lip, I murmur, "I'm not sure how I feel right now.
Maybe a little confused. I've never thought about you like that. I
mean..." My words trail off. He's being completely open with me. It's
difficult not to be just as forthcoming. "When I was younger, I had a
bit of a crush on you."

His lips hitch up at the corners. He brings one of my hands to his
lips and presses a gentle kiss against my knuckles.

"I know."

Surprise zings through me, and I grin. "You did?"

His smile intensifies. "It was very sweet. But that was just a crush.
You were a kid back then. This is different."

I nod. It feels different. A bit uncomfortable. And scary because I
don't want the foundation of our relationship to change.

He seems to sense my unease and the conflict coursing through me. His voice softens. "I'm not going to push you into something you don't want."

My mind is a tangle of chaotic thoughts. It's hard to keep them straight. "I need some time to think about it. To think about you in a different light." I hastily tack on, "To see if that's even possible."

"Of course. Take all the time you need. I'm not going anywhere, Gracie. And if you decide that a relationship between us isn't something you're interested in, that's fine. There won't be hurt feelings on my side. No matter what happens, we'll always be family. Just remember that."

He wraps an arm around my shoulders, pulling me into the heat of his body as we watch the waves roll in.

In the blink of an eye, everything between us feels different.

I feel blindsided by his words. By his feelings. I love Dominic. I can't remember a time when I didn't love him. But it's never been a romantic kind of love. Even when I had a silly teenage crush on him, it was nothing more than a phase.

Innocent and fleeting.

I'd be lying if I didn't admit that there's something comforting about the notion of him loving me. Of us being together. Of our relationship growing stronger. Of not having to worry about him falling for someone else and getting pushed aside.

Perhaps a fear of loneliness isn't the best reason to be with him, but it's there regardless, flashing like a beacon in the back of my mind.

Being with Dominic wouldn't be a hardship. We get along well and have so much history together. No one understands me the way he does. Sometimes I question if anyone ever will. And he's right, we have a lot in common. There's always been a special bond between us. My parents' death strengthened and deepened our relationship.

Deepened our love for one another.

Is it really a far stretch for our relationship to develop into something romantic?

I don't know.

That's something I need to think about.

CHAPTER TWENTY

One of my favorite things to do is stroll along Michigan Avenue and peek in all the brightly colored shop windows. This is exactly what Chloe and I are doing today. Chloe has been invited to a fancy work dinner and needs a cocktail dress. I would loan her one of mine, but she's six inches taller than I am and not as curvy.

Chloe has the body of a runway model.

Skinny bitch.

Know what's worse than that?

She eats like a teenage boy going through puberty and never gains any weight. It's so unfair. I don't like going out to lunch with her because she'll order a burger loaded with the works, chili cheese fries on the side, and a large Coke. She always polishes everything from her plate. I order a salad and a Diet Coke and am up a pound the next morning.

She's also allergic to working out. I've cajoled her into running with me along the lakefront a few times, but we always end up walking after two blocks. Whatever genes she inherited need to be cloned.

Pausing mid-stride, we stop to gaze at the gorgeous display of purses in the window of Salvatore Ferragamo, one of the many high-end shops lining this busy street. Chloe points to a tan and white snakeskin shoulder bag.

"Is that the most stunning handbag you've ever seen or what?"

I have to agree. It's beautiful. I could definitely see it on Chloe's arm. She would rock the hell out of a purse like that. I ask, "Do you want to go in and take a look?"

Her bubbly excitement fades as she shakes her head. "No, I've already been in there numerous times to drool. If I step foot in that store again, there is no way I'm walking out without it."

I shrug. "Okay."

With a conflicted expression, she casts one more wistful look at the handbag before pulling me along with her. It's a beautiful Thursday afternoon. I've already finished classes for the day, and I'm not on the volunteer schedule at the museum. I'm spending a few hours with Chloe before heading home to submerge myself in my studies.

"A few more months of shaking my ass at Covet and that purse will be as good as mine."

I make a quick mental note of the bag she's lusting over. Chloe's birthday is coming up, and I would love to buy her something special. She's been such a good friend, even after I pushed her away. It's been over a month since our reunion, and we've fallen right back into our old friendship as if there had never been a two-year hiccup.

I don't think Chloe has any idea just how meaningful her friendship is to me.

With the weather being so pleasant, we're certainly not the only ones out shopping today. Sometimes it's fun to walk around and watch tourists trying to navigate the city, professionals rushing from one place to another, not wanting to waste a single moment of their time, and people simply going about their daily lives. The energy on this street is infectious.

Chloe's eyes meet mine as we continue making our way up the block, heading toward Water Tower Place, a seven-story mall on the Magnificent Mile. "You mentioned something about Dominic on the phone. What were you going to tell me?"

I stifle a groan.

Right... I'd started to tell her about what happened between us at The Field Museum before we were interrupted.

Now that I've had more time to think, I'm not sure I want to bring it up. I can imagine how she'll react if I tell her everything Dominic confessed. I'm not sure if I want to hear it right now. Because I know Chloe, and she'll tell me to go for it.

She doesn't understand that it's more complicated.

Ever since Dominic revealed his feelings, I haven't thought about much else. I keep vacillating, thinking that there's no way we can just begin a romantic relationship. I don't want to risk ruining our relationship and losing the only family I have left.

He's right about us getting along so well and having so much in common. We have a solid friendship. I think that's why I'm having such a tough time with this decision.

I already love him.

But it isn't *that* kind of love.

Is it possible for the love we have to bloom and grow into something more?

At this point, I haven't come up with a definitive answer. It sucks, because I know he's patiently waiting for one.

Maybe I do need Chloe's advice on this matter since I'm so confused.

Inhaling deeply, I force the breath out before I can change my mind. "Dominic said that he's interested in exploring a romantic relationship with me."

I didn't realize what a relief it would be to say the words out loud.

One moment Chloe is walking beside me and the next she's not. The couple behind us nearly crashes into our backs. They grumble under their breaths and shoot us dirty looks. But Chloe couldn't care less. She doesn't pay attention to them. Her saucer-like eyes are fastened on me.

She practically bellows, *"Shut the fuck up!"* A few people swing around, gaping at her.

I grimace in embarrassment.

Grabbing my hand, Chloe stalks towards Saks Fifth Avenue, which is a few stores up the block. Once we're inside, she drags me behind her like a rag doll until we reach the shoe department. She finds two chairs and drops into the first one, staring at me expectantly.

"Park it, sister. Then you're going to fill me in on every single juicy detail. And I'm sure there are plenty." With a gleam in her eyes, she rubs her palms together in anticipation. "God, I hope this story ends with you two sweaty and naked in bed."

Maybe this wasn't such a great idea after all.

I sit next to her and chew my bottom lip until it feels like a slab of raw meat. Which doesn't take all that long since I've been chewing on it for days. It's a bad habit I've never been able to shake.

"I should have known something was up." She glares at me. "Your lip is a disgusting mess."

I release it from my teeth and gingerly touch it with my fingertip. She's right about it being a disgusting mess. "Yeah."

When I remain silent, she snaps, "Spill! I'm dying here!"

Chloe leans back and crosses her legs as though we're going to be here for a while.

Just as I'm about to open my mouth, a salesgirl approaches. "Is there anything I can help you with today?"

I wait for Chloe to tell her to beat it.

"Ummm..." Narrowing her eyes, Chloe studies the displays surrounding us. "Yeah. Actually, I'd love to see those black Manolo Blahniks with the crystal embellishments." She then points to a pair of black velvet Gianvito Rossi heels with satin bows. "And definitely those." Face filling with excitement, she gestures at a glittery pair of Monique Lhuillier suede sandals. "And those gorgeous little darlings."

They really are beautiful. Chloe has amazing taste.

Expensive taste.

What I admire most about Chloe is how she's willing to work for all the pretty things she wants to purchase. She doesn't need a man to buy them for her. She works as a paralegal during the day and dances at Covet a few nights a week.

"Eights, please."

With dollar signs in her eyes, the salesgirl skips off to do Chloe's bidding.

Chloe turns back to me and lifts her brows as if she's been waiting patiently for hours.

Unsure of how to explain the situation, I bottom-line it. "Dominic and I went to the Field Museum on Tuesday, and afterward, we sat by the lake." I shake my head. I still feel blindsided by the declaration days later. "He said that he's always loved me, but his feelings changed over the past year or so. They've become more," I pause, *"romantic* in nature."

Chloe's hand flies to her mouth. "*No!* Are you serious?" In the next breath, she says almost threateningly, "You'd better not be screwing with me!"

I give her a look.

Still shocked, she shakes her head. "I can't believe he actually said that to you!"

"I know." I collapse in the cloth-covered chair.

"Have you slept with him?"

How could she even think that? It's Dominic for goodness sake. *Dominic!* "No! Of course not."

"Well, that's a pity. I bet he's amazing in bed. Lord knows he has a ton of experience under his belt."

Yes, a ton of experience is right. He's probably slept with hundreds of women. The man is forty-five years old.

The salesgirl returns carrying four boxes, carefully setting them down on a chair next to Chloe.

"We had the three you asked for in your size. I also brought another pair that just arrived today."

Chloe perks up at the words *just arrived today*. They're like music to her ears.

The girl dramatically lifts the cover from the box and removes a beautiful sandal. Almost reverently, she whispers, "Jimmy Choo."

Chloe's eyes widen as she takes in the crystal-studded silver leather.

"Oh my God," she breathes, "those are stunning."

"They really are," I agree, feeling slightly awed.

She nibbles at her lower lip and asks, "How much?"

"Twenty-four hundred."

Chloe shoots the girl an exasperated look. "You're seriously killing me right now."

The girl grins evilly in response. "I'll leave these here for you to try on. Let me know if there's anything else I can help you with."

As she walks away, Chloe mutters, "Bitch."

With a small smile, I shake my head. "It's like they see you walking in and just know."

She huffs in irritation. "Tell me about it."

She zeros in on the Jimmy Choo sandals first. All talk of Dominic goes on the backburner as she slips a foot into each one. She reminds me of Cinderella trying on the glass slipper. Standing, she struts back and forth a few times before turning her foot from side to side.

Sighing, she says, "I love them."

I snort. "Of course you do. They're twenty-four hundred dollars. Did you really think you wouldn't?"

"I kind of hoped they wouldn't fit. Or they'd be uncomfortable. Or not look amazing on my feet." Her lips turn down at the corners. "But they fit perfectly and are super comfortable." She gives me a determined look. One I've seen many times before. "I want them."

"Maybe you should try on the others before rushing to any decisions."

Sitting down, she lovingly removes them and opens one of the other boxes.

Picking up where our previous conversation left off, she adds, "A man who's slept around and gotten the whole *I can't keep my dick in my pants phase* out of his system is the perfect candidate for a long-term relationship. He's seen what's out there and is ready to focus on being a good boyfriend or husband."

Boyfriend? Husband?

Yikes.

This conversation is moving at warp speed. I'm not even sure if I want anything romantic with Dominic and she's already talking marriage.

Wearing another pair of shoes, she walks along the row of chairs and poses in front of a mirror. I can tell she doesn't like them nearly as much as the first one.

"I don't know..."

Sitting back down, she unwraps the third pair. "What are you going to do? Have you talked with him about it yet?"

I shrug and pick at my thumbnail. "We've texted back and forth. I don't want it getting weird between us."

"Yeah." She grimaces. "That would definitely suck."

Taking a deep breath, I ask, "What do you think?"

She gives me a look that says, *Ummm, duh!* "That you should go for it."

No surprise there. Which is why I hesitated to bring it up. The ramifications could be disastrous if it doesn't work out between Dominic and me. I'm not even sure if I can mentally shift gears and think of him as a love interest.

It just seems... I don't know... *weird.*

There, I said it.

It feels weird to think of Dominic like that.

The question tumbles out of my mouth before I can rein it back in. "You don't think it's icky that he was my father's friend? That he's known me since I was in diapers?" A shiver zips through me as those disturbing thoughts bounce around my brain.

It just sounds so... *pervy*.

"Listen, if you were still in diapers, then I would say- yeah, it's totally creepy. But you're not. You're a twenty-three-year-old woman. He's forty-five. And hot as hell. I would be all over that if I were you."

Yes, I know she would.

"I'm not sure if I can get past the fact that he's my godfather. The person who my parents set up as my guardian. The man who's supposed to take care of me."

She grins and winks at me. "Oh, he'll take care of you, all right. No doubt about it."

I shake my head. "That's wrong on so many levels."

She rolls her eyes. "Well, I guess that's something you need to consider. No one can help you with this decision. You're the one who needs to be comfortable with it." Sounding more serious, she continues. "You've always loved Dominic." She waves a hand in my direction before I can interrupt. "Yes, yes, I know. It isn't *that* kind of love. I got it." She shrugs as if that's hardly problematic. "There's an undeniable bond between the two of you. Is there any reason that platonic love can't grow into something more? To me, it's a no-brainer."

What she said is true. I do love him. Maybe it *is* possible for romance to flourish from our current relationship. "I really don't know what to do."

Just when I think Chloe has become wise beyond her years, she leans closer and whispers, "Are you telling me that you've never touched yourself, not even once, while thinking about him?"

I'm sure a horrified expression mars my face. How could there not be? "Good Lord, no!"

She arches a brow and says, "I have. Lots of times."

My face crumples. "*Ewww.* Come on! I did not need to know that."

Unaffected by my reaction, she asks instead, "Are you attracted to him? Do you think he's hot?"

"On some level, I know he's handsome." I've always thought so. It's kind of like when you have a cousin or a best guy friend and you know they're good looking-hot even-but that doesn't necessarily mean you're attracted to them. Or that you want to jump their bones.

Starting a relationship with him would mean that I would have to change my perception of him.

Can I do that?

Chloe gets a little dreamy-eyed. "Yeah, he is. All that thick, blond hair shot through with silver and those gorgeous blue eyes. For a man his age, he has an incredibly buff body. I bet he works out every day." She licks her lips. I don't want to know what image is rolling through her head right now. "Yeah," she confirms to no one in particular, "I would do him in a minute."

"You already mentioned that," I remind her drily.

"I really do love older men. They last so much longer in bed and are way more focused on a woman's pleasure. I've been with too many guys under thirty who only think of themselves, the selfish bastards."

Matteo pops into my head. Maybe hookups with selfish men has been Chloe's experience, but it certainly wasn't mine. Matteo took his time. I've never orgasmed so hard or so many times in my life. But that was just sex. I doubt it will morph into a relationship. He doesn't seem interested in one. Plus, once again, he's disappeared. For all I know, he's purposely avoiding me.

Dominic, on the other hand...

He *is* interested in something more.

Chloe's eyes narrow as she studies me for a moment. "Are you sure you haven't slept with him yet? 'Cause you just got this look on your face."

I school my expression. "No. Nothing has transpired on that front."

"Well, maybe that should be your next step before deciding whether a relationship is worth exploring. I can't imagine him being a dud in the sack, but I guess it's always possible that the two of you might not click between the sheets."

"No! I can't just have a one-night stand with my *godfather*."

Again, I get a weird, jiggly feeling in the pit of my belly when I think about being intimate with Dominic. "I can't just jump into bed with him. What happens if we aren't compatible? What if things don't go back to the way they were? He isn't someone I can walk away from."

Not like the guy next door.

"I'd still sleep with him."

Now *I* roll my eyes. "Yes, I know. You keep telling me you would sleep with him at the drop of a hat. Or the drop of your panties."

She smirks. "I'll drop them right now if you want."

I hold up a hand. Chloe would do something that outrageous without a second thought. "Please, I beg of you... leave the panties securely in place."

The salesgirl sidles up to Chloe and sweeps her hand toward the boxes. "Have you made any decisions? Are there any other shoes I can show you?"

Shoulders slumping, Chloe sighs. "No, I've made up my mind. I'll take the Jimmy Choo sandals."

Looking pleased, the girl beams. "You won't regret it."

Chloe snorts. "Oh, I'm pretty sure I will when I open up my credit card statement next month."

CHAPTER TWENTY-ONE

As I leave the Art History building at the university, my eyes catch on obsidian-colored ones. My feet grind to a halt as thick shards of awareness slice through me. No matter how many times I see him, my reaction is always the same.

Always instantaneous.

Matteo.

There's no way him showing up here is a random coincidence.

First the Art Institute and now campus?

Unable to resist the urge, my eyes hungrily sweep over him. He really is gorgeous. How is it possible that every time I see him, he looks better than before? He's dressed in another dark suit that fits him to perfection.

I glance around, realizing that I'm not the only one checking him out. Girls slowly walk by the bench he's sitting on, trying to snag his interest. A group of five young women keep craning their necks to get a better look at him. They giggle while admiring him.

I can't blame them.

Lord knows I was tempted to blush and giggle the first time I saw him. Instead, I gawked mutely in the elevator.

So embarrassing.

Matteo doesn't pay the girls any attention, but I still feel jealous. His gaze stays fixed on mine. Realizing that I'm at a standstill, I scold myself for reacting like a deer in headlights and walk toward him. He stands as I approach him.

"Hello."

Ignoring his greeting, I blurt, "What are you doing here?"

His broad shoulders straighten as if preparing for battle. "I came for you."

Frowning, I shake my head. "How did you know I was here?"

Should this stalkerish behavior scare me?

Probably.

He always seems to know where I'm going to be and when.

How does he know this?

A better question would be- *why does he know this?*

"I was hoping we could talk. Maybe I can give you a lift back to the building."

I hitch my leather messenger bag higher on my shoulder, holding it like a security blanket. "I don't think we have anything to talk about."

He takes a step toward me so that I have to crane my neck to hold his gaze. "That's where we have a difference of opinion. I think we have a lot to discuss."

Feeling more emboldened, I wave a hand dismissively in his direction.

People may not recognize him or know who he is, but based on his appearance and the way he carries himself, they know Matteo is someone powerful. He has a magnetic aura that draws you to him like a scrap of metal.

"Look, we slept together," I say in a low voice to avoid giving the audience we have gained something to talk about. "It was nothing more than that. If you're worried that it'll be awkward running into each other in the building, don't be. I've already moved on and forgotten about it."

He doesn't need to know that unbidden thoughts and images of him still flit through my mind several times a day.

Cocking his head to one side, he studies me until I fidget. Just as the weight of his gaze becomes unbearable, he says, "Really, bella?

That's a shame. I've spent the last week thinking about little else other than you."

I rein in a snort. He must see the disbelief shining in my eyes.

"Are you angry that I haven't been able to see you?"

When I was nothing more than a booty call in the middle of the night?

Hardly.

I'm not delusional.

"We had fun together." I shrug as if one-night stands are my specialty. "But that's all it was."

"What if I told you that I wanted more?"

I'd call him a liar.

And I would tell myself that I'm a fool for believing him.

His limo pulls up to the curb. A man in a dark suit and shades walks around from the other side and opens the door, giving us an expectant look. If Matteo's presence hasn't drawn enough attention, this does the trick. Speculation over who he is runs rampant through the gathered crowd.

"Perhaps we can finish this discussion in private?" When I don't budge, he tacks on, "Please."

Because I'm not stupid and I learn from my mistakes, I know how dangerous getting in that car with him is to my well-being. My heart flips whenever he's near. My palms sweat profusely. My mouth dries. My tummy trembles. No one has ever affected me the way this man does. Glancing around, I see I'm not alone. Plenty of girls are soaking right through their panties while watching him.

That thought is enough to harden my resolve.

"No."

"No," he repeats the word as if it's completely foreign to him. "You won't accept a ride from me?"

I shake my head. I can't be alone with him. I'll spread my legs in minutes. Who am I kidding? More like seconds. Distance and detachment are the only armor I have against him. And they're flimsy at best.

"Why?" he asks.

"Because you and I have nothing to discuss."

He takes another step closer and strokes my cheek with his knuckles. "That is where you're wrong. We have much to talk about."

How can one touch melt my insides like ice cream on a hot August day?

"Do we?"

His voice drops as his eyes glimmer with fire. "Most assuredly."

Inhaling a shaky breath, I fight to hold firm in my stance. It seems vital to the power struggle taking place between us. "If you have something to say, we can talk right here." I glance at the driver who is still waiting patiently. "But I'm not getting into that limo with you."

Humor wars with hunger in his gaze. "Are you afraid to be alone with me? Afraid something will happen between us?"

There's no point in lying, is there?

"Deathly."

Looking thoughtful, he swipes his tongue over his teeth and shrugs. "Then I'll have Victor drive you back to the building."

Surprised by his capitulation, my brows knit together. "What about you?"

"After he drops you off, he'll return for me."

I peek at the gathered crowd of women. It's as though a rock star is in their midst. I'm sure they would love to have Matteo all to themselves. Before my mind begins to spin with jealousy, his fingers slide under my chin, turning my head until my eyes once again meet his.

He says softly, "You have nothing to be concerned about."

I think of the girl he screwed on his patio and the other one with him at the club. I've never been the jealous type, but it's hard not to be when woman gawk at him everywhere he goes.

"Have dinner with me."

That sounds much safer than being stuck in the limo with him.

"Just one dinner," he cajoles. "That's all I'm asking for. We'll have a nice meal and talk. Nothing more than that."

Biting my lip, I feel myself wavering. "When?"

"Tonight." His eyes stay locked on mine. I could lose myself in their bottomless depths.

"Do you promise to behave?"

One side of his sexy mouth hitches before he says solemnly, "I promise that nothing will happen that you don't want."

"That doesn't make me feel better." Closing my eyes, I ask quietly, "What time?"

"Six."

I know damn well that going out with him will more than likely lead to me orgasming, and I still can't say no.

"Okay. I'll see you tonight at six."

He pulls his phone out of his suit jacket pocket. "Want to text me your address?"

A gurgle of laughter escapes me, breaking the tension between us. His lips lift in response.

"I don't think I want you to have my cell number."

Unoffended, he shrugs and slips the phone back into his pocket. Our gazes hold as I slide into the limo. Victor severs the connection by closing the door. Just as I huff out a relived breath for getting away with my panties intact, my phone chimes with an incoming message.

Already have it, bella.

My breath stalls as I gape at the screen.

Seriously, who is this man?

CHAPTER TWENTY-TWO

The doorbell rings at six o'clock on the dot. I lay a hand across my lower abdomen as a thousand tiny butterflies take flight.

Inhaling a deep breath, I tell myself to calm down.

It's just dinner.

Nothing more.

A small thrill zings through me as I open the door. Matteo's dark eyes slide over my body, giving me the once-over. He never specified where we were going and I didn't want to open up a line of communication by texting him, so I chose an outfit consisting of white shorts, a navy-blue blouse, and silver sandals with a short heel.

I'd normally wear a skirt, but that option was a no-go after what happened in the limo the night he gave me a ride home from the club. Wearing an extra layer is a weak defense mechanism, but I have to protect myself any way I can when it comes to this man.

Apparently, casual was the way to go because Matteo is dressed in jeans and a pink button-down shirt. The sleeves are rolled up, exposing his forearms. It's a departure from what he normally wears.

Yet it's just as sexy as the suits.

And the athletic gear.

Although naked is my favorite look on him. Sculpted muscles on full display...

Mmmm.

As that inappropriate thought flickers through my head, my gaze shifts back to his.

A satisfied smirk twists his lips indicating that my perusal has not gone unnoticed. I should be irritated for already melting into a puddle of goo.

But I'm not.

I'm learning to accept that this man scrambles my brains whenever I'm around him.

"Are you finished eating me up with your eyes?"

Heat stings my cheeks. Trying to brazen out the situation, I shrug as if it's no big deal. "Stop looking so good, and maybe I'll stop staring."

His eyes widen, and a deep chuckle rolls off his lips. "Already this evening has become more interesting."

Before I can reply, he holds out an arm. "Ready?"

That one word makes me suck in a breath. "As I'll ever be."

"Don't worry, I promise that tonight will be relatively painless."

I grab my purse from the credenza and place my hand against his forearm. Since his sleeves are rolled up, my fingers rest against his olive-toned flesh. A shiver of awareness zips through me at the intimate touch.

He moves closer and says in a low voice, "Unless that's something you're into."

If he weren't holding onto me so tightly, I would stumble at the purred-out words and their implied meaning. At the arrow of heat that explodes like a firework in my core. Those slaps he gave to the woman on the balcony echo through my head. My eyes dart to his, but he only gives me a teasing wink.

We leave and make our way toward the elevator. There aren't more than fifty residents in the building, so we don't have to wait long. Which is a relief, because I'm a bundle of pent-up, restless energy. When the elevator begins to rise instead of descending to the lobby, I glance at Matteo in question.

He smiles smugly.

"I thought we were going to dinner?"

"We are. But I never said where, did I?"

Before I can ask any more questions, the doors slide open. We step out on the rooftop where the pool and gardens are located. As we make our way toward the flower beds, I notice that one of the tables has been covered with a thick, white tablecloth. A hurricane candle sits in the middle. Two sets of silverware and stemware glint in the flickering light.

"I hope you don't mind that I've arranged for us to have a private dinner up here." He glances around before his eyes finally make their way back to mine. "The gardens are beautiful, aren't they?"

"Private?" That single word resonates throughout my head. The rooftop terrace is *not* private. Residents from the building can use it at any time.

"Tonight, it's just for us. If someone tries pressing the elevator button, it will not work. They won't be able to gain access."

My mind spins as Matteo leads me to the table and pulls out one of the wrought iron chairs. Once I'm seated, he slides into the chair across from me. His gaze never strays.

I feel as if he's trying to decipher the myriad of expressions that must be flitting across my face. I've never been good at concealing them.

A man who looks as though he works at a fancy restaurant appears. "May I pour you a glass of wine, madam?"

"Please," I croak. I need a drink even though the wine will only amplify the off-kilter feeling coursing through me.

He fills my glass before doing the same for Matteo. "Appetizers will be out shortly."

Matteo's eyes remain riveted to mine. "Thank you, Roberto."

With a slight nod of acknowledgement, the waiter leaves.

I shake my head to clear it. What's going on here? "You arranged all this?"

"Does that surprise you?"

Does it surprise me that he would go to all this trouble? "Yeah, it does."

With a trembling hand, I pick up my glass and take a small sip. My eyes close in appreciation. Oh, that's good. *Really good.*

"I love how expressive your face is."

My eyes fly open to find that Matteo has closed some of the distance between us. My fingers grip the edge of the table, thankful for the circular object sitting between us. I need the separation.

"Why are you doing this?"

He has to know that this seduction isn't necessary. I was his from the moment I opened the door and set eyes on him.

Tilting his head to one side, he considers my question and replies with one of his own. "Why?"

"Yes..." I don't want to point out the differences between us, but he isn't leaving me a choice in the matter. Matteo could be with any women he wants. Probably several. At the same time. I see the way they watch him. And yet, I'm the one he's actively pursuing? It doesn't make sense, especially when I take into account that he doesn't *date* women.

"Why are you doing this? We already slept together."

Instead of answering my question, he picks up his glass and takes a sip of wine. My eyes drop to his mouth.

Why am I so preoccupied with it?

I have no idea, but I am. Wildly so. I want to drag a fingertip over that sexy top lip and sweep it across the lower one. Memories of Matteo's mouth licking and sucking my flesh make me shiver.

I shake myself out of my stupor, jerking my gaze back to his. My breath catches from the stark hunger filling his dark eyes. He knows what's been cartwheeling through my head and is just as turned on as I am. The way he continues to watch me ignites a firestorm of lust deep in my belly.

And lower.

Most definitely lower.

I squirm in my chair. But there is no relief to be had. Not yet anyway.

"Is it so difficult to believe that I would like to get to know you better, Grace?"

Shaking my head, I will myself to stay focused on the conversation and not the way his eyes continue to seduce me. I fling his own words back at him. "Aren't you the one who said that you don't date women?" I pause and add, "You fuck them."

Matteo inclines his head in acknowledgment. "Normally that's exactly how I go about things." He pauses as if considering his next words carefully. As if considering me with an equal amount of caution. "However, there's something about you. Something that intrigues me." He leans closer. "Don't you feel it? The energy that hums between us? The attraction?"

I nod.

Of course, I feel it.

How could I not? It's all-encompassing. I feel it from the tip of my head to the bottom of my toes. Every time I'm with Matteo, I feel more alive than I've felt in a long time. Do you know how addictive that is? He's like a drug pumping wildly through my system. I know he's not good for me, but I still want more. I can't help myself.

"There's a pull between us. One that begs to be explored. I'm not making any promises. I just want to spend more time together, to figure it out. Is there any reason we can't do that?"

Yes. I'm scarred enough. Getting involved with him will only leave more indelible marks upon my soul. I'm trying to heal, not put myself through any more unnecessary pain.

But can I walk away from him? From what he makes me feel? Should I deny myself something that has the power to make me feel so incredibly good because the chance of a happily ever after is nonexistent?

Because he isn't trying to whitewash the situation?

Or lie about his true intentions?

I should appreciate his honesty and simply accept it for what it is. I'm not going into this blindly. I understand exactly what's going on.

"Okay."

With a small smile playing around the edges of his lips, he lifts his glass toward mine. I do the same.

A predatory gleam fills his eyes. "To getting to know one another."

I clink my glass against his as a shiver of apprehension scuttles through me. Sipping my wine, I wonder what I've just set in motion.

CHAPTER TWENTY-THREE

Standing by the railing that overlooks the city, I breathe deeply as the cool night breeze ruffles my hair. Willis Tower rises above the other lit-up building. I take in the skyline, admiring the breathtaking beauty surrounding me. I've seen the lake from my patio at night. But this is something altogether different. The bright city lights stretch like grasping fingers into the distance. I realize just how much I missed Chicago.

Matteo stands behind me with his front lightly pressed into my back. His arms are loosely wrapped around me. His warm breath fans against the side of my face. As always, his proximity sends shivers scampering down my spine.

Slowly he runs the tip of his nose across my neck.

I struggle to resist the urge to close my eyes and roll my head back, allowing him greater access. I want to feel his mouth kissing and nipping my skin. Instead, I focus on how the brightly lit buildings punctuate the dark sky.

I try not to lose myself in him too quickly.

When it comes down to it, I know nothing about Matteo.

I know that he's ridiculously good looking. That he dresses well and lives in an expensive building. He obviously has the power to dig into my background and find out all sorts of information.

But who is he really?

If we venture into relationship territory, I need these questions answered.

"Have you always lived here?" I ask.

For a long, silent moment, he continues caressing me with the tip of his nose. My stomach sinks as I wonder if he'll use his power of seduction to avoid sharing personal details with me. How can I give any more of myself when he won't open up at all?

"Yes, I was born here."

"But you have an accent." It's light, but noticeable, always threaded through his words.

"I've spent a great deal of time in Italy. My mother's parents are still in Padova, as are many aunt, uncles, and cousins."

The crumbs he shares whet my appetite for more. "Do you have any sisters or brothers?"

My eyes shut as his lips touch my neck. "Yes. Two sisters, two brothers."

One of five...

I can't begin to fathom what growing up in a family with so many siblings must have been like. Then add in all those cousins, aunts, and uncles. Grandparents, too. With a swiftness I'm unprepared for, longing cuts through my heart. I'm jealous that he can lay claim to so many people.

I have no idea what being part of a large family feels like.

Although I was content with my parents and had a happy, well-adjusted childhood, I secretly longed for a sibling. More than one. Of course, I loved having my parents' undivided attention. Who wouldn't? I accompanied them everywhere they went, but still felt lonely as the only child in a room full of adults.

I don't remember hearing them talk about having more kids. I think they enjoyed parenting and still being able to live their lives the way they wanted- working, traveling, and visiting friends.

Mom and Dad loved the law and their jobs at the District Attorney's office. They liked the challenges and rigors of their careers. They were passionate about giving back to society. They felt that what they did protected people. That it mattered and gave their lives intrinsic meaning.

They always made time for me despite their demanding careers. Our family may have been small, but we lived large and had many adventures together. It never felt as though something was lacking.

Or missing.

If my mother and father had glimpsed the future and saw how they'd be abruptly taken from me, would they have done things differently? Would they have given me siblings?

Matteo seems to sense the morose direction of my thoughts. His arms tighten around my waist as though he's anchoring me to him. Does he feel how close I am to floating away into oblivion?

Blinking hard, I'm back in the present instead of tangled up in the past.

"You still miss them."

We've never discussed my parents or their death, but I know what he's referring to.

"Every single day," I whisper.

"Being alone must be difficult."

He has no idea.

How could he?

He's been surrounded by family his entire life. He couldn't begin to understand how lonely it is to have no one.

Unbidden tears flood my eyes. Other than Dominic and Chloe, I never talk about my parents. I keep all the pain associated with them locked in a box, buried deep inside. To constantly take it out and hold it in my hands is excruciatingly painful.

I stay busy with school, volunteering, and going out with Chloe and her friends. I spend time with Dominic. When my mind is engaged with other things, I don't dwell on the loss as much. At least, I try not to.

But the stone-cold reality is that the sadness is always festering in the back of my mind.

"Don't cry, bella. I don't like seeing you sad."

This evening began with me trying to figure out who this man is and has turned into me dwelling on my past. "I'm fine. It's been two years now. It doesn't hurt as much as it used to," I lie.

Needing a distraction until I can get my emotions under control, I say, "Tell me about Italy."

I accompanied my parents on trips to France, England, Germany, Greece, Africa, India, and China. They loved exploring new places. Mom and Dad enjoyed immersing themselves in rich cultural histories and learning about how other people lived. It was important to them that I not take the life I had for granted. And I didn't. I had a different perspective than a lot of my classmates. I realized that not everyone lived the way we do. Even in our own country, I was shown that life could be a vastly different experience.

"Each summer, my mother would take all of us to Padova for three months so that we could spend time with family. And then around Christmas, we would go back for a few weeks. Italy has always felt like a second home to me."

I smile while imagining Matteo's entire family gathered together in Italy to celebrate the holidays. "That sounds lovely."

"It was." He's quiet for a moment before asking, "What was it like growing up for you? Did you have a happy childhood?"

I keep my gaze on the city lights shining brightly as far as the eye can see. "Yes, very happy. But it was just the three of us. Sometimes my godfather would spend the holidays with us, and that was always nice."

"There are no aunts or uncles? Grandparents?"

Sadness rushes through me as I shake my head. "No. It was just the three of us. And of course, Dominic, my godfather. He's the closest thing I have to family now." I feel the need to explain that even though it sounds lonely, for the most part, it wasn't. I don't have any complaints about how I was raised. "My mother and father were wonderful parents. They spent a great deal of time with me. I think they both hoped I would follow them into law, but I've always loved art. They took me all over the world. We visited natural history and art museums, along with castles and churches. The love I have for art and architecture is because of them. Because they fostered it within me. I'm the person I am today because of them."

"I'm sorry. To lose your parents at such a young age is a huge heartbreak to suffer."

His words send another thick shaft of pain slicing through me, almost cleaving me in half. "Yes."

Thankfully, he asks no more questions about them. "Your godfather lives here in Chicago?"

"Yes. He's one of the reasons I moved back. I wanted to be near him." I shrug. "Neither one of us have family."

"Will you introduce us?"

Surprised by the request, I turn my head to look at him. "I don't know," I say truthfully. "I haven't given it any thought."

"I'd like to meet him."

Feeling confused, I ask, "Why?"

"I want to meet the most important person in your life."

I try steeling my heart, but it melts a bit from his words.

Matteo turns me around and pulls me closer until my breasts flatten against his chest. I tilt my head to meet his dark gaze.

"I thought we were taking this one step at a time."

"Meeting your godfather would be moving too swiftly?"

"Maybe." Dropping my gaze, I sink my teeth into my lower lip.

"Is there a reason I shouldn't meet this man?"

"Of course not," I say hastily. The last conversation I had with Dominic flashes through my mind. Introducing the two of them will have to wait for the time being. I admit softly, "You're confusing me. I'm not sure what to think of you or what's going on with us."

His lips ghost over mine. "Maybe that's a good thing. Maybe you need to stop thinking so much and rely on how I make you feel."

That's exactly what happens when I'm around him. My brain automatically clicks off and I'm reduced to a mass of quivering hormones.

"Would you like to use the pool?"

Smiling, my brows draw together. "I didn't bring a suit."

"Do we need them?"

That question makes me laugh. "Ah, yeah. I think we do."

"Have you forgotten that I've already seen you naked?" Leaning forward, he brushes his lips over mine. "You're a delicious sight, all pressed up against the glass with the city in the background."

Heat fills my cheeks. "We can't," I whisper.

"Of course we can. No one is allowed up here until I allow it."

Grasping at straws, I murmur, "I'm sure there are cameras." Am I tempted to give in? Tempted to skinny-dip with him?

Yeah, I am.

"The cameras have been disabled for the time being."

His answer makes me pull away. I frown. "How do you know?" Is he telling me what I want to hear so that I'll give in? A month from now, will I find a video clip of me swimming in the buff or doing a lot more? That thought cools some of ardor rushing through me.

"I know the owner of the building," he explains. "Call it a special privilege."

I raise a brow, wondering how many other women have been treated to a night on the rooftop.

"You do this often?" I blurt.

A knowing smile slowly spreads across his face. It makes me want to deck him.

"Jealous?"

I snort, trying to sound haughty. "Hardly."

Maybe.

A little.

He settles his fingers under my chin and tips my face toward his. "I've never brought a woman up here. I told you- I don't date. I fuck. But for you, I'm willing to make an exception."

His words make my belly quiver.

Do I believe him?

Studying him, I realize that- yeah, I do. Matteo has to know that he doesn't have to wine and dine me so that I'll have sex with him.

Yet here we are, standing amid the beautiful gardens on the rooftop deck after enjoying a decadent dinner prepared just for us.

Of course I'm wavering.

"You're absolutely sure the cameras have been turned off?"

Hunger burns his eyes. "Positive."

Feeling nervous and unsure, my tongue darts out to moisten my lips. His eyes drop to them, and a groan rumbles up from deep within his chest.

"Okay."

An instant later, he pulls me to him. His lips descend for a kiss so consuming that I feel drunk from it. Mouth rising from mine, he backs away. Still dazed from the kiss, I watch as he sinks onto one of the deck chairs.

"Strip for me."

A ball of apprehension forms in my gut. I've never stripped with the intention of seducing or turning someone on. I've peeled off my clothing while someone else did the same so we could jump into bed. But no one has ever sat down and simply watched me undress.

I stand frozen in place, unsure what to do. I watch Matteo's face. The way his eyes roam over my body makes my pulse pound.

Moving back to Chicago, re-starting my life, I didn't realize it at first, but a theme has emerged. It's one of me stepping out of my comfort zone. Pushing my own limits. And this is just another example.

I could say no.

But I don't want to.

I have no idea what will happen with Matteo in the long run, but I want to enjoy our time together while it lasts.

I step out of my sandals. My fingers hover over the buttons of my blouse. I can't stop them from trembling as I slip one button free from its hole before moving on to the next.

The noise from the city below fades into the background. I'm only aware of Matteo sitting in front of me, watching every single brush of my fingers against my body. Having his undivided attention makes me feel sexy.

When I reach the last button, the material parts before I slip it off my shoulders, allowing it to fall to the ground. I can almost feel the way his eyes caress my naked flesh. The way he continues watching as I bare more of it for him.

My fingers move to the waistband of my shorts and pop open the button. I lower the zipper and wiggle the fabric over my hips until it meets the same fate as the shirt. Eyes locked on his, I stand before him in pale pink panties and a lacy bra.

Reaching around my back, I unhook the clasp. The straps slide down my shoulders, and the cups fall away.

What Matteo said before is correct. He *has* seen me naked. That knowledge doesn't vanquish the skittishness pounding through me. My fingers slip beneath the elastic band of my panties, but I don't immediately remove them.

Holding his gaze, I silently beg him to take over.

He takes pity on me and stands, his gaze never faltering from mine.

His fingers go to the top of his shirt and begin unfastening the buttons. When he reaches the bottom, his shirt hangs open, displaying a strip of olive-toned skin. He shrugs it off and makes quick work of his jeans, revealing tight black boxer briefs.

In the blink of an eye, those disappear as well.

My breath catches at the sight of him... all that firm, muscular flesh.

He's gorgeous.

Matteo walks toward me with a hand extended. I take it without hesitation. We move to the edge of the pool, and he smiles at me before we jump in.

CHAPTER TWENTY-FOUR

I wake the next morning to memories of what happened last night with Matteo flashing through my mind. Stretching, I smile and sink further into the soft covers.

The other side of the bed is empty.

I push the pang of disappointment from my mind. Just because he said all the words I wanted to hear doesn't mean that we've somehow become embroiled in a relationship.

I told myself that I would enjoy whatever this is between us and that's exactly what I plan to do. I refuse to overthink or overanalyze the situation. If all we do is have fantastic sex-and make no mistake, the sex has been mind-blowing-I'll enjoy the ride for as long as it lasts.

There's no reason why I shouldn't.

I'm a grown, single woman. I have nothing to be ashamed of for indulging in a relationship solely based on sex.

A noise from the kitchen makes me sit up. Holding the white comforter to my naked breasts, I strain my ears and listen for the slightest sound.

Just as I start to relax, chalking it up to an overactive imagination, I hear it again. Someone's moving around in the kitchen. That last noise was *definitely* the closing of a cabinet door. The fine hair on my arms stands at attention. As I'm about to get out of bed and throw on some clothes, Matteo fills the doorway looking rumpled.

The tension filling me instantly fades. I smile, realizing that he's naked and holding two cups of coffee.

"I'd be careful with that, if I were you. One stumble and you could be permanently scarred for life."

His cock hardens as I stare unabashedly at it.

"Trust me, the thought occurred to me once or twice."

My eyes move back up to his. "Thank you for bringing me coffee in bed."

Sauntering closer, he holds out one mug like an offering. I slip my hands around the ceramic and bring it to my lips for a small sip. The dark, aromatic roast scalds my throat.

Perfect.

"I brought you something else as well."

Setting his mug down on the mirrored nightstand, his erection juts out at me. I can't remember seeing anything so tempting. I'm fascinated by its length and girth. I lean closer and lick the tip like it's a lollipop. One hand wraps around his thick shaft as the other settles under the heavy weight of his balls. Gently I begin massaging his sac. My fingers curl around the circumference, gliding up and down his cock before I bring the bulbous head to my lips and suck him deep inside my mouth. I flatten my tongue against the bit of sensitive skin where the head and shaft meet as I move up and down. His fingers tunnel through my hair and sink into my scalp, holding me firmly in place. Hearing his low moan of pleasure makes me hasten my pace.

Just when I think he might be close to coming, he gently pushes me away. A popping sound fills the room as I release his cock. I glance up at him in question. He continues towering over the side of the bed, his eyes burning into mine. Disappointment surges through me that he won't allow me to finish the job.

I want to make him come.

I want him to fall apart.

I want to bring him to his knees.

Matteo is always composed. Always perfectly put together. Even when he's working out. He's not a man who easily loses control.

"Turn over," he bites out, sending my heartrate skyrocketing.

I scramble to do his bidding. Doggie style has never been one of my favorite positions. I've only done it a few times. It was lackluster at best. My boyfriend seemed to enjoy it, but I couldn't get off.

If anyone can change my opinion about being on all fours, it's this man. The sound of him tearing into a condom package breaks the silence. As soon as I'm on my hands and knees with my ass in the air, Matteo grabs me by the hips and drags me to the edge of the bed.

"Spread your legs."

I oblige.

"Further."

I widen them more. A hand lands on the middle of my back and pushes my chest toward the mattress. I feel open and exposed.

Matteo cups my cheeks and massages the firm globes. My eyes close. His touch feels incredible. I'm not comfortable with the position, but I like what he's doing. My inhibitions start to dissolve.

A hand slips between my legs and strokes my pussy lips before zeroing in on my clit, rubbing it in tight little circles. I arch against his hand, seeking more contact. His blunt-tipped fingers are pure magic. As I start to spiral, he dips a finger inside my wetness, eliciting a groan.

I've never met a man who knows how to work a woman's body the way he does.

He pumps his finger inside me until my core pulses around him. I want to feel his hard length buried deep inside my pussy, filling me to the brim. Making me lose control. Removing his finger from me, he trails it over the cleft that divides my cheeks. I freeze because no one has ever touched me there.

I gasp when his teeth sink into one of my ass cheeks. The bite isn't painful, but will leave a mark. His breath feathers over my heated flesh. His tongue darts inside me and I arch, wanting only to get closer.

His hands once again grip my cheeks. The head of his cock brushes against my lower lips. He coats himself in my wetness and enters me. I let out a keening wail as he slides all the way in to the hilt.

He keeps a firm hold on my hips as he continues moving in and out of me. He's not slamming home, but slowly stoking the fires within, pushing me higher and higher until we both explode with pleasure.

Curling his body around mine, he nips at my shoulder and pulls away. The moment his cock slides free, he delivers a sharp, stinging slap to my bottom. I yelp and turn to glare at him. He grins, his eyes still holding remnants of simmering heat.

Matteo heads to the bathroom attached to my bedroom to dispose of the condom. Reappearing moments later, he pulls on his boxers. My heart sinks and I wonder if he stuck around this morning just to get in another round before disappearing for good.

I hate myself for feeling disappointed.

Maybe even hurt.

I need to get better at this whole *just sex* thing. If his normal pattern holds true, I won't hear a word from Matteo for at least a week. I could kick myself for believing him when he told me that he was interested in something more. For being seduced by a romantic dinner. For believing that I was different than the other women who came before me. I want to laugh as that thought slams into my brain. How stupid am I for falling for such an obvious and unoriginal line?

Gathering the sheet around me, I pray that he'll just leave. I'm not in the mood for any more lies.

"So, I was thinking we could go for a run. Then maybe grab some breakfast afterward."

The disappointment and hurt that had been bubbling up in me instantly vanishes.

"Sure. That sounds good." I hold back a grin. I can't allow myself to get too jacked up. Breakfast and a run don't necessarily mean anything.

"All right," he pulls on his jeans, "I'm going home to change. I'll be back in about ten minutes." He holds my gaze. "Is that enough time for you?"

"Yep." I throw off the sheets I'd just gathered around me and hop out of bed. His eyes smolder as they track my movements.

He covers his gorgeous chest by yanking on a shirt. "You'd better get some clothes on," his words are low, tinged with a hint of a growl, "or we won't be going for that run. Instead, you'll find yourself flat on your back for another hour."

Hmmm.

Sounds tempting.

CHAPTER TWENTY-FIVE

Matteo and I spend the entire weekend together. Much like Saturday, I wake up the next morning to coffee in bed. Before I can enjoy my java, Matteo's face is between my legs, licking and nibbling until I scream his name. I don't have a chance to catch my breath before he buries his cock deep inside me, making me orgasm again.

There's no denying that Matteo is a fierce, demanding lover. He has pushed me outside my comfort zone, but I can't say that I regret it. Boneless and completely sated, we hit the streets again to jog along the lakefront.

Even though everything seems fine between us, I keep waiting for him to pull away. To tell me that he needs to take off before disappearing from the face of the earth again.

But he doesn't.

We spend Sunday afternoon strolling along the streets of downtown Chicago, just meandering through the different shops lining Michigan Avenue. There's no particular destination for this outing. And no time constrictions or restraints. He holds my hand the entire time we're together.

Matteo asks question after question about my childhood, as if he's trying to delve deeper into what events have shaped me into the person I now am. It gives me cautious hope that whatever is unfolding between us isn't just a casual weekend fling.

As we grab sandwiches from a food truck late Sunday afternoon, it occurs to me that I'm the one who's been doing most of the talking. That needs to change.

"You mentioned that you were raised here, do your parents still live in Chicago?" Opening the red and white checkered wrapper, I take a huge bite of my Italian beef sandwich. My eyes almost roll up inside my head. The shaved beef, soft bread, and hot peppers hit my taste buds at the same time.

Mmmm, delicious!

"Yes, they're still here."

I wait for a moment, hoping he'll elaborate. He doesn't.

The only thing I know about Matteo is that he grew up in Chicago, has four siblings, and spent time in Italy as a child.

Does he still visit Italy on a regular basis?

I have no idea.

He hasn't divulged any other tidbits. He hasn't mentioned anything personal at all. A little voice inside my head wonders if his evasiveness is a red flag.

If he didn't live next door, I'd be convinced that he had a wife and kids stashed away somewhere. I don't believe that for a minute, but the thought is sobering. The high I've been riding on all weekend begins to evaporate.

"Do your siblings still live in the area as well?"

"Yes."

I can't imagine what it would be like to have a large, boisterous family or a houseful of people during the holidays. Even when my mother's parents were alive, it was just the five of us. There weren't any loud, animated dinners at our house. My grandparents were stoic Germans.

"You ready to head back?"

Jostled out of my thoughts, I realize that the weekend is almost over, and I still have school work to complete. I'd planned to put in five or six hours on Saturday afternoon, but I pushed it off when Matteo and I ended up spending the day together. I can't continue to procrastinate. I'll have a long night ahead of me even if I start an hour from now.

I sneak a peek at Matteo as we continue walking side by side.

If I'm up until two o'clock in the morning, spending the weekend with him has been worth it. I have zero regrets.

As we head back to Lexington Place, I keep thinking about how there's still so much that I don't know about him. When I try to ask questions, he gives me the bare minimum in response.

Is it on purpose?

I don't want to believe it is, but...

Tired of stewing over his secrecy, I finally blurt, "You don't talk about yourself very much." If he's unwilling to open up even a little bit, I don't know how much more of myself I can invest in this relationship.

His dark eyes shift in my direction. "What is it that you want to know?"

I shake my head, unsure of what to ask. I want him to share bits and pieces of himself with me because he wants to, not because I extracted it through an interrogation.

"What is it that you do?"

I always see him in expensive suits, so he's a professional of some sort. But he's never mentioned a job or career. It strikes me as odd that I've spent the weekend in bed with him, and I don't even know what he does for a living. A sliver of unease pierces me.

I don't even know his last name.

I almost stop short at that realization.

"I own a few businesses, along with some real estate."

Okay... that's not vague.

"Oh?" I ask, hoping a sign of interest will encourage him to elaborate.

He remains silent.

Fueled by frustration, I prompt, "What kind of businesses?" Maybe what he does isn't legal. I almost laugh at myself for being ridiculous. Of course, it's legal. I've never consorted with anyone involved in criminal activities. Dear Lord, my parents would roll over in their graves if I did.

That thought makes me wince.

"I own three restaurants and some commercial properties."

Air whooshes from my lungs in relief. I hadn't realized just how tense my body had become.

Restaurants.

Completely legal.

"Wow." That seems normal enough. Although I wouldn't have pegged Matteo for a restaurateur. Maybe a stockbroker? Or a fortune five hundred business owner. What I do know is that he lives in a posh building and is driven around in a limousine. So he obviously does quite well for himself.

"Would I know them?"

Silence stretches out between us before he says in a clipped tone, "Osteria, Trattoria Bartelone, and Osprey."

My feet grind to a halt at the names he's just thrown out. "You own *those* restaurants?"

He stops a few feet away and pierces me with a sharp look. "Yes, they're mine."

I shake my head in wonder. "Those are three of the most exclusive restaurants in the greater Chicago area." My mind tumbles back to our first dinner together. "You took me to Osprey." It's always booked at least six months in advanced.

I'd marveled at how we waltzed in and were immediately shown to a table. A nice one, at that. Then there's the deferential treatment he received from the staff. I just assumed that's the way Matteo is normally treated. Power radiates from him. Even if he hadn't been the owner, people would still give him a wide berth. Women would still stare with pent-up longing. I see it in the people we pass every time we're out together.

"Yes."

I frown in confusion. "Why didn't you say something then?"

He shrugs. Even outfitted in jeans and a gray Henley, he looks elegant. "It didn't seem important at the time. We were just getting to know one another."

I'm not sure how to respond.

Should he have clued me in?

Maybe.

Maybe not.

It wouldn't have made a difference to me. I've been enamored since I first laid eyes on Matteo. Whenever we come into contact with one another, those feelings only seem to intensify.

"You're right," I finally say, "but it makes me realize that I know next to nothing about you. We've spent the entire weekend together and I couldn't tell you anything more than what I already knew." My eyes continue holding his, begging for some answers. Begging him to let me in.

As soon as I finish speaking, a shield falls over his eyes. Instead of acknowledging my words, he jerks his head in the direction we've been walking. "Should we continue?"

Stunned by the dismissal, I start moving again. The little crumbs he shared continue to churn in my head.

Should I feel hurt by the fact that he isn't willing to be real with me? We may not be an official couple, but it's hard to trust someone when you think they're keeping secrets.

Who is Matteo?

Who is he *really*?

I don't have the slightest clue.

And that, I realize with a pang of regret, is a deal breaker for me. He's peppered me with questions all weekend long, and I've answered them honestly. Even when it dredged up painful memories.

If he hadn't tried to get inside my head, I probably could have let his behavior go. I could take our relationship at face value. Keep it light and airy. Less personal. Strictly sexual.

He's the one who insisted on taking things further.

Not me.

When we're about a block from the building, I stop walking. Again, he gives me a questioning look. The openness I'd been privy to all weekend is long gone. A closed off expression has taken up residence on his handsome face.

I don't understand it.

And I don't understand the reasons behind it. Why does he feel the need to be so guarded with me when I've been nothing but forthcoming with him?

Not only with my past but sexually, as well. I've given him more this weekend than I ever gave Eric. I've let him in when I haven't been able to do that with another human being in two years. For reasons I can't begin to fathom, I've put myself out there. I've allowed him to get close. I've allowed myself to be vulnerable with him.

But none of that has been reciprocated.

"If this is going to go any further, I need to know more about you. I've let you into my life, but it doesn't feel as if you're willing to do the same in return." I take a breath. "If this is just sex, tell me." Because that's not what this weekend felt like at all. Even though I'm lying through my teeth, I force myself to say the words. "I'm fine with it. Just have the courtesy to be straight with me. Don't pretend this is more than what it is. I assure you, the pretense isn't necessary."

I don't want to develop feelings for Matteo when there's no chance of a future with him. I need to know if we're just sleeping together so I can protect my heart.

With two quick steps, he swallows up the concrete between us and takes me into his arms.

"Is that what you want, Grace?"

I shrug, afraid to give voice to my thoughts. Afraid to lay myself completely bare.

"Because that's not what I want," he says. "I apologize if that's the impression I've given you. That's not how I wanted to come across."

His words fill me with relief, but caution and unease continue to swirl within me. Until he gives me more, how can I trust him?

"I'm used to keeping people, women especially, at arm's length. Just give me time."

Somewhat reassured that I'm not making more of this relationship than is warranted, I give him a small smile. "Okay."

He responds by crushing his lips down onto mine. Drawing my body closer, my breasts flatten against the solid wall of his chest. My arms automatically loop around his neck.

All too soon, he breaks the kiss.

"How much work do you have to finish up tonight?"

"Not much," I lie.

Hunger ignites in his eyes. "Good."

Hands linked, we quickly stride up the last block. Mikey, the weekend doorman, opens the heavy glass door as we approach. His eyes twinkle as he watches us step into the lobby. As we head toward the elevator, I see Chloe at the front desk. Our gazes collide before hers dart to the man at my side.

"Chloe! What are you doing here?"

Eyes on Matteo, her face pales. Then she looks at me. For an uncomfortable moment, she doesn't say a word. None of us do.

My brows knit together as I try to figure out why she's acting so odd.

"Chloe?"

She shakes herself out of the mental stupor she's fallen into and forces a tight-lipped smile. It doesn't reach her eyes.

When she remains quiet, I ask, "Is everything okay?" I've never seen her this edgy and tense before. I don't know what to make of it.

"What? Oh, um, everything's fine. I was in the neighborhood and thought I'd stop by." Again, her green eyes shift to Matteo before moving back to mine. "Obviously, you're busy." She shrugs as if it's no big deal. "I should have texted first. I didn't realize..." Her face colors as she takes a step toward the door. "I better get going. Call me later, okay?"

Before I can introduce her to Matteo, she flies out the door. I frown. I have no idea why she acted so strangely. You'd think Chloe would be ecstatic to meet someone I'm spending time with. But that wasn't the case at all. It's like she couldn't get away from me fast enough.

"I take it that was a friend of yours?"

"Um, yes. My best friend, Chloe." I've told him all about her. Since this is potentially turning out to be more than just sex, I would have liked to introduce them. I want Matteo to meet the people who are important to me.

Guess it will have to happen another time.

Matteo lifts my hand to his mouth and presses a light kiss against it. "Ready to head upstairs?"

My heart melts at such a sweet gesture.

"Yes."

As we board the elevator, he reels me to him. All thoughts of Chloe disappear in the blink of an eye as we head up to our floor.

CHAPTER TWENTY-SIX

"Hey, thanks for meeting me," Chloe mutters.

I can tell something is wrong because Chloe is abnormally subdued. Hoping I'm just reading into things that aren't there, I smile. "Of course!" I set my purse down on the table. "I'm glad you could get away from work for a quick lunch."

She doesn't smile. "Me, too." In fact, she avoids eye contact.

We slide into opposite sides of the booth near a window that overlooks the busy street. Cars and people race past. A waitress stops by with a pitcher of water and takes our order. Feeling concerned, I watch as Chloe fidgets with her phone.

I haven't talked to Chloe in a few days. Since I didn't get a lot completed over the weekend, I've spent Monday, Tuesday, and Wednesday submerged in my coursework while trying to keep up with my volunteer schedule. Matteo has been tied up with his restaurants.

Which is probably for the best.

I don't think I could handle having him around when I have so much reading to catch up on. His presence is distracting. I can't focus when he's anywhere near me.

Thinking about him puts a dreamy smile on my face. I can't help it. The man makes me feel giddy. We have yet to label our relationship, but knowing I'm more than a booty call is enough for now. We agreed to take it slow and see where it goes.

After a few moments of silence, Chloe shifts in her seat. What's going on with her? Ever since I ran into her at my building Sunday evening, she's been acting strangely.

I don't like the awkwardness between us. It feels foreign. When I first saw her after not speaking for two years, it didn't feel this uncomfortable. "Chloe?" The growing silence continues to stretch my nerves to the breaking point. "What's going on?"

I don't expect the words that tumble from her lips.

"Are you seeing Matteo Valentini?"

Valentini?

Is that his last name? I didn't know. I can't remember if I asked that question while we were out walking Sunday afternoon.

Val-en-tini.

Slowly I repeat his last name in my mind.

Wait a minute…

I sit up a little straighter. "You know him?" I had the weirdest feeling when I saw her in the lobby that something was up. I assumed she was taken aback to see me with someone. Especially when I hadn't mentioned it before.

I'm beginning to realize it's more than that.

The way she keeps watching me and the cautious look in her eyes has all my muscles tensing up. Air gets clogged in my throat as I wait for her to drop a bomb.

Maybe Matteo is married.

Maybe he has a family tucked away in the suburbs.

I'm surprised when disbelieving laughter bursts from her lips. "Um, yeah. *Everyone* knows who Matteo Valentini is."

I blink, trying to play mental catch-up. What am I missing here? It must be something huge from the way she's behaving. "They do?"

Leaning toward me, Chloe says in a low voice, "He owns Covet."

For a moment, I stare at her while processing that information. Details about the nightclub flood my brain. Each time I was there, he was as well. I thought it was a coincidence. Guess not.

I slowly say the words as if trying them on for size. "Matteo owns the place where you work?"

Eyes wide, she nods. "Yeah."

My mind whirls. "But he didn't know who you were the other day." He looked right at her and didn't say a word. At least he pretended not to have a clue. The pit of my belly tightens. Would he do that?

"I've only been working there for a few months. And it's just a couple times a week. He owns the place, but a manager handles the staff. We see Matteo around the club, but he rarely deals with personnel issues. He leaves that to Rocco."

I shake my head, trying to absorb what she just told me.

Is this discovery really that big of a deal?

No. Although I don't understand why Matteo didn't tell me himself when we talked the other day.

"Okay. So, he owns a nightclub, a few restaurants, and some commercial real estate."

Blowing out an exasperated sigh, she whispers harshly, "Grace, the Valentini family owns half the damn city of Chicago."

Needing to distance myself from her and this conversation, I sit all the way back against the padded bench. "What are you talking about, Chloe?"

"Don't you know who the Valentini family is?"

The Valentini family?

I shake my head.

The name means nothing to me.

"Should I?"

"They run the city. They have their hands in all of the politician's pockets. There's even talk that they own the police, which explains why they're never brought up on charges. Everything they're investigated for seems to roll off their backs. I've heard some of the lawyers at work talk about it. These aren't people you should be involved with."

Frustrated and confused, I ask, "What does that mean? How does one family wield that kind of power?" It sounds ludicrous. *She* sounds ludicrous. I want to laugh and roll my eyes, but I can tell by her frightened expression that she's serious. She wholeheartedly believes what she's saying.

Eyes wide, she mouths the words, *"They're mafia."*

Unable to control myself after hearing that crazy reply, I laugh until tears leak from the corners of my eyes. Out of the two of us, Chloe has always had the more vivid imagination. I think it's completely run away from her this time.

Mafia.

Give me a break.

The man isn't a criminal. He's a businessman. A restaurateur.

When I'm calm enough to string words together again, I say, "Come on, Chloe. Matteo owns a few businesses. Restaurants. A club. Real estate. Just because he's Italian doesn't mean his family is involved with anything illegal or are part of some underground crime organization." Rolling my eyes, I add, "You sounds ridiculous."

Undaunted by my skepticism, Chloe places her hand over mine. I wince as her fingers bite into my flesh. "Grace, please, you need to be careful. That's all I'm saying." Her eyes search mine. "Why didn't you mention that you were seeing him?" She shakes her head. "When did this even start?"

"It's a recent development," I say evasively. "I didn't mention anything because it wasn't serious."

Concern shines from her wide green gaze. It pricks something deep inside me. "But it's getting serious?"

I shrug, unsure of how much to reveal. "I don't know. We spent the weekend together."

Her eyes widen as if something has just clicked in her brain. "Oh my God, *he's* the one you slept with two weeks ago!" She whisper-yells the words.

Heat floods my cheeks as I glance around the diner. Thankfully no one is paying us any attention. "Shhh! You don't have to yell it!"

"It was him, wasn't it?"

I still don't understand why this is a big deal. It sounds like Chloe has been listening to idle gossip. "Yes, okay? It was him."

She's silent for a beat, as though she's piecing everything together in her head. "So, you slept with Matteo on Friday, and then, during the week, Dominic told you that he has feelings for you and wants to explore a relationship. A few days later, you end up spending the weekend with Matteo. Do I have it right?"

If my face weren't beet red before, it is now.

That sounds so bad.

Chloe murmurs, "Look, I'm not judging you." She snorts at that idea. "I'm the last person to judge anyone. I thought you were contemplating a relationship with Dominic." Chloe looks as confused as I feel. Before this weekend with Matteo, I did give serious consideration to the idea. "What happened to *that*?"

Glancing away, I look out the window, watching as people walk by while gathering my thoughts. "I love Dominic. He will *always* be my family, but I don't have romantic feelings for him. They're just not there."

"Does he know how you feel? Have you told him about Matteo?"

I shake my head. "No. I haven't discussed any of this with him. When Matteo and I first slept together, I assumed it would be a one-time thing. I never dreamed it would turn into something more. That's why I didn't bother mentioning it."

"I don't even know where you would meet a man like him." Her brows furrow. "Was it at Covet? Is that where it happened?" She sounds upset, as if this predicament might inadvertently be her fault.

I shake my head. "No." I don't tell her about the times I ran into him there. "He lives next door."

Her eyes bulge from their sockets as her voice rises a decibel. *"Matteo Valentini is your neighbor?"*

"Yes." I take a sip of my Diet Coke before continuing. "We ran into each other a few times around the building. One thing led to another."

She looks incredulous. "You never said anything!"

I shrug. "I didn't know his last name, Chloe. I didn't think you would know him." And I definitely didn't expect her to flip out like this either.

"I don't know. I... I just wish I'd been able to warn you sooner. Maybe then..." Biting her lip, she glances away and asks, "Do you like him, Grace? Is this serious?"

Sidestepping the question, I say instead, "It's too early to tell."

Wanting her to understand, I add, "I just know that being with him feels good. For the first time in two years, I feel alive again."

My words have the intended effect. Her eyes are still filled with concern, but they soften. "I just wish you were with someone..." She pauses, trying to choose her words more carefully. "I wish you were involved with someone... *safer*."

I laugh. "Matteo is perfectly safe."

I feel secure and protected when I'm with him. He doesn't feel dangerous to me. Powerful, yes. Commanding, for sure. But I don't think he would ever hurt me.

Continuing to chew her lower lip, she says, "Sometimes I see him at the club. He makes me nervous. I don't like the idea of you being with him. You've been so *insulated* and now you're seeing a mob boss?" She shakes her head. "It doesn't make sense."

I sigh. "I am not seeing a mob boss." That sounds preposterous. "I think you've heard too many rumors. Plus, how dangerous can he be if you work for him?"

"I don't have anything to do with the man! He hasn't said two words to me. I think he's at the club during the day. When I'm there, I just do what I'm paid to, which is dance. That's it. The money is good, and I'm not doing anything wrong. I keep my nose clean, and I mind my own business." She gives me a sharp look and adds, "And I sure as hell don't ask questions."

A shiver scuttles down my spine. Matteo's reluctance to answer the most innocuous of questions comes to mind out of nowhere.

"Just promise me that you'll be careful, okay?"

I give her a reassuring smile. "There's no reason for me to be careful. Whatever you've heard about Matteo and his family are nothing more than lies." They have to be.

Her gaze skitters away from mine. "I don't think so, Grace."

CHAPTER TWENTY-SEVEN

I don't tell Matteo about the ridiculous gossip Chloe has brought to my attention. I'm not trying to bury my head in the sand, but I think Chloe has watched *The Godfather* one too many times. Or maybe she's read too many mafia novels with far-fetched plotlines.

I've toyed with asking him the questions buzzing around in my brain, but I haven't seen much of Matteo since last weekend. I've been overloaded with coursework and volunteering. And Matteo isn't home during the day or evenings. His hands are full with the restaurants.

And Covet.

The only real time we spend together is when he slips into my bed around two in the morning. Waking up with him next to me is the best feeling in the world. And the way it feels when he's buried deep inside my body is even better. When we come together, the chemistry that flares to life between us is undeniable.

Without tangible evidence regarding the concerns Chloe voiced, I can't confront Matteo. He's finally starting to open up to me. I can't fling far-fetched accusations at him about his family. That will only shut him down.

I need someone else's opinion on the matter. Which is why I ask

Jonathan to take a walk when we have a much needed fifteen-minute break between tours.

Jonathan and I have become fast friends over the past few weeks. Right from the start, it felt as if I'd known him for years. Which is unusual for me since I don't normally click with people so quickly.

He invited me to his house to meet Jamie, whom I adore. The two of them are so good together. Jamie is quieter and more reserved, but warm and caring. He allows Jonathan to soak up all the attention while watching from the sidelines. They balance each another out perfectly, and I love spending time with them.

As busy as life is, I still lie awake at night thinking about what Chloe divulged. I listen to the sound of Matteo breathing next to me, asking myself if any of the allegations could be true. I've done a few internet searches, but found nothing damning. Just innuendo. Gossip. Mostly the same rumors Chloe brought to my attention in the first place. It does nothing to lend credence to all the speculation. Which means I'm in the same place as before.

"What did you want to talk about, doll face?"

I smile at the term of endearment as Jonathan slings a wiry arm around my waist and tugs me closer. The wind whips off the lake, blowing over us.

Stalling, I ask teasingly, "How do you know that I want to talk? Maybe I just wanted to spend a little time alone with you."

He rolls his eyes. "Undoubtedly. But I can tell there's something on your mind. You've been a bit preoccupied lately."

Pushing away, I search his face. "You could really tell?"

His normally humor-filled eyes brim with concern. "I see it because I know you."

I nibble at my lower lip. I love volunteering at the museum, and I love leading guided tours. It bothers me that I haven't been giving one hundred percent to the people who come in to learn more about the art currently on display. I don't want to appear unprofessional by allowing my personal life to interfere with my professional one.

Jonathan tugs me back into the warm comfort of his arms. Because we've gotten to be so close, he knows what I'm thinking.

"No one else has noticed. Don't give it a second thought. Now tell me what's going on in that pretty little head of yours. We've got roughly ten minutes until we need to head back inside for our next tours. So spill. Tell Uncle Johnny all about what's bothering you."

I laugh. "*Uncle Johnny?* That makes you sound like a pedophile."

He sighs dramatically. "Come on. Tick-tock. I'll need at least ten minutes to give you my best armchair analysis of the situation."

He's right. I'm procrastinating. Maybe I don't want to give voice to the ugly whispers that have been filling my head. Maybe I'm afraid that Jonathan will confirm everything Chloe said. If that ends up happening, I'll have no choice but to pop the bubble Matteo and I are living in by bringing it up to him.

I hedge, "You know the man I've been seeing..."

"Umm-hmm." He drawls out the sound.

"I told you that his name was Matteo." I pause for a moment as my heart pounds. "Matteo Valentini."

Jonathan doesn't say a word, but every muscle in his body goes whipcord tight. A deafening silence fills the void between us. I realize that what I've refused to believe- all the rumors, the online innuendo- is true. Matteo isn't simply a restaurateur and nightclub owner. Or someone who owns commercial real estate.

We keep walking, but Jonathan's body remains stiff. The longer the uncomfortable silence stretches between us, the more I panic.

"Jonathan," I whisper, "say something."

He stops and turns to me. His face has lost most of its color. "I didn't realize that's who he was." Heaving a breath, he mutters to himself, "I should have."

Though I dismissed Chloe when she voiced her concerns the other day, it's more difficult to do after a second person reacts similarly. "My friend thinks that his family is part of the mafia."

He laughs, but there's no humor in the sound. Which is odd because Jonathan is always laughing. Always happy. Always cracking jokes. The man doesn't have a serious bone in his body. It's one of the reasons I love being around him. His humor is infectious. He has the rare ability to make the dourest person smile. The fact that his normal, sunny disposition has fled is telling.

It frightens me more than I want to admit.

"Oh honey, his family isn't just part of the mafia. They *are* the mafia."

A chill of unease slithers down my spine at the seriousness of his tone.

Looking concerned, he shakes his head. "What the hell have you gotten yourself involved in?"

That question hits me like a punch to the stomach. This situation is much worse than what I allowed myself to believe.

"I don't know," I finally whisper. "I didn't have a clue as to who he was."

"How could you *not* know?"

Breathing through waves of nausea, I shake my head. "I haven't lived in Chicago for a long time. Matteo is my next-door neighbor. I ran into him a couple of times and then we started…"

His solemn expression transforms into a smirk. "Yes, I can just imagine what you two started doing. The man is completely gorgeous." Sounding more flippant, he adds, "Hell, knowing who he is, *I* would still sleep with him."

Those words break the thick, stifling tension that had fallen over us with the mere mention of *Matteo Valentini*.

Feeling torn, I ask, "What should I do?"

He looks sympathetic. "I don't know what to tell you, doll face. This is unchartered territory."

"Do you think I should talk to him?"

Jonathan squares his shoulders. "All right, by my estimation of the situation, you have three options."

I nod, feeling better that he's taking control and giving me some much-needed advice.

"Option number one is that you end it and walk away." His blue-green gaze turns solemn. "And you don't say one damn word about anything you heard."

Knowing everything I do, that's exactly what my next move should be. Why would I knowingly want to get involved with someone who has a notorious reputation and a shady past attached to him?

So why does the thought of breaking things off with Matteo make my heart ache?

"Option two is that you let the relationship run its course. I mean, how long will this thing between you two really last? A few weeks? A month or two?" He looks thoughtful. "I don't remember ever hearing of him being involved in a relationship before."

Chewing the inside of my cheek, I contemplate the merits of that choice. Can I feign ignorance for as long as it takes? Is it possible to screw Matteo out of my system? Or will I only grow to care about him more?

"Option three is that you talk to him. But only do that if you've lost your ever-loving mind and truly believe you two have a future together."

An arrow of dread pierces me at the idea of discussing these rumors with him.

We fall silent, both lost in our own private thoughts.

"No matter what you decide, you need to be careful. The Valentinis are a powerful family. No one knows for sure what they're involved in because nothing is ever publicly discussed. There are no loose ends to tie up," he raises his eyebrows, "if you catch my drift. It's all specula-tion and conjecture. Everyone in this city knows not to cross them, including the police and the DA's office. Nothing touches them, Grace. Do you know how powerful you need to be for your name to carry that kind of clout?"

Everything he says swirls around in my head. Jonathan is right. The Valentinis must be extremely influential to wield that kind of power.

Pulling me in for a hug, he whispers, "Is Valentini having you followed?"

Brows jerking together, I pull away. "No." I try to swallow down the rising paranoia. "I... well, I don't think so." Panic laces my voice as it continues to rise. "Why?"

He jerks his chin to the right. "You see that guy over there? He was inside the museum earlier today. He trailed behind our group at a discreet distance. I figured he was a cheapskate and didn't want to pay for the tour. But then, when we came outside, he followed. Now he's sitting where he can keep an eye on us. I'm willing to bet that when we head inside, he'll end up there as well."

I glance toward the parking lot. Sure enough, there's a man sitting on one of the benches. He's not turned directly toward us, more to the side as if he's looking at the Art Institute, but we're in his line of sight. I want nothing more than to discredit Jonathan's wild claims, but...

I think he's right. I think that man is following me.

And the only logical explanation is that he works for Matteo.

CHAPTER TWENTY-EIGHT

The rest of the afternoon creeps by. All Jonathan has done is reconfirm Chloe's concerns. I'd hope to dismiss these rumors as nothing more than outlandish gossip but now that I've heard a nearly identical story from a different source, how can I?

I can't.

The thought of Matteo having me followed makes goose bumps rise across my arms.

As much as I want to dismiss everything I've heard from my friends, I can't. Matteo is a Valentini. Enough insinuations have been made for me to question whether Matteo is someone I should allow into my life.

Jonathan is right. There are three options for me to consider.

I end things between us.

I ride this out and enjoy the sex until we part ways.

Or I tell him what I've heard and pray he'll be honest with me.

All the times I've tried asking questions flood through my mind. Matteo has never been forthcoming with personal information. Getting him to share anything is like trying to squeeze blood from a turnip. If I'd been smart, I would have listened to my instincts and questioned why he was so tight-lipped. Instead, I let it go, thinking that he would open up when he was ready.

The real question is, *can I continue to be with someone, continue having sex with him, if I can't trust him?*

I don't think I can.

Not even for a short period of time. If Matteo and I are going to be together—*really be together*—he needs to be honest with me.

For the first time since I've begun volunteering at the Art Institute, I'm relieved when the day ends. I need to go home and think. I need to figure out how to approach Matteo. Right before I leave, Jonathan wraps me up in his arms and tells me to take care. Those words take on more meaning than ever before.

As I push out through the doors, I get a text from Dominic saying that he'd like to see me for dinner tonight, and that his driver will be waiting outside for me.

Glancing around, I spot Henry waiting at the curb with the Range Rover.

I haven't seen Dominic in two weeks. Since he shared his feelings with me, things have been more strained between us. I want our relationship to shift back to the easy way it's always been. I don't want it to feel weird.

When he first mentioned us getting together, I was willing to consider it. *Us* being together is comfortable. Safe. In a way, it made sense.

But the more I thought about it, the more I realized that my feelings for him weren't romantic in nature. I love Dominic. I have *always* loved him. I may have crushed on him when I was a kid, but that's all it was. A harmless teenage crush. It wasn't rooted in reality.

What I need right now is for Dominic to be my godfather. The man who's been a permanent fixture and a pillar of strength in my life. Dominic is the closest thing I have to a father figure. I don't think I could bear to have him pull away because of my rejection.

The thought of losing him is scary.

I didn't plan to speak with Dominic tonight, but maybe it's best to straighten out one situation before tackling another.

The drive north takes more than an hour. But I'm grateful for the solitude. There's nothing I can do other than stare out the window as we move through the city toward the North Shore.

By the time we pull into the circular drive in front of Dominic's house, I feel more settled than when I first stepped into the car. Henry opens the door as I climb out. Then I head to the steps that lead to the mahogany front door. Maria greets me with a smile that lights up her weathered face. Seeing her sends a feeling of home flooding through me. It makes me realize that I shouldn't have waited so long to speak with Dominic.

"Mr. Grimaldi is on a call in his office. He says to make yourself at home on the terrace and he will join you as soon as he is able."

I nod in response.

"Would you like a glass of wine brought out to you, Miss Grace?"

After the stressful day I've had, a glass of wine sounds heavenly. The ride here relaxed me, but I'm anxious about speaking with Dominic. I don't want to hurt his feelings.

I set my purse on the credenza in the front hall. "Yes, a glass of wine sounds wonderful. Thank you, Maria."

As she heads to the kitchen, I add, "I'm going upstairs to change. I'll be down in a few minutes."

"Take your time." She glances toward Dominic's home office. "I think he may be a while."

Maria has managed Dominic's household since I was a kid. She's a warm woman with three children of her own. Her husband died ten years ago from a heart attack, and Dominic helped put her kids through college. Maria thinks the world of him.

Toeing off my heels, I head up the curving staircase. I've had my hair pulled up all day, so it feels good to loosen the band holding it in a bun. I run my fingers through the strands and lightly massage my scalp.

I change into a pair of yoga pants and a T-shirt. Using the back staircase, I hit the first floor and walk out onto the terrace. A glass of wine waits alongside a tumbler of amber colored liquid on the rocks.

Apparently, it's been a stressful day for Dominic as well.

Picking up the tumbler and my glass, I take a sip of the white wine before heading inside. I bet Dominic is still working in his study.

The door to his office is cracked open an inch. When I'm about a foot away, he snarls, "Well, that's not good enough! I told you this needed to be taken care of immediately!"

The tone of his voice sends a shiver of dread racing down my spine. My father often said that Dominic could be a vicious opponent who went for the jugular in the courtroom. In all the years I've known Dominic, I've never seen that side of him. I don't like the barely leashed violence in his normally teasing voice. It scares me.

There's a pause as I stand frozen in place, our drinks still clutched in my hands, unsure of what to do.

"No, goddamn it! You listen to me, you little bastard! You'd better find a way to remedy the situation, or I swear," his voice drops further, filling with a malice I never imagined him capable of, "I'll kill you with my own bare hands. Have I made myself clear?" There's another pause before he snaps, "Good. I expect to hear from you in the morning. No later than eight."

Without a goodbye, his phone hits the polished wood desk as if he slammed it down or threw it. I've never seen Dominic lose control. He's always calm and professional. I can't imagine what would cause him to act this way.

My heart beats wildly under my breast as I stand outside the office door. I should sneak out to the terrace to wait for him. Hopefully he'll be in a better mood by the time he gets there.

If not, dinner will be an uncomfortable affair. Thinking about it fills me with dread. I wonder if it's too late to find Henry and ask him to drive me back to the city. Just as I take a hasty step backward, the floorboards creak beneath my feet. In the silent hallway, it sounds like a gunshot.

There's no way Dominic didn't hear it.

Sucking in a deep breath, I paste a smile on my face and push open the door. I'm kicking myself for not staying outside and enjoying the sunset. Why did I think this was such a good idea? Dominic is the only person in the large, dark wood-paneled study, yet the thick tension hanging in the air is enough to choke me.

Surprised by my presence, his brooding blue gaze meets mine. As he pins me with a hard look, I stop in my tracks. It feels like the oxygen has been sucked out of the room. He stares at me in silence with a razor-sharp edge to his eyes. I stand rooted in my spot, shivering as a wave of apprehension slams into me.

"Gracie?" He barks out my name. "I thought Maria instructed you to wait on the terrace." He's never spoken to me in such an abrupt tone before.

Clearing my throat, I whisper, "I'm sorry." It takes effort to keep my voice steady. I have to remind myself that this is Dominic. *Dominic*. My godfather. The man I trust above everyone else. "You're always working so hard. I thought you might like a drink while you wrap business up. I didn't mean to intrude."

I don't want him to know that I overheard part of his phone call. I'm not sure why that feels imperative, but it does. Dominic has never made me feel nervous, scared, or uncomfortable, but I feel all of those emotions now.

On wooden legs, I force myself to close the distance separating us before setting his drink on the desk. He continues to hold my gaze until his eyes drop to the chilled amber liquid. He wraps his fingers around the glass before lifting it to his lips and downing a third of it. As the alcohol slides down his throat, he closes his eyes and sighs. He fills his lungs with a breath of air and releases it. When he opens his eyes again, all the tension and anger that had been darkening them disappears.

It's almost as if he'd never been agitated in the first place.

"Thank you, sweetheart. I really needed that."

My lips tremble as I fake another smile. I want to forget about the conversation I overheard. I want to escape the lingering unease that continues to permeate the atmosphere in this room. A hint of cigar smoke tinges the air. I've always found the masculine scent comforting, but right now it does nothing to alleviate my discomfort.

"I think dinner is ready." I hesitantly step toward the door, wanting to flee his presence. Which is something I've never felt before. These feelings are so strange and foreign that I don't know how to deal with them. "Should we go?"

He makes no move to rise from his chair. "If you wouldn't mind taking a seat, I'll have Maria hold dinner for a bit longer. There's something we need to discuss."

His words make my belly pinch with more unease. Before I can agree, he gets on the phone and calls the kitchen, instructing Maria to keep dinner warm until we're ready.

I have no choice but to stay.

His office feels claustrophobic. Almost as if the walls are pressing in on me. Bookshelves line one entire wall from floor to ceiling. A bar on the other side holds an assortment of fine liquor. A leather couch and two chairs sit in front of a fireplace. I normally love the view of the front gardens, but not today. The brightly colored mums bring me no joy.

I'd hoped that we could sit at the more informal arrangement with its couch and chairs. When Dominic makes no move toward the grouping, I slip into one of the chairs across from his desk. The silence that follows ratchets up my already taut nerves.

Picking up the tumbler, he takes another sip before setting it down again. "It's been brought to my attention that you've been keeping company with someone who, shall we say, is rather unsavory in character."

My mouth falls open in shock. *"What?"*

I squirm beneath his relentless stare. "Matteo Valentini." He pauses and studies me with his head tipped to one side. "You've been seeing him?"

The words may be arranged to form a question, but he isn't asking one.

I gulp as fresh nerves prickle in the pit of my belly. "Yes. We've seen each other a few times."

He continues to pin me in place for a long moment before finally looking away. My body deflates in relief. From the middle drawer, he pulls out a thick manila envelope and places it between us.

My eyes fall to it.

When I make no attempt to pick it up, he says, "Go on. Take a look."

My eyes lift to his in confusion. I moisten my lips. "Just tell me what's inside." When he remains silent, I add, "I don't want to play this game."

Instead of giving me an answer, he grabs the envelope, opens the fastener, and dumps the contents out onto his desk.

Photographs.

He picks up a black and white one. They all look to be eight by ten in size. The first one is slightly grainy. Dark. He glances at it and holds it out to me. I have no choice but to take the picture. I don't want to look, but I can't help myself.

My breath stalls as I stare down at the snapshot.

There's no mistaking the people on the glossy paper.

Matteo.

And me.

At Covet.

One of his hands is wrapped around my throat. The other sits high on my rib cage. His thumb rests beneath my breast.

The picture looks *erotic*.

The expression on my face...

Heat stings my cheeks.

Before I can explain the situation, another picture is handed over. This time, the image is sharper and brighter. I'm stepping into the limousine with Matteo. I try to take in every detail of the photograph, but my eyes are drawn to Matteo's face. His eyes are filled with an intensity, a burning desire, as he stares up at me from inside the vehicle.

Dominic holds out a third photo.

This one shows us running along the lakeshore.

Before I can process anything more, another is shoved into my hands.

It's one of us eating at Osprey.

A snapshot of us walking around the city slides in front of me. We're holding hands. I'm smiling at Matteo. I look happy. Instead of focusing on Matteo, I marvel at the happiness on my face while running a finger across my image.

How long has it been since I've smiled like that? Or had that sparkle in my eye?

Almost two years.

Matteo is the first person to make me feel lighthearted and free.

For the first time since walking into Dominic's office, anger roils through my veins. Who I see is none of his business. I'm a grown woman. He had no right to spy on me.

Glancing up from the photographs, I give him an incredulous look. "You had me followed?"

I'd allowed myself to believe it was Matteo's doing. I had no reason to assume Dominic would do such a thing. But he did. My godfather paid someone to tail me and snap pictures of private moments that weren't meant to be witnessed by a third party. The fact that Dominic would do something so sneaky shocks me.

Leaning forward, his eyes stay fixed on mine. He doesn't look the least bit regretful. Resting his elbows on the desk, he steeples his hands. "Damn right I did."

Unable to wrap my brain around what's happening, I shake my head. "Why would you do that?"

"I was concerned." He glances down at the photographs spread out across his desk. "Obviously I had good reason to be. Matteo Valentini is a dangerous man." When I don't reply, he continues with, "He's not someone you should be involved with."

Dominic is the third person to say that to me.

"Do you have any idea who his family is or even half the shit they're involved in?"

Biting my lower lip, I shake my head again. "I've heard some rumors. Until I figure out the truth for myself, that's all they are. Rumors."

Exasperated by my response, he runs a hand through his hair. "Oh, Gracie. You may be twenty-three years old, but you're too damn innocent and trusting. You take everyone at face value. You think everyone is like you- honest, with the best of intentions." Pausing, his eyes soften. "I don't want to see you get hurt or taken advantage of."

"Dominic-"

He cuts me off. In the blink of an eye, all the tenderness disappears. "Do you think Matteo Valentini is the kind of man your father would have wanted to see you with? Someone with ties to the mafia?"

I feel my face grow cold as every ounce of color drains from it. Bringing my dad, the one man I idolize, into this conversation is a low blow. Even for Dominic. My spine straightens and I snap, "My dad taught me to withhold judgment until I have all the facts. That's what I'm doing."

Drawing in a sharp breath, he exhales as if fighting to hang on to the last vestiges of his patience. "Gracie, please. I'm trying to protect you. I only have your best interests at heart."

I cringe when he pulls out another envelope. This time he hands it to me. "Open it."

Reluctantly I push the metal flaps together and slide the top open. Instead of dumping the contents like Dominic did a few moments ago, I slip my hand inside and pull out a sheaf of photographs.

Swallowing down a fresh bout of nausea, I look at the top one. It shows Matteo and a gorgeous woman with long, glossy dark hair clinging to his side.

Not wanting to continue staring at it, I flip to the next one.

Again, Matteo has been captured on film. This time he's with a beautiful blonde. She's tall and leggy.

Hardening my heart, I shuffle it to the bottom of the pile. The next picture is of him at a fancy function. A theme is emerging. Another woman is wrapped around him. Getting the gist of the pictures, I scan the rest. There are about fifteen in total.

Different women.

Different venues.

I throw down the stack and glance at Dominic, who still sits behind his desk. His gaze never leaves mine.

"I don't want you hurt by this man, and I'm afraid that's all he'll end up doing. Matteo Valentini has no intention of being faithful to you." He gestures at the photos. "Clearly."

I force down the bile rising in my throat.

"We aren't serious," I say. I don't want him to know how wounded I am by seeing Matteo with other women.

Dominic stares for a minute before he rises from his seat, coming around the desk, and squatting down in front of me. He takes my hands in his and gives them a squeeze.

Unable to meet his gaze, I stare at my lap.

"Look at me, Gracie."

I lift my eyes until they lock on his.

"It was never my intention to cause you pain. I think your parents would want me to protect you any way I see fit, even if it means having you followed. I know you don't like what I did, but it seemed necessary. I needed to know what was going on in your life since you weren't telling me."

Hearing him admit that he was aware of my withdrawal makes me feel worse. "I wasn't trying to keep this from you."

The edges of his lips lift fractionally. He doesn't believe me. "Things have been a bit strained between us lately. What I suggested to you," a hint of vulnerability enters his voice, "obviously isn't something you want."

"I needed some time to think about it." But he's right. I don't want our relationship changing.

Thankfully I don't have to say anything more. Dominic seems to understand. Smiling, he squeezes my hand again. "It's all right, Gracie. I told you it would be. The last thing I want is for our relationship to become awkward. Let's forget I ever mentioned anything and keep moving forward. Sound good to you?"

I feel as if a huge weight has been lifted from my shoulders. One I never realized was there. "I'm sorry."

With a sincere expression on his face, he shakes his head. "You have nothing to apologize for. At the time, I thought a relationship between us was worth exploring, but we both have to want it."

I nod. "I never intended to hurt you."

"You haven't." In the next breath he says, "But us not having the close relationship we've always enjoyed, does."

Bridging the gap between us, I wrap my arms around him and hug him tightly to me. "I should have told you right away when I realized how I felt. I shouldn't have let it linger. All it did was make everything uncomfortable when it didn't have to be."

"Enough said. We're putting this behind us. There's no reason for us to discuss it again, okay?"

Relief suffuses me. I give him a smile. "That sounds good."

With his arms loosely wrapped around me, he leans back so that his eyes can meet mine. "I know you won't agree with what I'm about to say, but you need to trust me on this." Dominic pauses. "I don't want you involved with Matteo Valentini. He's a dangerous man. You need to promise me that you'll steer clear of him from now on."

Sucking my lower lip into my mouth, I gnaw on it. "I need to at least talk with him." I owe him that much.

"He doesn't care about you." He points to the photographs strewn about his desk. "You're just a distraction."

A distraction.

Glancing at them feels painful.

I wonder how many of these women he's slept with since we've been together. All of them? Am I even surprised? I shouldn't be. Maybe Dominic's right. Maybe I am naïve.

"I can't avoid him," I say. "He lives next door to me."

Dominic's jaw tightens. "I know. That's why I think it would be best if you stay here until we can find a different place."

What?

Move?

No. I love my condo.

"Please, let me handle this." My gaze shifts to the glossy photos of Matteo with countless other women. "Obviously I don't matter to him." As embarrassing as it is to admit, I force out the words. "Whatever's going on between us is nothing more than a fling. Living next to him won't matter. He's barely home."

A look of doubt settles over Dominic's face. "Just stay here for a few weeks. That's long enough for him to understand that whatever was going on between you two is now over."

As tempting as it is to hide at Dominic's, I won't do that. I'm not going to alter my life to avoid having an adult conversation with Matteo. I went into our relationship with the understanding that if it turned out to be just sex, I would be fine with it.

I would enjoy it for what it was.

I need to hold myself to that vow.

I wish he'd been straight with me from the beginning and told me that he wasn't interested in being tied down.

He shouldn't have spent the weekend making love to me and walking around the city hand in hand. He shouldn't have led me on by pretending we were more than fuck buddies. The pretense was never necessary. I wanted Matteo on a physical level right from the get-go. I never made any bones about that.

"Gracie?"

Dominic's hands cradle my cheeks as I blink back to our conversation.

"The firm can send a letter instructing him that there is to be no further contact between the two of you."

A slight chuckle escapes me even though there's nothing funny about a cease and desist type of letter. "No. I don't want you involved in this." If everything I've heard about Matteo and his family is true, I don't want to drag anyone else into this breakup. I can handle Matteo on my own.

"You know I'd do anything for you."

My heart softens. I'm mad that Dominic had me followed and invaded my privacy but, I understand the rationale behind it.

Sort of.

"I'll take care of it on my own. Everything will be fine." God, I hope I'm right. "Our relationship was casual."

Those words shouldn't puncture my heart, but they do.

To me, what Matteo and I had was the start of something meaning-ful. Obviously, that was never really the case.

CHAPTER TWENTY-NINE

It seems easier to stay at Dominic's instead of going home. I know Matteo will show up in the middle of the night, and I need time to digest everything I've learned today.

When Matteo texts to ask where I am around midnight, I don't respond. There are so many questions bubbling up inside me.

Can I trust him to tell me the truth when he's done everything in his power to keep me ignorant?

He texts once. Then he calls. I turn off my phone after the second attempt and roll over to try to fall asleep. But I can't. My mind is too filled with Matteo. Like a specter, he haunts me for the rest of the night.

When I wake in the morning, my eyes feel gritty, and I'm exhausted. As much as I would love to stay in bed for a few more hours, I can't. I have two classes I can't afford to miss. I need to hustle home and take a shower before heading to campus.

By the time I make it down to the kitchen, Dominic has left for the day, and Maria has a steaming cup of coffee waiting in a to-go cup. Holding it, I savor the scent of roasted, freshly ground beans.

"Mmmmm, smells good, Maria. Thank you."

"Mr. Grimaldi wanted to make sure you had a cup to take with you. And Henry is waiting to take you downtown."

I nod. Dominic is so considerate.

If I were smart, I would accept the feelings he has for me. Is it possible for my feelings to deepen? Maybe. I can't deny the strong connection between us. We have a friendship that tightly binds us. Marriages have been founded on less than mutual love and respect.

As much as I wish I could love Dominic differently, I can't.

It doesn't feel right.

I think we're better off with what we have.

"I'm going to grab my purse, and I'll be on my way."

"Very good, Miss Grace."

There's a ton of traffic going into the city despite the early hour. My class doesn't begin until ten, so I have plenty of time. I can always skip the shower, run up, grab my bag for school, and have Henry drop me off on campus if necessary.

When we're halfway to Lexington Place, I fish my phone out of my purse. I haven't looked at it this morning. I'm afraid of what I'll find. But avoidance is no longer the way I want to handle the unpleasant parts of my life. I lived that way for two years. I can't do it any longer.

Pressing a button, I turn my phone on and wait as it comes to life. Once the home screen lights up, I see five missed calls and an equal amount of unread texts.

Not all of them are from Matteo.

Chloe texted twice to check in.

And Jonathan texted and called asking what I decided to do regarding my situation. He doesn't use any names and I wonder if he's worried that my phone is being tapped. After he realized someone was watching us, the notion isn't too ludicrous.

I'm still blown away that Dominic hired someone to watch me.

We roll up in front of Lexington Place shortly before eight o'clock. I thank Henry and hop out with my purse and coffee in hand. Normally I drink one cup, but I can tell this is going to be a morning when a second cup is needed to power through the day. I don't have to volunteer, so I can come home later and take a nap.

George opens the door as I rush toward it. I give him a smile before heading to the elevator. Minutes later, I'm inside my condo. I didn't expect to find Matteo waiting for me, but...

Okay, I don't know what I expected. I'm confused about where my feelings for him stand right now.

Stripping off my clothes, I jump in the shower. As hot water pours over my body, I feel my muscles loosen. The tension that had coursed through me goes down the drain. Closing my eyes, I lather my hair and let the spray rinse away the suds.

By the time I step out of the steamed-up glass enclosure, I feel more settled regarding what needs to be done. I grab a towel and dry my hair before rubbing my body. Then I wrap it around my chest, tucking in the end so the towel stays put as I walk into the bedroom to get dressed.

Partway to my dresser, my eyes land on the chair in the corner.

And the man sitting on it.

Clad in a black suit and wingtips, Matteo's long legs are stretched out in front of him. His body is angled forward, elbows propped on his knees. The tips of his fingers are steepled as his dark eyes pin mine.

My hand flies to my chest as if that will stop my heart from exploding.

"Matteo! What are you doing here?"

He doesn't say a word. I shift, uncomfortably aware that I'm wrapped in a towel that hits mid-thigh.

Ignoring my question, he asks one of his own. "Where were you last night?"

Everything I've recently discovered rushes back to me. Mafia connections, the pictures of other women, the possibility that he's dangerous.

Squaring my shoulders, I say, "I spent the night at Dominic's."

His expression darkens. "Tell me what you've found out."

My blood turns to ice. I didn't expect him to realize so quickly that something was wrong. Maybe I thought he would continue pretending that he's not keeping secrets from me. He's never been forthcoming with information, so why would that change now? Clutching my towel, I swallow hard.

Without thinking, I blurt, "Your family is part of the mafia."

Matteo's face is an emotionless mask. "What else?"

"I'm not the only woman you've been seeing."

He doesn't blink. "And?"

"You're dangerous."

"Is that what you think, bella?" His obsidian gaze continues holding mine from across the room. "That I'm dangerous?"

The questions are voiced calmly. And yet I hear the steel lurking below the surface.

Do I think that Matteo is dangerous?

Do I believe what Chloe, Jonathan, and Dominic have said?

My response is equally quiet. "I think you could be."

"Anyone is dangerous under the right circumstances." He pauses. "Even you."

Unable to move or breathe, I stand rooted in place. My toes curl into the area rug.

"Do I scare you?"

His question rattles around in my head. My shoulders slump as my guard drops. "No." Matteo does not frighten me. He probably should, but he doesn't. Maybe, like Dominic said earlier, I'm too naïve to see Matteo for who he truly is.

You know what does scare me?

The way I feel when I'm with him. The sheer addictiveness of it. The possibility that no one else will ever be able to make me feel this way again.

I don't want to lose that. Not yet. Not ever.

He leans back in the chair. "Come here, Grace."

I should keep my distance. He hasn't addressed any of my concerns. I know what will happen if he gets his hands on me. It's what happens every time I'm near him.

When I don't move, he repeats himself. *"Come here, bella."*

Another part of me-possibly my heart-overrides my brain and propels me forward until I stand in front of him.

His eyes sear mine, holding them captive.

"As for my family being involved in the *Cosa Nostra*, that's true. My father's great grandparents came over from Sicily in the late eighteen hundreds looking for work. But it wasn't easy for Italians in New York at that time. No one wanted to hire them. We were looked down upon, like dogs. So the family banded together and found alternative ways to protect their own and prosper. It started out with gambling and liquor and evolved from there. For a long time, the Valentini *famiglia* ruled New York. When Chicago began to grow, we sensed opportunity and expanded. My father's side of the family has been here ever since. During the 'twenties, bootlegging became a means of strength and money. And with it, our influence became even more far-reaching. That remains unchanged today. The Valentini name carries great power with it. I'm proud of who I am and where I come from, bella. Never doubt it."

I remain silent as I greedily soak up every word that comes out of his mouth. My body vibrates with the knowledge that he is allowing me a small glimpse into his world.

"I should have told you the truth myself so that you wouldn't have to hear it from others. I apologize for that. It's not the way I wanted you to find out. I thought I had more time." He runs a hand through his inky black hair. "I liked that you didn't have any preconceived notions about who I was. With you, I could be myself more than I have ever been with anyone else."

What he's revealed confirms all the rumors I've heard. Matteo's family is part of the mafia. *Matteo* is involved with the mafia. Or *the Cosa Nostra* as he called it. I have so many questions. But part of me is afraid of the answers I'll receive. I'm scared of the decisions they might force me to make.

Matteo continues, his voice dangerously low. "The Valentini family and the businesses we're involved in- they have nothing to do with *us*." His eyes search mine. "That part of my life has nothing to do with *you*."

My tongue peeks out to moisten my lips. My heart thuds against my ribcage. I can't believe we're having this conversation or that, up until a few days ago, I had no idea who Matteo was.

"If you have questions, ask them now. I can't promise to answer all of them. There are some things I can't discuss. This isn't me trying to keep secrets. This is me trying to protect you. Do you understand the difference?"

I nod. "What your family does... is it illegal?"

He gives me a hard stare. One that makes my entire body quiver. "Yes. Although, more of it is legitimized than it once was."

I really shouldn't ask... "What kind of illegal things?"

His expression darkens, becoming more closed-off. "That isn't a question I'm going to answer."

I nod again, knowing that I've stepped over the imaginary line he's drawn between us. "Okay."

"What else?"

It might push the limits, but I have to know. "Are you involved in anything illegal?"

"For the most part, no. Like I said before, I own three restaurants and some other properties."

"Covet," I interject. "You own that too, right?"

He doesn't seem surprised that I know about the upscale, risqué nightclub. "Yes. I own Covet." He pauses. "Your friend works there."

It's not a question. "Yes."

Just as I have found out information, so has Matteo. "Chloe Banks?"

I nod.

"Is she the one who told you about me?"

That's not a question *I'm* going to answer. Chloe is my best friend, and I'll protect her any way I can. "All that matters is that the person who should have told me about this didn't."

He dips his head. "Fair enough. I should have told you the truth about my family, about me, when I knew that you were someone I wanted to be with." He shrugs. "But I liked that you didn't know who I was. To you, I was just Matteo. I wasn't a Valentini. I wasn't someone to be feared, avoided, or fussed over."

My heart skips a beat. "Should I fear you?" It doesn't escape me that everyone who cares about me feels exactly the way he just described. They're scared for me. They don't want me involved with him.

Eyes on mine, he shakes his head. "Have I ever given you any reason to fear me?"

"No," I reply without hesitation. "Never."

"Then I think you have your answer."

I close my eyes to gather the courage to ask one more question. In light of everything he's revealed, maybe this shouldn't matter, but it does. "Are you seeing other women?"

"Not anymore."

Which means he was in the beginning. Those pictures are real.

I hate the jealousy that crashes through me with his admittance. "When did you stop?" Just as Matteo is holding back information from me, I do the same. I have no intention of telling him about Dominic hiring someone to follow him or the photographs that were taken.

The evidence that was used to persuade me to turn against him.

"After we spent the weekend together." He watches me closely, trying to gauge my reaction. "Do you believe me?"

I don't know what to believe anymore. What I saw in those photographs broke my heart. They made me feel expendable. And that's a deal breaker for me.

"I don't know."

"Bella," sounding stripped bare, the word slides from his lips, "there is no one else. Only you. I knew you were special the first time I saw you. I tried fighting the feelings you roused in me, but I couldn't." He sweeps his arms out wide. "I'm begging you to overlook all the ways I've fucked up. You're the only woman I want. This..." his gaze burns into mine, "all these feelings are new to me. I'm not comfortable with them yet. But I want you, Grace. I want to make *us* happen."

I want to believe him.

God, I want so badly to believe that he's telling the truth. That he's opening his heart to me.

With his eyes locked on mine, he reaches up and tugs off my towel. It falls to the floor.

And then I'm completely naked.

"This body," his eyes greedily rove over every inch of me, "is the only one I want." Matteo takes hold of my fingers and reels me toward him. I should resist and take time to digest everything he just told me. But I don't because I still want him.

What kind of person does that make me?

He settles me on his lap and bands his arms around me, holding on as if he'll never let go.

"I haven't given you much reason to trust me. But you need to know that I would never hurt you. Nor would I put you in harm's way." He brushes his lips over mine. He doesn't seek entrance, but I open for him, silently begging for more. Instead of delving in, he teases me with soft strokes.

"Do you believe me?"

Out of the corner of my eye, I catch a glimpse of us in the mirror leaning against the wall. Matteo is fully dressed while I sit naked on his lap, held tenderly in his arms. I feel the moment he also sees us. His arms tighten around me.

"You're so beautiful."

His lips graze my throat. I arch, allowing him greater access. With one arm under my legs, he lifts them until my lower lips are visible in the looking glass. I gasp when his fingers dip between my legs.

He whispers, "Don't ever run from me, bella. You're mine now."

CHAPTER THIRTY

"Are you sure I look okay?"

I twist and turn in front of the mirror, trying to get a better look at my behind. I'm wearing a sleeveless navy-blue linen dress that hits right above my knees and is belted around my waist.

I'm going for demure.

"You look beautiful."

As always, my insides liquify. The slight accent melts my panties, making me want to climb right back into bed with him.

But that's not going to happen.

Matteo has invited me to his parents' fortieth wedding anniversary party. I'm touched that he wants me to meet his family, but I'm a bundle of frayed nerves.

We haven't discussed the *Cosa Nostra* since that morning when I found him in my bedroom after my shower. Boundaries regarding certain subjects that cannot be discussed have already been clearly established.

In the back of my mind, I understand this is for my own protection. I also realize he can't discuss situations that put the people he loves at risk. Even if he wanted to disclose everything to me about his family, I don't think I'd want to know all the details.

The relationship I have with Matteo is unlike anything I've ever dealt with before. I'm trying to navigate it the best I can. There are times when I wish I'd never found out about him so that I could have remained blissfully ignorant. But I know that sooner or later, reality would have reared its ugly head.

It was only a matter of time.

I often play a game of What If in my head. If I'd known who Matteo was from the beginning, would it have made a difference? Would I have steered clear of him if I'd known about his family? Would my attraction to Matteo been lessened if I'd allowed fear to control my feelings?

I doubt it.

I've never experienced this kind of desire. It feels all-consuming, as if it could swallow me whole if I don't tread carefully. That scares me because I have no idea what the future holds for us. Or if we even have one.

The only thing I can do is take this relationship one day at a time. For the time being, that works. But I have no idea if that will be the case three months from now.

Or six.

Or a year.

Won't all the secrets eventually put a strain on our relationship?

I haven't forgotten that Matteo said his family is *mostly* legitimate.

I grew up knowing there was a right and a wrong. When I was in high school, I never strayed from the straight and narrow. I didn't befriend classmates who pushed the limits or dabbled in illegal activities. I never wanted to do anything that would reflect poorly on my parents.

The world Matteo grew up in was nothing like mine.

Neither is the one he lives in now.

I question whether a relationship can work whenever I dwell on our differences. I don't know if I can turn a blind eye to all the nitty-gritty details.

I'm so lost in my thoughts that I jump when Matteo wraps his arms around my shoulders and pulls me to his chest. He buries his nose in my hair. I've left it down the way he prefers it.

"Having second thoughts?"

I wonder if that question isn't just about the party, but our relationship.

A guilty expression flickers across my face in the mirror. He notices it as well.

"You don't have to accompany me this afternoon." He presses a kiss to the side of my neck.

"I want to."

There's no way I would pass up an opportunity to peek into the world Matteo tried to hide from me. But I'm nervous. I want to meet his family, but it would be much less stressful if I knew next to nothing about them.

With unhurried movements, he caresses the curve of my neck with his lips, eliciting a moan from me.

"Matteo..."

My voice trails off on a lusty sigh. It boggles my mind just how much I want him. How easily he's able to turn me on. We rolled out of the bed two hours ago after he did the most sinfully delicious things to my body, and already he's able to stoke the flames of my desire to life with the simplest of gestures.

I never feel sated with Matteo. I always want more.

"Are you wearing panties?"

I laugh. Is he crazy? I'm about to meet his entire family. There's no way I'd leave home without them. "Of course."

"Take them off," he whispers in my ear.

Eyes widening, I meet his dark gaze in the mirror. "What?"

My heart stutters in response when I realize that he's not joking. Reaching around, he cups my breasts in his palms. I whimper as he plays with me.

"Take off the panties."

When I hesitate, he says, "No one will realize. Your outfit is very ladylike. I want to know that you have nothing on beneath this very prim and proper dress you've chosen to wear."

His talented hands slide down my ribcage and settle on my hips. Inch by inch, he gathers up my dress until my panties are exposed. Mesmerized, I watch in the mirror. His eyes are also focused on the silky material.

Or what lies beneath it.

When all the linen has been collected, Matteo transfers it to one hand, freeing up the other. He dips his fingers into my lacy panties, zeroing in on my clit. He rubs small circles over the tiny bud until my eyelids fall and my head lolls against his chest.

His touch drives me crazy.

There isn't anything I wouldn't do to feel his hands and mouth on me. I would beg and plead. Cry for more.

"Mmmm, so wet. I think you're much too greedy for the pleasure only I can give you."

The thought has occurred to me as well.

It's never been like this before.

I've never been like this before.

He torments me by manipulating that little bundle of nerves.

"Now, be a good girl and take them off."

Through the fog clouding my brain, I understand how he's trying to persuade me to do something I'd rather not do. "Matteo, no..."

"Yes." He doesn't let up on his ministrations as he buries his face in the side of my neck, gently nipping my skin with his teeth.

Gahhhhh.

I'm soooooo close to coming.

It's there.

Right there.

Just a bit more...

I thrust my pelvis forward, wanting more. He pulls his hand away so that the pressure on my clit remains the same. When I whine in protest, he chuckles. "If you want to come, take off the panties. That's all you have to do. Simple, isn't it?"

I want to scream in frustration because we both know I can't stay aroused like this until we get home tonight. I'll go mad. I wiggle out of the underwear and kick them away. Heaving out a breath, I wait for him to finish me off. I'm so wound up that it feels like I'm going to claw my way right out of my skin.

"There!"

His lips curve into a satisfied smile. My eyes narrow. I'd love to slug him, but I'm much too focused on my own pleasure to take a swing.

"So very beautiful."

My eyes shift to the mirror and I watch as he drags his fingers across my sensitive flesh. My clit pulses.

I need him to touch me.

A small whimper escapes before I can stifle it.

He kisses the side of my neck, nipping at my throat. I have no idea why that's such a turn on, but it is. It jacks up everything inside me. I'm so distracted by his lips that it takes a moment to realize that he's touching me everywhere but that one throbbing spot.

"Please, Matteo."

His hooded gaze meets mine in the mirror as he lowers the front of my dress and smooths his palms over the material a few times to flatten the wrinkles. I stare in confusion. I'm on the verge of exploding and only his touch can push me over the edge.

With his hands resting on my shoulders, he turns me so that we face one another. I crane my neck to make eye contact.

He kisses the tip of my nose. "I don't trust you not to put your panties back on before walking out the door. This will give me some assurance."

"What!" I shriek in a voice so high it hurts my own ears. "You're just going to leave me like this?"

My outrage seems to give him pleasure. "No, bella, I wouldn't do that to you. Grab your purse and let's go. It will take more than an hour to arrive at the compound. That's plenty of time to make you come." He gives me a wink. "Several times, if you're a good girl."

Grumbling at his underhandedness, I stomp off to find my purse. My core is pulsing with need. My legs are shaky. Narrowing my eyes, I glance over my shoulder and sneak over to the mirrored dresser. Inching out the top drawer, I grab a pair of underwear. One last look in his direction shows that he's busy adjusting his cuff links.

I slip the panties into my purse. Had Matteo done what he said, I would have attended the party without panties. Since he broke his word, it's only fair that I break mine in return.

The man is entirely too certain of himself. I want to knock him down a peg or two and show him that he can't control me as easily as he assumes.

I give him a superior look from the bedroom door. "Ready to go?"

"Yep. One last thing to take care of and then we can leave."

In my head, I'm smug.

Sure, my lady parts ache, but Matteo thought he could manipulate me into doing something he wanted and my pride's not having it. Once we return home, he'll realize his mistake.

Standing next to the bed, his dark eyes find mine. My libido jumps to attention. He crooks a finger. "Come here."

I don't question his motives. I move until I'm standing before him. Silently he lays his hands on my shoulders and turns me around so that my back is aligned with his front. He skims his hands over my arms before locking his fingers around each of my wrists. His body curves against mine. I feel the length of his erection as he bends me over until my hands are stretched out on the bed and my chest is pressed into the mattress. My heart flutters in response. I turn my head so that the side of my face rests against the comforter.

"Don't move."

He kisses my cheek and then his body disappears. A question hovers on the tip of my tongue when he flips up the back of my dress, exposing my naked backside to the cool air in the room. His hand slides over my ass. Eyelashes fluttering closed, I sink into the pleasure of his touch.

Crack!

My eyes spring open and I yelp at the sting left in the wake of his palm colliding with my bare flesh. He smooths his hand over the area he just smacked.

"The panties. Take them out of your purse."

The slap has rendered me breathless. And exposed. I'm aware of the vulnerable position I've been stretched out into. Gulping, I say, "What are you-"

I don't get the denial out before he smacks the other cheek. Fire ignites. I hiss out a sharp breath at the flare of pain before his fingers slide over the smarting area.

"Bella?"

"Okay," I grumble. "I'll take them out."

"Good girl."

I close my eyes as his hands stroke over my stinging backside. I won't admit it to him, but I like when he spanks me. There's something very *dominant* about it.

A groan bursts from my lips when his finger dips inside me. His touch is magical even when he's inflicting pain.

"It turns me on to see my handprint on your ass. I like it," he muses darkly. *"A lot."*

I bite my lip, trying to stifle the whimper his words summon.

Sex with Matteo is light years away from the relationship I had with my college boyfriend. Eric now seems like an untried boy. After only a few months, sex between us became routine. Whereas everything Matteo does is new and full of untold pleasure. I'm eager to explore all these different facets with him.

I want him to push past all my limits.

I want him to touch me in ways that feel foreign, but exciting.

I just want... *Matteo*.

"This is exactly how I'm going to have you tonight. With your ass high in the air. By then, my handprints will have faded, and I'll have to mark you again."

His fingers glide across my clit. My pussy drips. I'm so turned on by the way he's touched me. Even the spanks excite me. They make me ache in ways I didn't imagine possible.

"Do you want that?"

Unable to lie, I say, "Yes."

"Good." His fingers circle one last time before slipping deep inside my sheath. I groan, bearing down against his hand.

"Turn over."

I roll over onto my back, spreading my legs before he can tell me to. His eyes dart to my center and he licks his lips in anticipation.

"I'm hungry, bella. I don't think I can wait for the limo."

Neither can I.

My eyelids drift shut as his mouth settles on my pulsing clit. He gently suckles me, and I explode in seconds. A scream tears from my throat. Long after I crash back down to earth, Matteo continues to lick me as if he can't get enough of my taste.

"Delicious."

He gives my lower lips another long, slow lap with his tongue and lifts his head, piercing me with his gaze.

"I hope you've learned your lesson."

I smile and stretch like a content cat lying in the afternoon sun. "I like your lessons."

Chuckling, he buries his face in my softness and nuzzles my clit. "Yes, I can see that you do. I have a feeling you're going to need lots of discipline. I'm more than happy to give it to you."

I think I could live with his head between my thighs for the rest of my life.

"You have me all worked up. I hope you're ready to return the favor once we're in the limo."

The thought of taking him into my mouth as we speed through the city is so sexy that I groan. "More than ready."

Straightening his suit, he laughs and holds out his hand. "Then we should get going."

CHAPTER THIRTY-ONE

Matteo's parents live about an hour north of Chicago. The cosmopolitan, bustling city with all its high rises and concrete slowly gives way to wide-open spaces scattered with red-barned farms as the limo travels down the highway. Trees in the middle of turning fiery red, breathtaking orange and deep, rich yellows dot the landscape. It's an idyllic sight. I'm reminded of how much I missed the change in seasons while living in Seattle. Driving through the countryside during autumn is one of life's little pleasures.

Leaving the freeway, we head east on country roads toward Lake Michigan until we turn onto a private road flanked by mature trees. We stop at the guardhouse to gain clearance. The driver speaks with security before the gate is opened, and we're allowed on to the property.

I may have been distracted by Matteo before leaving the condo, and I was certainly busy reciprocating the favor on the way over, but now I'm reminded that Matteo's family is unlike any other I have come across.

It's one that has guards in place and takes security seriously.

As we roll toward the lake, the thick greenery opens to reveal a magnificent stone mansion nestled among lush, gently rolling hills that are perfectly manicured. The breath stalls in my lungs as I stare at it with wide eyes. I think Matteo referred to the estate as a compound. He wasn't lying. It's massive.

My parents came from money, and we had a very nice house here in Chicago and then in Seattle, and Dominic has a gorgeous house on the North Shore, but they're *nothing* compared to the sight before me. I'm bowled over by the sheer size of it. It's as if someone took a country manor house in England and dropped it down on this beautiful piece of land near the water.

"*This* is where you grew up?" I shake my head in amazement. I imagine it would take at least a day to explore all the nooks and crannies of this place.

"Yes. Welcome to the Valentini family compound."

A shiver of apprehension skitters through me as the limousine continues to our destination. When we're about half a mile away, I notice cars parked in the circular drive and along the side of the road. There's at least forty of them.

"This house has stood for over a hundred years. During prohibition, my family used the lake for bootlegging. It was an easy place to hide liquor. The property was so far out in the country, that it was considered safe." He smirks. "A hideout."

"That's really interesting." I can picture the period in time he's describing. Sure, it only took us an hour to drive here, but in the early nineteen hundreds, it would have taken the better part of a day. The estate would have been difficult to access.

He gives a little shrug. "There's a lot of interesting history here at the house. Perhaps later, we'll take a tour."

I smile. "I would love that."

My eyes fasten on to the house. I can't help the nervousness bubbling up inside me. Matteo slips an arm around my body and pulls me on to his lap. The closer we get, the more massive and overwhelming the building becomes. Gently he presses his lips against my temple.

"Don't worry. They'll adore you." He adds, "Just as I do."

Is he crazy? Of course, I'm going to worry. I'm riddled with anxiety.

Meeting someone's parents for the first time is nerve-wracking enough without layering on everything else I know about them.

"Have you told them anything about me?" I have no idea what Matteo might have said. Maybe nothing at all. Maybe they think I'm nothing more than a random girl he's bringing along today.

That thought makes my belly churn even more than it was moments ago.

"I told them that I was seeing a woman who is smart, beautiful, and strong."

Surprised, I rip my gaze away from the house. "Is that how you see me?" I ask, looking at him.

It's not how I view myself, especially with the toll the last two years have taken. Much of the time, I feel like a baby bird nursing a broken wing. As if I constantly have to fight through the pain just to push forward.

Just to persevere.

And yet, when I'm with Matteo, it doesn't feel that way at all. The dull throbbing pain, the heartache that continually gnaws at me, falls away.

His brows furrow. "How could I not?" His fingers stroke over my face. "You're gorgeous. You captured my attention from the moment I stepped onto the elevator. I couldn't get you out of my head, no matter how much I tried. Even with all that you have lost, you're still warm, ever willing to open yourself up to new things and take chances with your life. You've been to hell and back, but that hasn't changed who you are at the core. You've moved across the country to start a new life. You're attending a prestigious university, working toward fulfilling your dreams." His eyes turn curious. "How could I not find all that incredibly sexy?" He sweeps his thumb across my lower lip. "As much as your beauty and strength turn me on, it's what is up here," his fingertips tap the side of my head before dropping to my heart, "and here that I find most fascinating."

His words leave me breathless. Lifting my lips, I seek out his. We break apart when the car comes to a stop.

"Mmmm." He smiles devilishly. "That needy look in your eyes... I like that most of all."

Heat blooms in my cheeks as I try to compose myself. In a matter of minutes, I'll meet his family. I have no idea how long this relationship will last, but I want them to like me.

Victor opens the door for us. Matteo slides out first and reaches in to assist me. I self-consciously sweep a hand over my dress, immediately remembering that I'm not wearing underwear.

Pulling me closer, Matteo whispers against my hair, "All day I'll be thinking about you bare under that demure dress. Can you still feel the imprint of my hand upon your perfect little backside?"

My cheeks pinken at the reminder of what he did an hour ago. And at how much I enjoyed him bending me over and assaulting my bottom. I squirm and he lets loose a low chuckle that arrows to my core.

"Perhaps I'll check in a bit."

"Don't you dare!" I intend for the words to come out sounding crisp and haughty. Instead they're breathy and full of need. Most of the time, I feel ill-equipped to deal with a man like Matteo. As if I'm no match for him. As if I will never be a match for him.

Matteo hands me the flowers I brought for his mother before we head to the house. The door swings open as Matteo reaches for the handle. As soon as I catch sight of the grand foyer, all the commotion from inside comes spilling out. In a house this magnificent, I expect a butler to greet newcomers since I'm sure the hosts are busy circulating among their guests. Instead, I find a tiny woman with inky black hair and a face full of laugh lines. Her eyes settle on the man next to me as she smiles ear to ear.

She grins broadly. "I'm Teresa. You may call me that or Mama."

I couldn't possibly refer to Matteo's mother as *Mama*. What to call her swirls through my head as more people trickle into the foyer. Hugs are exchanged, slaps on the back are given, and introductions are made.

"Welcome to our home," Teresa says. "We're thrilled you could join us!"

"Thank you so much for having me." I hand over the small bouquet I picked up from the store. "Congratulations on your anniversary."

Taking the flowers, she buries her nose in them and inhales deeply.

"Thank you, they're lovely. Matteo must have mentioned how much I enjoy having fresh flowers around the house." I'm breathing a quick sigh of relief that I've made it over the first hurdle when she takes firm hold of my hand. "Come, there are many people who would like to meet you."

Surprise and confusion color my voice. "There are?"

"Of course!" She gives me a knowing look and lowers her voice. "It's not often that my son brings home a woman. And such a beautiful one, at that!"

I almost snort in disbelief, but rein it in at the last moment. I don't want to offend this wonderful woman.

I've seen the type of woman Matteo goes out with. They look like supermodels. I, on the other hand, look nothing of the sort. All the photographs Dominic had taken flash through my mind.

I know what Matteo said in the limo, but still, doubt creeps in at the edges.

She nods approvingly to her son. An amused smile tugs at the corners of Matteo's lips. He's on the cusp of laughing. I narrow my eyes at him. He's lucky he got a blow-job on the way over because he won't be getting one during the ride home.

"I'm going to take Grace around and introduce her to the family." She waves a hand at him. "I'll return her later."

Um... what?

I throw a pleading look over my shoulder before being dragged through the house and then out to the patio where most of the guests have congregated. A huge white tent has been set up on the lawn. Little girls in over-the-top fluffy dresses and boys in polos and pressed khakis race around squealing and laughing. There must be at least a hundred and fifty people in attendance. Waiters and waitresses in black uniforms pass around silver platters loaded with food and beverages. A girl stops by with a tray of drinks. Teresa grabs two flutes and hands one to me.

"Champagne," she says, taking a sip.

Nervous about being hijacked by Matteo's mother, I hold the glass to my lips and take a taste. As I do, people flock to Teresa. She greets each one of them warmly, making a point to introduce me to everyone as if I'm an honored guest. It feels surreal, like being stuck in a never-ending reception line at a wedding. I'm not used to so many strangers pressing in on me. Most of the people Teresa presents me to are related to the Valentinis in one way or another. It could be distantly, three or four cousins removed, but it doesn't make a difference. Here, everyone is family and made to feel welcome.

It boggles my mind just how large this family is. After a while, faces begin to swim before my eyes. I have no idea where Matteo is. Feeling overwhelmed, I plaster a smile on my face while continuing to shake hands politely. At least an hour passes by when a tall, curvy woman with an exotic face and long hair links her arm through mine.

"Mama, I'm going to take Grace to get some food."

A smiling Teresa waves us off. It's easy to see that she's in her element and enjoys being surrounded by family and friends. "Good idea, Sofia. Make her a plate. I'm sure she must be starving."

Sofia whisks me over to a long, rectangular-shaped table laden with every kind of Italian dish. Pastas, meats, seafood, soups, antipasto, salads, and breads beckon to me. A separate table holds an array of delicious looking desserts. I feel just as overwhelmed by the food choices as I did by the amount of people I've met today.

The younger woman gives my arm a gentle squeeze to capture my attention. "We met earlier." She smiles. "You probably don't remember."

"I'm sorry, I don't, "I admit. "There are so many people, it's all kind of a blur."

She laughs. It's a deep, husky sound. "I'm Sofia, Matteo's younger sister."

That explains why she's so beautiful. "It's nice to meet you."

I glance over at Teresa, who is still greeting people, laughing and hugging everyone she comes in contact with. In all the scenarios that ran through my head earlier, I never imagined that Matteo's family would go out of their way to make me feel at home. "Your mother is wonderful." Being at her side for the last hour has made me long for my own mother. It's hard not to miss Mom when I'm around someone so warm and nurturing as Teresa.

"She is," Sofia agrees without hesitation. "She's ecstatic that Matteo has finally brought a woman home to meet her."

I shouldn't pry...

"That doesn't happen very often?"

She snorts. I don't know her at all, but I like her easy, carefree manner. "Are you kidding? The closest we get is the occasional photograph that turns up in a magazine of him at some event or function with a skinny socialite on his arm." She gives me one of *those* looks. "I'm sure you know the type."

Yes, I most certainly do. I have about a dozen pictures of Matteo with women who look like that.

She arches a brow. "Hardly the kind of girl you take home to meet your mother." She nods at her parents. I notice that her father, Enzo, has joined Teresa. His arm is wrapped around his wife. Looking content, she leans her head against him. They look happy together.

And so completely normal.

It's hard to believe that the people I've met today are involved in underground criminal activities. Being here with them, being so easily accepted by them, makes me feel more conflicted.

Pushing those thoughts away, I force a smile.

"Exactly how did you and Matteo meet? My brother tells us nothing."

Part of me wonders how honest I should be with Sofia. If her brother wanted them to know about our relationship, wouldn't he fill them in himself?

"We both live at Lexington Place. We ran into one another in the elevator and..." my voice trails off as I remember my first glimpse of Matteo and how enamored I was.

It's been two months, and those feelings have yet to wear off. I doubt they ever will.

"I love that!" Stepping closer, she rubs her palms together as her voice drops. "Now tell me more."

Her laid-back manner puts me at ease. I chuckle. As close-mouthed as Matteo is, his sister seems to be the opposite. It's a refreshing change. I know that if given half a chance, we could be friends.

As I open my mouth to ask a question of my own, a fine shiver races across my flesh right before a set of hands settle on my shoulder. I don't have to turn around to know who they belong to because I'm so attuned to him.

"I hope you're not badgering Grace with questions," Matteo says with a hint of amusement.

His sister's eyes light up with mischief. "Of course I was. How could I possibly resist the opportunity?"

Not wanting to encourage her, I stifle my laughter by biting my lower lip.

I can only guess at Matteo's expression, but I hear exasperation in his deep voice. "Keep it up, and this will be the first and last time you see her."

Unaffected by his words, she continues teasingly with, "So what you're really saying is that even if we don't see Grace, *you* will."

I turn my head in an attempt to gauge his reaction. He's not looking at Sofia, though. His eyes have already settled on mine. A possessive look fills them.

"Yes, I would have to say so."

Despite what I know about him and his family, I can't stop the tiny bubbles of happiness that burst within me in response to his answer.

Ignoring her brother, Sofia says, "I'll give you my number before you leave. That way we can grab lunch in the city."

Matteo groans, as if the notion of me spending any time alone with his sister is painful. This only brightens Sofia's smile. Before he can say anything more, she gives a little wave and disappears into the crowd of friends and relatives.

Matteo's arms slide around me, pulling me close. We haven't been together long, but being with him feels right. As if this is where I truly belong. Oblivious to all the noise and chaos surrounding us, we stay wrapped up in one another.

I sigh contentedly and look around the tent, taking in all the people who have gathered to help Teresa and Enzo celebrate their anniversary.

The Valentinis are nothing like what I imagined. Maybe I've watched one too many *Godfather* movies. Maybe I was expecting murder and mayhem, but these people are normal. They could be any close-knit family. If Matteo hadn't confirmed the rumors himself, I don't think I would have believed them. Part of me still wants to deny the truth.

As I watch silently from the sidelines, it's obvious how much love is shared between them. I secretly long to be part of the madness.

"What are you thinking, bella?" His warm breath rustles the hair around my ear.

Shrugging, I give him a smile. "Just that you're very lucky to be surrounded by all this family."

His eyes never leave mine. "Yes, I am. Family is everything."

Those words break my heart because mine is no longer here. I've never experienced anything like this before. It's overwhelming, and yet I feel drawn to the chaos. I want to soak it up and be part of it. I don't think Matteo understands how alone I feel.

Being surrounded by his family, all of whom have welcomed me with open arms into their home, exacerbates my despair because once I return downtown, I'll be even more aware of my loneliness.

It's a bitter pill to swallow and not something I want to discuss because it sounds like I'm indulging in a pity party for one. And I don't want that. Not today. I want to enjoy the rest of the afternoon and Matteo's company.

"Did you get a chance to eat?"

Relieved to leave those heavy thoughts behind, I shake my head. "No, not yet. But I'm starving."

He gathers the hair from the side of my neck and presses a kiss to the delicate flesh. As always, his touch awakens hundreds of nerve endings within me. "I'm starving as well, but not for anything that's being offered over there."

A shiver slips down my spine as he continues to nibble at my neck. I remember that I'm completely bare under my dress.

"Perhaps later, we can take the tour I mentioned earlier, and I can spread those pretty thighs and have my dessert."

CHAPTER THIRTY-TWO

George tips his hat while holding the door open as I exit the building. "Have a good run, Ms. Castile."

I give him a smile along with a wave. "Thanks, George, I'll see you in an hour!"

I take off down the sidewalk, heading toward the lakefront. Over the past few days, the weather has turned chilly. Autumn is thick in the air. The breeze is cool, but I know that once I warm up, it'll feel invigorating.

Normally Matteo and I run together, but today I needed some time to myself. He seemed to understand that even though I never told him that I wanted to be alone. Which, in a way, makes everything more difficult. He pushes me when I need it, and takes a small step back when sensing my inner conflict.

How am I supposed to walk away from a man who is so finely attuned to me?

People spend their entire lives searching for someone who understands them. Someone they can connect with on a fundamental level. Someone who feeds their intrinsic needs and desires. That is precisely what I've found in Matteo.

Each night we spend making love, I find myself falling for him. Every morning when I wake in his arms, I fall a bit harder. And each kiss he gives me before heading back to his condo to get ready for work makes me count down the minutes until we're together again.

And yet I have to make an agonizing choice.

I have to decide if I can be with Matteo.

Can I ignore everything I know about him? About his family?

If I can't, I need to walk away now before this relationship progresses any further and I'm unable to pull myself out.

It's been just under a week since Matteo brought me to the family compound for his parents' anniversary celebration. I was nervous about meeting his relatives, but everyone was wonderful. So warm and welcoming. Sofia called me a few days ago, and we set a date to meet for lunch the following week along with a shopping excursion on Michigan Avenue. As happy as forming a bond with Matteo's sister makes me, a niggle of worry keeps creeping into the back of my mind.

Whether they refer to it as the *Cosa Nostra* or the *mafia*, it still means the same thing. Illegal activities. Criminal. Unlawful. People are sent to prison for what the Valentinis are involved in. My parents spent their careers prosecuting people like them. And here I am, involved with someone who is entrenched in that lifestyle.

Whose entire *family* is involved in that lifestyle.

Going back generations.

We may be in the early stages of our relationship, but I know how I feel about Matteo. Already he's left an indelible mark on my soul.

And that worries me.

I never expected to fall this hard or feel torn over making the *right* choice. My parents may not be alive, but I know what they would expect me to do. This decision shouldn't be difficult. But it is. The *right* choice doesn't necessarily feel *right* to me in this case.

Because my mind is so preoccupied, it feels like I reach the lake in record time. But I know that's not true. I'm so stuck in my own head right now that I'm not paying attention to where I am. I'm operating on autopilot.

I wish there were someone I could talk to about this situation.

But there's no one.

I can't discuss it with Chloe or Jonathan.

And definitely not Dominic, who doesn't think I should be seeing Matteo in the first place. I can't broach the subject with Sofia either. Her loyalty belongs to Matteo. I would expect nothing less.

I guess the person I need to speak with is Matteo.

Once my mind latches on to the idea, I know it's the right one.

I'll do it tonight.

Matteo and I can discuss everything over dinner. I can't invest any more of myself if we don't have a future together. And if we do, then I have a decision to make. I either choose to be a part of the world Matteo occupies, or I walk away.

Feeling settled with a plan, I turn back toward Lexington Place. Class starts at eleven, so I need to get moving.

Dominic's disapproval invades my thoughts. *Do you think Matteo Valentini is the kind of man your father would have wanted to see you with? Someone with ties to the mafia?*

As those words echo through my head, I pick up my pace trying to outrun them. My breath comes faster now. My legs ache. They feel like limp noodles, but I don't stop pushing.

Neither of my parents would understand Matteo's world. Nor would they understand how I could turn my back on my upbringing.

As I prepare to turn onto the street where Lexington Place is located, I notice a car careening down the asphalt, weaving in and out of traffic. Instead of slowing, the driver guns the engine. I'm safe on the sidewalk, but my pulse accelerates until it feels like my heart is pounding against my ribs.

Paralyzed by fear, my eyes stay fastened on the vehicle. It looks like it's speeding right toward me. Adrenaline spikes through my veins, making my skin prickle with awareness.

Just as the sedan jumps the curb, I leap out of the way. My feet get tangled, and I trip, tumbling to the cement before rolling toward one of the buildings. Stunned, I lay on the sidewalk for a moment as chaos breaks out around me.

Feet pound against the pavement.

The edges of my vision grow blurry as a sense of shock fills me.

I stare sightlessly at the crowd gathered around me. Raised voices babble with disbelief. A few individuals crane their necks, looking up and down the busy street, trying to locate the vehicle that almost hit me.

But it's gone.

It never even slowed.

"Miss? Miss? Are you okay?" The man talking to me pauses and asks, "Can you hear me?"

My eyes lock on him as he fills my line of sight. Thankfully he blocks out all the others, allowing me to focus on him.

Sucking in a shaky breath, I nod weakly. That's when I realize that I'm still sprawled out on the sidewalk. My hands scrabble to find purchase. As I struggle to sit upright, he gently pushes me down.

"You need to stay where you are. Don't try getting up just yet. We need to make sure that your spine and head haven't sustained any injuries. An ambulance is on its way."

I hurt all over. My hands and knees have taken the brunt of my fall. I don't think anything is seriously wrong, though. I don't remember actually being hit. But it was a close call. *So close.* I don't know how I managed to escape unscathed.

"I'm-I'm okay." I moisten my lips. My mind is spinning. I can't think about anything other than the fact that whoever was behind the wheel of that car didn't even stop to see if I was okay.

I tremble as that thought continues to fester. I gingerly touch the back of my skull because it's throbbing. I can't remember if I knocked it when I fell to the ground.

The man hovering over me has taken control of the situation. I wonder if he's an off-duty police officer. He has an authoritative demeanor about him. Nothing feels okay right now, but the power he exudes calms me.

I feel safe even though I'm still lying on the walkway.

He runs his hands over me, probing for injury. "Tell me if anything hurts when I touch it."

His hands are huge, but his touch is tender. As if he's aware of his own strength.

"I'm okay." My voice trembles. "Just a bit shaken up."

"You took a nasty spill when you dodged that car. It's better to wait until the ambulance arrives." He gives me a reassuring smile. "Just to be safe."

I nod.

Tears fill my eyes as the gravity of the situation hits me. I can't believe this has happened. If I hadn't jumped out of the way when I did, I could have been seriously injured.

I could have been killed.

Thank God I saw it coming.

My eyes dart around the crowd, which now looks three people deep. "I think I'm okay." Using my hands, I lift myself up again. But like before, he gently pushes me down.

"You need to stay put, Grace. I have experience in these kind of situations, and it's best not to move. I hear the sirens now. It won't be long, I promise. Then the EMT's can decide what to do. But I think they'll want to take a closer look at you at the hospital. Maybe take a few X-rays, too. They can call a family member for you."

That last comment brings more tears to my eyes. Other than Dominic, there's no one to call. But this stranger doesn't know that. Resigned, I squeeze my eyes shut to block out everything around me. "Thank you for staying with me."

"It's not a problem. Hopefully one of these bystanders got the license plate. I hate to see that asshole get away with a near hit-and-run." He asks, "You didn't happen to notice the plate number, did you?"

In my mind, all I see is a nondescript car speeding toward me.

I don't know what color the vehicle was, let alone what was on the license plate. I couldn't even tell if it had an Illinois plate. I only remember the feeling of panic that filled me when I realized the car wasn't veering away, but barreling straight toward me.

Opening my eyes, I shake my head. "No, I don't remember anything."

Looking sympathetic, he nods. "I wouldn't expect you to."

I'm still trying to make sense of what just happened. "Do you think it was a drunk driver?"

"It's possible." He glances up as the sirens become louder. "Looks like the bus is here. They'll get you to the hospital and checked out."

It's hard to believe that I left my building less than an hour ago for a run to clear my head. I never could have imagined that I'd be heading to the hospital instead of back to Lexington Place after almost being hit by a reckless driver.

CHAPTER THIRTY-THREE

I lay balled up on my bed, watching Matteo as he paces back and forth in front of me. He hasn't said much since we've gotten home from the hospital. Other than a few scrapes and bruises, I'm fine.

I'm more shaken up than anything else.

I tried declining a one-way ticket to the hospital, but the paramedics were having none of it. They seemed to take orders from the guy at the scene. At the emergency room, the doctor decided to run a battery of tests. I don't think I've ever been so thoroughly checked over in my life.

Matteo was already waiting for me when we came through the ER doors.

The weird thing is that I don't remember calling him.

But I must have, right?

Then again, I was out of it after the accident. So, it's possible that I called or texted. Maybe I asked the guy who stayed with me to contact him. Everything is still fuzzy. The doctor said that was normal. Apparently, shock can do that to you.

My eyes gravitate toward Matteo again. Not knowing how to make this better, I watch from my curled-up position on the bed. He drags a hand through his hair and shifts his gaze to me.

"You don't remember anything about the car? Nothing sticks out in your mind?"

Exhausted from everything that has taken place today, I shake my head.

I'm done talking about what happened. I rehashed the story several times for the police at the hospital. I can't remember anything other than the sedan being dark. I don't know if it was a man or woman behind the wheel.

"Nothing?" He looks frustrated by my response. "It's all just a blank?"

I sigh as irritation sets in. Does he think I'm lying? I have no reason to do that. I want the psycho who almost hit me off the streets as much as he does. "I'm sorry, but I can't remember."

I've had enough Tylenol to choke a Clydesdale, yet I still have a pounding headache.

"It was an accident. Probably a guy coming home from a night out drinking." Wanting it to be that or something else equally innocuous, I add, "Or a teenager who was texting."

He levels a hard-edged stare in my direction.

After a long silence, I ask, "You don't think so?"

"I'm not sure," he says slowly, as if he's choosing his words carefully. Which is odd.

All of my sore muscles clench. "You think what happened was on purpose?"

He stares flatly before speaking. "I think it's possible."

Goose bumps break out across my flesh.

"Why would you say that?" I shake my head, wincing from the pain that movement causes. None of this makes sense. "Why would someone want to hurt me?"

He plows a hand through his hair again. A few seconds of silence ensue before he mutters, "Maybe they were trying to get to me. I don't know, bella. That's the problem. I just don't know." Turning toward me, his eyes meet mine. The look he gives me is gut-wrenching.

Ignoring my body's protests, I pull myself into a sitting position. "You think that what happened today is somehow related to *you*? To your *family*?"

He closes the distance between us and carefully lays a hand on me. His dark gaze continues holding mine. Anger radiates from him in heavy waves. "I don't know."

My mind snaps back to him waiting at the hospital for the ambulance to arrive. No matter how hard I try, I can't remember contacting him.

"Did I call you after the accident?"

His brows pinch together. He seems thrown by the question. "No." His fingers softly trail over my face. "You didn't call." Before I can ask any further questions, his arms band around me, gently pulling me closer so that my cheek can rest against his chest. "I should have been there." Pain seeps into his raspy voice. "I never should have let you run by yourself."

His previous comments continue to rattle around my head. I focus on the one question I can't shake. "If I didn't contact you, how did you know I was at the hospital?" I pull away, needing some distance so that I'm able to think clearly. "You were at the hospital before I arrived. How did you know?" Another shiver creeps through me as I wait for a rational explanation.

Matteo doesn't say a word.

My mind somersaults. The pit sitting at the bottom of my belly continues to grow with each passing second of silence. How could he know what I was doing or what was happening unless...

"Did you have me followed?"

Guilt flickers in his eyes, and I know my suspicion is correct. The thought of being watched makes my skin crawl. I went through a similar situation with Dominic. I can't do it again.

"Why?" My blood starts to boil. The physical pain pressing in on me recedes as mental anguish takes over. "Why would you do that?"

Reaching out, he tries to stroke his fingers across my cheek. I flinch and his hand stops midair. His eyes flare wide, as if I've struck him. All I've done since meeting Matteo is seek out his touch. This is the first time I've refused it. My response leaves him stricken. Tamping down my inner turmoil, I scoot backwards, away from him.

"Why would you have me followed?" I pause, my voice dropping dangerously low. "Do you not trust me?"

His eyebrows shoot up in surprise. "No! Of course, I trust you. It was more of a protective measure. I'm just trying to keep you safe." He moves toward me and tries to scoop me up into his arms. I press my hand to his chest to stop him.

"Why would you do something like that behind my back?"

"Because my world is a dangerous one, and I need to protect what's mine," he answers without a hint of regret. "And make no mistake, bella, you are mine."

I wrap my arms around myself for comfort as a feeling of unease grows inside my chest. "You should have told me," I accuse.

"Would you have willingly agreed to a security detail?"

"Of course not," I fire back.

Who would want someone skulking around after them? Spying, then reporting back on every move they make. It creeped me out when Dominic did it, and it creeps me out now knowing that Matteo couldn't be bothered to discuss the situation with me. He had no right to sic a watchdog on me without consulting me first.

He straightens to his full height. The hard expression on his face proves that he has no remorse. "I thought it was better this way. You go about living your life, but I take the necessary measures to make sure nothing happens to you."

Frustrated by this conversation, I stare out the window. It feels like my life has imploded. My mind replays everything that happened this morning, and something clicks in my head.

I'm such an idiot.

I murmur, "The man who stayed with me until the ambulance arrived... that was him, wasn't it?" I don't know why I'm asking. It makes perfect sense. I'd thought he was an off-duty cop from the way he'd taken control of the situation. He was also the first person to reach me.

He'd been close.

Just not close enough.

Stone-faced, Matteo nods once. "Yes. That was Devon. He's your protection."

My temper flares. "I don't need protection!" At least I never did before.

Thinking I'd been involved in a random accident is one thing. Knowing someone purposefully sought me out with the intention of harming or killing me because of who I'm involved with is another matter altogether.

I'm beginning to grasp the full gravity of the situation I've become embroiled in. Being with Matteo means giving up certain personal freedoms. It means allowing myself to be watched and followed wherever I go and never being completely alone. It also means accepting the possibility of becoming a target for anyone with an axe to grind against the Valentini family.

Am I okay with giving up so much?

Can I live my life under lock and key?

"Bella?"

These chaotic thoughts rush through my mind until my head aches even more than before.

I... I can't do this.

Not now.

Not with the way I feel.

"Grace, please talk to me. Try to understand that what I did was for your own protection. It had nothing to do with trusting you. I was trying to keep you safe. You have to understand that."

If Matteo's assumption is correct, his preventive measures turned out to be necessary ones.

That thought makes me feel sick to my stomach.

"You should have told me," I whisper. "I don't like the idea of someone watching me." Another painful thought slams into me. "How long has Devon been following me?"

He holds my gaze and releases a long, slow breath. "Since I decided that I wanted you."

That's not an answer.

I shake my head, needing more information. *"How long, Matteo? How long has this been going on?"*

"Almost a month." He quickly adds, "You wouldn't have known had this incident not happened. But he couldn't leave you there, Grace. Devon's job is to keep you safe. He's not there to interfere with any of the choices you make."

I glare at him. "But he reports to you on everything I do. Everyone I have a conversation with. He doesn't work for *me*. He works for *you*."

Matteo's silence is telling.

Yes, I'm an idiot. My voice sounds deadened as I say, "That's how you knew where I was. You had me followed."

"It was purely for the sake of protecting you. The fact that you didn't know who I was made it more dangerous for you. When you're here in the condo, I know you're safe. George watches out for you."

I'm going to lose my mind.

Is he serious right now?

"*George?* Why would he tell you anything? Isn't that against the rules of this building?" I'm angry, and even though I would never do it, I bite out, "I could have him fired for that!"

"He works for me, bella."

"What? No! He's the doorman, he works for the building."

Matteo drops another bomb. "I own the building."

I stare speechlessly. The wheels in my head spin out of control as I try to play mental catch-up. One stark revelation after another keeps falling on me. I feel blindsided and lied to.

Matteo owns Lexington Place.

Again, it all makes sense.

I felt so safe moving here because of all the security measures. I felt as though George took care of everyone the same way. But it wasn't like that at all. Nothing is what I thought it was. That notion is a frightening one. Panic sets in and I inhale a deep breath to stave off the feeling of the walls closing in on me. But it doesn't help.

I can't breathe.

I need to get away from Matteo.

Maybe Dominic was right after all.

Maybe I should have moved in with him for a while and taken my time finding a place. I slide out of bed and make my way toward the floor to ceiling windows. I stare outside, trying to find my bearings.

"Why didn't you tell me about Lexington Place?"

Nothing is what it seems. Worse, I have no idea how much more I still don't know.

He doesn't touch me, but I feel him step behind me. My entire body yearns for contact with his. I want to feel his strong, protective arms wrapped around me. But I can't allow that to happen. I can't allow Matteo to cloud my judgment any more than he already has.

"It didn't seem important. I told you that I owned a few businesses and real estate."

Drawing in another fortifying breath, I try steeling myself before turning to face him. He's closer than I anticipated.

Tears fill my eyes. "Throughout our entire relationship, you've kept secrets from me." What I'm about to say is painful, but nonetheless true. And that's what hurts most. "You've carefully picked and chosen what to tell me. Every so often, you would drop a breadcrumb, making me think that you were opening up and letting me in. But you haven't at all." I cut him off when he opens his mouth to interrupt. "And then you have the audacity to dig into *my* past! Into *my* life." Anger tinges every word. "To have *me* followed!" I shake my head in disbelief.

Matteo jerks forward to touch me, but I stumble until my back hits the window. I press against the glass in an attempt to evade his reach. A whimper escapes my lips as I cringe. His eyes widen. His face pales, losing some of its golden color. Holding up both hands, he steps away from me.

I know Matteo would never hurt me. I believe it in my heart, but it's still not enough. Not after everything that has come to light today.

Overcome with exhaustion, I whisper, "You should leave. I want to be alone right now." I massage my throbbing temples. "I need time to think. And I can't do that with you here."

"Grace."

It breaks my heart to hear so much agony in his voice.

"Please, Matteo," I gasp when he makes no move to leave. "I need to think everything through. You have to give me that. You can't control everything."

With a tortured expression, he reluctantly takes a step away from me.

His face hardens, and he growls, "I'm not going anywhere. You're mine. You were mine from the very beginning."

I don't respond to that statement because somewhere deep inside, his words strike a chord. I'm just not sure if I want them to. "You need to call off the guards. I can take care of myself."

His jaw tightens. "You need protection. Your safety is all that matters."

Not knowing what else to do, I unleash the words that have been rolling around in the back of my head for days. "I don't belong in your world, Matteo." Tears flood my eyes. "I'm not sure if I can live this way. And I'm not sure if I can trust you. Since the beginning, I've laid myself completely bare." It hurts to continue, but I don't have a choice. He needs to accept the harsh truth. "You've kept important information from me. You had me followed even though you knew I wouldn't want it. And now someone might have tried to hurt me to get to you or your family."

The torture filling his eyes pierces my heart. I feel like I'm callously cutting the damn thing from my body.

"Everything would've been different if you had just been upfront with me. But you refused to do that."

"Bella..."

He sounds fractured. I've never heard Matteo sound like that before. As if his heart is breaking just as much as mine. *"Please. Give me a chance to explain-"*

"*No!* I can't deal with any more tonight." I cover my face and close my eyes, fighting to stay calm. "I want to go to bed. Please..."

My request is met with silence.

"Please, Matteo," I whisper, "just do as I ask."

"Okay." There's so much defeat in his normally commanding voice. "I'll go." I hear him trudge toward the bedroom door, then stop. I tense while waiting for what he's going to say.

I can't bear much more.

"It was never my intention to hurt you. From the moment I saw you, I wanted you. Even when I tried keeping my distance, I couldn't. I wanted to be near you. I wanted to bask in your light." His voice deepens, growing stronger as it picks up momentum. *"You are mine.* Nothing will change that, bella. I'll give you tonight. I see how exhausted you are. The last thing I want is to leave you. But if that's what you need, then I'll walk out the door. I'll give you the space you're asking for. Come the morning, I'll be back and we *will* talk this out."

And there he is.

The Matteo Valentini I've come to know.

Powerful.

Commanding.

Arrogant.

I hate the tiny thrill that hums through me in response to his promise. I may be pushing him away, but he refuses to go willingly.

I've been granted a reprieve.

But that's all it is.

A chance for me to regroup.

I lift my head until our gazes lock. "I don't want your men watching me."

He nods. "I'll release Devon for the night. But until we know more about this hit-and-run, I don't want you going anywhere without protection."

The chinks in his armor I'd caught a fleeting glimpse of have disappeared as if they'd never been there to begin with.

"Understood?"

The fact that he's reiterating that what happened this morning may not have been an accident sends a fresh wave of nausea crashing over me. I just want my bed right now. I want to sleep until everything in my body stops aching.

Especially my heart.

"Yes, I understand."

Before I can react, he closes the distance between us until a few inches separate us. His unique scent invades my senses, and I have to brace myself so that my body doesn't rock toward his. His fingers snake under my chin and lift it until my eyes meet his. Intensity swirls in his obsidian gaze. It makes a lump form in my throat. Pushing this man away hurts more than anything I've suffered through today. It goes against every fiber of my being.

"I won't allow you to run from me." His quietly spoken words have a razor-sharp edge to them. I don't doubt for a moment that he'll find me wherever I go. "Do not misinterpret what's happening between us.

This is not me walking away. I am in no way letting you go." I gasp as he tugs my chin closer and whispers harshly, "I doubt that I will ever let you go."

My tongue darts out to moisten my dry lips. I see the truth of his words shining brilliantly in his eyes. "I know, Matteo." And I do. I understand everything he's saying to me. "But you can't force me to be with you. Not if I don't want you."

His eyes fall to my lips before slowly climbing up to my mine. "Should I prove how much you still want me?"

Before I can scoff, he leans down and feathers a soft kiss against my parted lips. I can't deny that part of me wants him to push this further. To take what he wants. To make me forget everything that transpired today.

But he doesn't.

All too soon, he pulls away and stalks toward the bedroom door.

"I'll see you in the morning."

And then he's gone. On shaky legs, I make my way to the bed and slide underneath the covers.

What the hell am I going to do?

The thought of leaving him, walking away, makes me feel like I'm gasping for air. As if I'm nothing more than a fish out of water. I don't know if I can do it.

But can I live with someone who is tied to the mafia?

I almost laugh at that question.

Matteo Valentini isn't just involved with the Chicago mafia.

His family *is* the Cosa Nostra.

CHAPTER THIRTY-FOUR

"Do you realize," with each word Dominic bites out, his voice grows more thunderous, "that you were almost *killed* today? What more has to happen for you to understand that this man is dangerous?" His booming voice echoes throughout the cavernous family room.

I don't know what to say to him. Nor do I know how to calm the tirade he's bent on having. I knew he would be angry, but I never suspected that he would blow his top.

Chewing my lower lip, I stare at Dominic from the sleek white couch I'm huddled on. He sits across from me on a matching chair. His body vibrates with barely suppressed rage.

I never should have come here. Had I been smart, I would have stayed put at the condo. After kicking Matteo out, loneliness quickly set in. Dominic's house has always felt like a second home, so I called a taxi and headed here.

"He's a menace! Mark my words, Gracie, you're going to end up dead if you stay with him. I hate to say it, but it's the truth!"

I don't necessarily believe the words poised on the tip of my tongue, but I force them out nevertheless. "What happened this morning could have been a random accident. I have no concrete evidence that it's linked to Matteo or his family. And neither do you.

So please, stop jumping to conclusions until the police give us more information."

Dominic levels me with a look of disbelief. "Tell me that you don't believe the words coming out of your mouth right now. Tell me that you haven't been brainwashed by that bastard."

I don't want what happened this morning to be linked to the Valentini family. But it seems much too coincidental to be random. After replaying the incident over and over in my head, I now think the driver had been gunning directly for me. Maybe I'm filling in the blank holes in my memory with what I think happened.

I don't know.

I don't know anything anymore.

I haven't felt this lost since...

"I haven't been brainwashed. Until there's evidence that proves it was a premeditated act, I don't have anything else to go on."

His blue eyes drill into mine. He looks torn between throwing his hands up in the air in frustration or wringing my neck. Changing tactics, his entire demeanor softens. "Look, sweetheart, I don't want to be the bad guy here. I really don't. If I thought this guy was good for you, I wouldn't have a problem with him or his family. But that's not the case." He shoots me another hard look. "And we both know it. The last thing I want is to see you get hurt by this man."

I blow out a long breath, trying to hold on to the last ounce of my patience. "Dominic, I'm fine. What happened today..." I shrug. Pain lances through my arm with the movement. I try not to wince because it'll just set him off again. "Until the police have more information, I'm treating this as an accident. You need to do the same." Trying to inject some levity into this heavy situation, I say teasingly, "You're a lawyer. You know how it works. Innocent until proven guilty, right?"

His eyes flatten. "Not where you're concerned. I'll protect you any damn way I can." He reaches over and slowly runs a finger along the curve of my jaw. "What kind of man would I be if I sat by and allowed you to make such a huge mistake?" His eyes darken, once again sparking with fire. "One that could cost you your life?"

"That's not going to happen. You're overreacting."

His fingers continue stroking my face. His gaze burns into mine with renewed intensity.

"Your parents entrusted me with your care and well-being. I'm trying to do what they would have wanted. I'm trying to protect you."

His words prick at my heart like a knife.

"Please, Dominic, I can't do this right now."

Looking contrite, he nods. "I'm sorry. It's been a long day. How about I pour you a glass of wine? I'm sure that will help settle your nerves. Then you can head upstairs and get a good night's sleep. You'll feel better in the morning."

I give him a grateful smile. "Thank you, that sounds lovely."

He heads into the kitchen. I hear the pop of a cork being pulled free from its bottle. There's the familiar clink of glasses and then he's rejoining me in the family room. He hands me one of the half-filled glasses before settling next to me. His arm slips around my shoulders and he tugs me toward him. Burrowing into his side, I take a sip of wine.

Cuddled up on the couch with Dominic, I realize this is what I came here for. All I wanted was for someone to hold me, to tell me that everything would be okay. I take a drink, and my body loosens. My eyelids droop. Dominic is right- it's been a long day, and heading up to bed sounds like a good idea.

I'm startled back into consciousness when he says, "I'm worried about you, Gracie." His voice turns rough. "It would kill me if anything happened to you."

It takes effort to lift my head to meet his gaze. Both love and concern swim around in his eyes. I force a reassuring smile. "Nothing is going to happen to me. I promise." Wanting to lighten the mood, I say, "You worry too much. You're like an old woman."

He chuckles, and his voice takes on a somber tone. "Something almost happened today, and I feel like you're turning a blind eye to the situation you're in." He pauses. "I know you like this guy, but he's not right for you."

I take another sip of fresh and fruity white wine. "You've been listening to gossip. You don't even know him."

"I know enough. As soon as I realized that you were involved with Matteo Valentini, I had him investigated."

I'm taken aback by the confession, but I'm not surprised. After finding out that Dominic had someone follow Matteo and snap photographs of him with other women, it makes sense that he would take it one step further.

But still...

I don't like it.

I don't like that he's taken it upon himself to interfere with my life. I'm not a child. I'm a grown woman capable of making my own decisions. And my own mistakes, if that's what this turns out to be.

What he's done is unsettling. I can't imagine my parents doing this. They would have trusted me enough to make good decisions.

"Be honest, not only with me, but with yourself. Aren't you concerned about what he's involved in?"

A denial sits perched on the tip of my tongue, but I can't force it out. It's one of the reasons I asked Matteo to leave my condo earlier. I needed time to think about what it means to be with a man like him. One who may never be able to tell me everything that he and his family are involved in. One who constantly needs to protect what's his so that no one takes it from him.

Stalling, I take another sip from my glass. When Dominic continues to wait for an answer, I admit the truth. Not only to him, but to myself. "Yes, it concerns me."

Surprise morphs across his handsome features. "It *should* concern you, Gracie. These are dangerous people we're talking about. They don't care about anything or anyone."

His words make me think about Matteo's family. His mother, Teresa. His father, Enzo. His sisters and brothers. All the aunts, uncles, and cousins. A few nieces and nephews, as well. So many people, that I'd had a hard time keeping them straight. All of whom I instantly liked. I can't imagine any of them deliberately trying to harm me. Or hurting anyone, honestly.

"They would never hurt me," I murmur, more to myself than him.

His harsh laughter startles me. The wine in my glass sloshes around.

"Oh, sweetheart," his tone is patronizing, "one of your best qualities is your naïveté." Dominic shakes his head. "They would hurt you in a heartbeat. You're not one of them. You will *never* be one of them." He holds up a hand to silence me when I open my mouth to argue. "Let's assume for the sake of this conversation, that you're right and none of the Valentini family would harm one beautiful blond hair on your head. They have enemies, Gracie. There are people who would go to great lengths to inflict pain to them. You're what they call- *collateral damage*."

A shiver snakes through me in response to his tirade.

I'm suddenly overcome with exhaustion. I can't take any more of Dominic's ranting. "But I like him," I whisper.

Maybe love him.

Sighing deeply, Dominic kisses the top of my head and pulls me in for another hug. "I know, sweetheart. I know. But you need to trust me when I tell you that he isn't the right man for you."

"How can you say that?" I snuggle closer, trying to get comfortable. My eyelids are on the verge of closing. It's been such a long day. "You don't know him."

"Because I know the kind of people who raised you." He allows those words to whirl through my muddled mind before asking, "Do you think either of your parents would approve of Matteo Valentini?"

A lump forms in the back of my throat. I've asked myself the same question a hundred times and the answer is always the same. In my heart, I want to believe that Mom and Dad wouldn't judge him by what his family has done, but I suspect that Matteo hasn't strictly been on the legal end of things either.

"We both know that they wouldn't want you involved with someone like him. Nor would they understand how you could turn your back on your upbringing. Are you forgetting that they prosecuted and locked up scum-bags like him?" He pauses. "That it was their life's work?"

I wince. Opening my eyes, I struggle to sit up, realizing that my glass is no longer in my hand. Instead, Dominic holds it.

Is it weird that I don't remember him taking it from me?

"Did you want to finish your wine?"

"Please." I need something to wash away the bad taste his words have left in my mouth. A few swallows later, the glass is empty. He plucks it from my fingers and sets it down on the coffee table. Needing distance, I lean against the couch cushions and close my eyes as a bone-tired weariness sets in. I don't open my eyes when Dominic's fingers trail over my cheek and cup the side of my face because I'm too tired.

"My poor girl. I think this has all been too much for you. You need a good night's sleep. Everything will look so much clearer in the morning. It always does."

I silently agree with him. I need to sleep. I don't think I could pry my eyelids open if I tried. I'm tired of dwelling on the situation, and I don't want to hear any more of what Dominic has to say either.

I need to figure out my relationship with Matteo on my own.

Dominic will have to accept that I'm a grown woman. He can't hire someone to follow me around. Nor should he investigate the man I've chosen to spend time with.

Dominic kisses my cheek. "I love you, Gracie."

Those are the last words I hear before my mind clicks off, and I get sucked under a thick blanket of mental fog to a place where I no longer have to think.

CHAPTER THIRTY-FIVE

Arggggh... my head.

It's killing me. It feels like someone is pounding inside of it with a hammer.

I should roll over and go back to sleep, but I need some water. It feels like a big ball of cotton has been wedged inside my mouth. It takes effort to pry open my eyelids. Bright sunlight pours through the windows. I blink, trying to adjust to the intensity.

A strange fuzziness fills my head. Needing to make sense of what's happening, my mind tumbles back to yesterday. It takes a moment for the memories to coalesce and then solidify.

The accident–or near hit-and-run–is the first thing that flashes through my sleep-addled brain.

Is that why I feel so crappy this morning?

Is this the aftereffect of the fall I took? Now that I think about it, I remember being checked over at the hospital. I'm pretty sure the doctor examined my head and said I hadn't hit it. Matteo was there. He was so upset about the accident. I don't think I've ever seen him that distraught.

With a suddenness that catches me off guard, the memories return one on top of another.

Matteo was afraid that he was the reason someone tried hurting me.

The man who stayed with me after the accident works for Matteo.

Matteo owns the building we live in.

God, it's all coming back to me. No wonder I feel like crap.

After all the secrets came to light, I asked Matteo to leave. Before walking away, he told me there was nowhere I could run. No way to escape him.

I was his.

I'd packed an overnight bag and fled to Dominic's. The moment he laid eyes on me, Dominic knew something had happened. I was all scraped up. Bruises had already formed on my skin. He'd enfolded me in his arms and walked me in to the house. As I explained what happened, he'd grown more and more incensed.

I remember having a glass of wine and talking for a bit. With the way I currently feel, you'd think I'd knocked back the entire bottle myself.

Did I drink more than one glass?

If I recall correctly, it wasn't even a full glass. Everything's so fuzzy, like my mind is sifting through buckets of sand. I don't like this feeling. Running a hand over my face, I haul myself up into a sitting position. Shock spikes through me when I realize that I'm in Dominic's master suite.

How did I get here?

Glancing down at myself, I yank the comforter up to conceal my bare breasts. I peek beneath the covers with a sense of dread.

Totally naked.

What the hell happened last night?

Why aren't I wearing pajamas?

I search my brain, desperate for answers. Anything that would explain the situation. But I keep drawing blanks. I don't remember changing my clothes last night. There are no memories after falling asleep on the couch in the family room.

Some of the muzziness clouding my brain falls away. Eyes flying around the room, I search for Dominic, hoping he'll be able to shed light on what happened, but he's nowhere to be found. The bathroom door has been left ajar, and the shower is running. I sit frozen in place with the covers clutched against my breasts. The water shuts off a few minutes later, and I hear the swish of the shower door sliding open.

This can't be happening. It has to be some sort of bizarre dream.

Questions brim at my lips.

Every single one of them flees my mind as Dominic strolls out of the bathroom rubbing his hair with a towel. Nothing covers his body.

He's as naked as I am.

My mouth drops open as I stare at him in shock. I've never seen Dominic without clothes on. Sure, I've seen him in swim trucks, but I've never seen... I gulp.

I've never seen *that* before!

It takes a few seconds to realize that I'm staring. This can't be happening.

Why is Dominic parading around naked in front of me?

And why can't I rip my eyes away from his penis?

A small squeak escapes me when it begins to thicken, and I'm jolted back to the present. Scorching heat floods my cheeks.

"Morning, sweetheart. I hope you're feeling better." He rubs the towel through his blond hair and stands there like being naked in front of me is an everyday occurrence.

Confused and uncomfortable, I clear my throat, while trying to keep my focus on the far wall. I can still see him in my periphery, but at least I no longer have a head-on view.

Dominic chuckles. "There's no reason to be shy. Not after last night," he says, his voice low and husky.

My eyes dart to his.

The floor may as well have just dropped out from under me. "What do you mean?" I croak.

Grinning, he closes the distance between us. I'm no longer distracted by his jutting erection. My heart thrashes against my rib cage.

Desperately I try to recall even the minutest detail from last night. A tiny fragment that will clue me in on what he's implying took place between us. I don't need it spelled out, though. The fact that I'm in his bed naked says it all in gigantic neon letters.

He settles on the bed next to me. There's a tenderness in his gaze as it holds mine. His fingers feather across my cheek. I stare, praying that my suspicions are wrong.

He searches my eyes before asking, "You don't remember anything?"

I shake my head.

He sighs. "That's too bad. What happened between us was beautiful. So much better than I could have ever imagined." His voice drops an octave. "About an hour after we turned in last night, you knocked on my door, asking if we could talk."

Nothing he says jogs my brain.

There are no flashes of memory.

Only an empty void of nothingness.

My face remains blank. As does my mind. I don't even recall getting off the couch. Or going to bed. My mind trips back to the last memory I was able to hang on to. And that's sitting with Dominic, finishing my glass of wine, and resting my head against the back of the couch before closing my eyes.

Is that why I can't remember?

Because I was so exhausted?

What other rational explanation could there be for waking up like this?

"You climbed into bed with me and we talked about everything that's been going on in your life." His thumb sweeps across my bottom lip. "It was such a good talk, Gracie." A look of disappointment settles over his features as his brows beetle together. "I'm surprised you don't remember."

Talking in bed doesn't explain why I'm now naked in it.

He shrugs. "One thing led to another, and we ended up making love last night. I have to say, it was well worth the wait." He smiles and leans toward me, brushing his mouth over mine. I don't shy away from the kiss because my mind is still cartwheeling.

Swallowing down the rising bile, I whisper, "You're telling me that we had sex last night?"

He taps a fingertip against my nose. "We made love, Gracie. It wasn't sex. What happened between us was love."

My belly drops to my toes.

Shaking my head in disbelief, I suck my lower lip into my mouth. What happened yesterday felt like a nightmare. I thought everything would feel normal again when I woke up this morning. But that hasn't happened.

Today is more screwed up than yesterday.

How is that possible?

"We really..." it takes a moment for me to wrap my lips around the words, *"made love?"*

Dominic strokes the side of my face before his fingers trail down the side of my neck, dipping beneath the covers. He caresses my left breast. My nipple tightens in response. A deep groan of appreciation slips from him and I brush his hand away from my body.

His touch doesn't feel right.

"I would be more than happy to give you a repeat performance. I've got some time until I have to head into the office." He grins and gives me a flirtatious wink. "Hell, maybe I'll call in and let them know that I'll be working from home today. Would you like that, Gracie? We can spend all day in bed."

I blanch at that idea. *"No! We can't... I mean..."*

"I'm sorry you don't remember what happened between us," he says with a contrite expression. "It was really special. I've waited a long time for us to be together. Maybe I should have slowed you down last night..."

Slowed me down?

What the hell is he talking about?

"When you stripped and started kissing me, I couldn't resist." His eyes darken with hunger. "You're a hard woman to say no to, sweetheart."

With tears springing to my eyes, I bury my face in my hands. God, what a mess... "Dominic, I'm sorry, but I don't remember any of this. I don't..."

He wraps me in his arms, holding me against his chest. "Shhhh, it's okay. We have time to figure this out. There's no rush." He drops tiny butterfly kisses along the side of my face.

Dominic and I sleeping together last night was a mistake. It should have never happened. Even thinking about it makes me nauseous. I need to get out of here. I can't stay in this house another second longer.

Pulling myself together, I chance a look at him. "I need to go home." Everything from yesterday has slammed into me, yet my mind is still fuzzy around the edges.

What day is it?

Thursday?

Friday?

Regardless... "I have to get to class." I'm sure he doesn't want me to miss school.

"No problem. I'll have the car brought around. We can hash this out tonight, okay? I'll send Henry to pick you up around five o'clock," he says nonchalantly, as if my world hasn't been tipped upside down.

It's weird.

What else can I do but play along?

When I remain silent, he asks, "Does that work for you?"

Not sure what to say, I nod in agreement. I would do almost anything to get out of this situation. The sooner, the better. My throat feels tight, as if I'm suffocating very slowly.

When he makes no move to leave, I blurt, "I have to get dressed."

"Of course." He releases me from his grasp and stands. I'm still keenly aware of his nudity. His penis is *right* there, less than a foot away from me. And he's still erect. Averting my eyes, I draw in a shaky breath and wait for him to leave. I've never been so uncomfortable in my life.

"Gracie."

I continue staring straight ahead, hoping to avoid further awkwardness.

His fingers slide under my chin and lift my head to bring us eye to eye. "Please don't be embarrassed about this. It's been a long time coming."

Unsure how to respond, I nod.

He quietly says, "I think your parents would approve. Don't you?"

I blink hard, not wanting to think about Mom and Dad right now. I have no idea if they would approve of me sleeping with my godfather, the man they chose to protect me. Who has known me since infancy.

Maybe they would.

Or maybe they'd think it's weird.

Which is what I think.

Clearing my throat, I repeat, "I need to get dressed."

He nods and strolls over to his walk-in closet. I leap out of the bed when he disappears from sight. As soon as my feet hit the floor, everything wavers. I have to close my eyes and inhale a deep, steadying breath.

My body aches more than it did yesterday. Additional bruises have blossomed along my thighs and torso. Shaking off the fogginess, I stumble from Dominic's room toward the one I've always considered my own.

I close and lock the door, leaning heavily against it.

I need a shower.

Once the water warms, I step under the spray and wet my hair, face, and limbs. I lather up and gently rub my body, mindful of the bruises and scrapes marring my flesh. Ten minutes later, I step out feeling more alert. My mind is still somersaulting, though. What happened with Dominic doesn't make sense. I'm having a difficult time accepting that we slept together.

Guilt churns within me.

I considered a relationship with Dominic a while back, but that was before Matteo and I became involved. The only man I can imagine being with now is Matteo.

I rummage through my overnight bag, pulling on panties and a bra before finding a shirt and jeans.

A fresh wave of nausea rolls over me.

What am I going to tell Matteo?

How am I going to explain that I slept with another man?

My godfather, of all people.

Inhaling a shaky breath, I slowly release it as my stomach continues to roil. I need to get out of this house *now*. Hopefully Dominic has left for the office. I don't want to face him again.

How did everything veer so completely out of control last night? If

Dominic weren't so adamant that we had slept together, I would question it. But he has no reason to lie. I may not want to believe him, but I do.

Shoving my feet into a pair of ballet flats, I zip up my bag and hoist it on to my shoulder, wincing as my sore muscles throb. Then I'm out the door. I'm halfway down the staircase when the pounding begins. It rattles the front door on its hinges. My feet stall as Dominic strolls into the foyer, grabs the handle, and opens it.

Matteo stands on the other side.

Frozen on the staircase, the breath catches in my throat. My fingers bite into the banister. Matteo's dark eyes dart around before landing on me. The fury in them pins me in place.

CHAPTER THIRTY-SIX

"Matteo." My voice cracks as his name spills from my mouth.

He shoves past Dominic, taking the stairs two at a time. When he's close enough, Matteo yanks me toward him. I flinch as his arms wrap around me.

Hearing my hiss of pain, he loosens his grip. His fingers slip under my chin and tip my face toward his. "Sorry, bella. I didn't mean to be so rough." His lips brush over mine.

My breath comes out in shaky puffs. My heart drums against my ribcage. I thought I'd have more time before facing him. I'm nowhere near ready for a confrontation. I hope Dominic will give me the courtesy of telling Matteo what happened in private. The last thing I need is an audience. I already know that Matteo will be livid.

"It's okay," I whisper. "I'm okay." I just want to inhale his masculine scent and pretend that the last twenty-four hours never happened.

"Good. I was worried about you."

Although I want to run my hands over his face, I keep them to myself.

"Ah, Mr. Matteo Valentini, I presume. Nice of you to drop by," Dominic pauses, his tongue sweeping across his teeth, *"unannounced.*

Perhaps you might give some advanced notice of your impending arrival in the future. It's really only polite."

My eyes dart from Matteo to Dominic. A wave of anxiety crashes over me. Matteo's embrace tightens.

"Gracie, darling, why don't you tell your boyfriend what happened last night. He has a right to know."

I stare at Dominic in shock, floored that he is bringing this up in front of Matteo. Doesn't he understand that I want to break this news to him myself?

In private.

Without him looking on.

Matteo tenses, and his eyes shift from where Dominic stands by the front door to me. "What's he talking about?"

I swallow the bile rising in my throat.

Before I can think of a rational explanation, Dominic continues, "You have to understand that I've known Gracie her entire life. When her parents died, they entrusted me with both her care and well-being. Obviously, it's a responsibility I gladly accepted. Gracie's a special young woman. Her heart is as pure as gold. She deserves a man who is her equal." He pauses. "You are *not* the kind of man her parents would have approved of. The Valentinis are the kind of people her parents spent their careers prosecuting and locking up behind bars. You have no future with my godchild."

Every muscle in Matteo's body clenches. His jaw ticks as he glares at Dominic. He doesn't loosen his hold on me. "You're right." The barely suppressed violence within his words is audible. "I could be the most perfect man in the world and I still wouldn't be good enough for her."

Dominic's eyes slide to mine. "This is a rather indelicate subject to be discussing with you but obviously, it needs to be said so that you understand the gravity of the situation. Last night, Gracie and I consummated the love we feel for one another."

Horror floods my entire body.

No.

Why is Dominic doing this? For the first time since Matteo stormed through the front door, a flicker of doubt crosses his face.

His eyes turn frigid. "Is that true?" he rasps, his voice riddled with disbelief and tinged with hurt. "Did you sleep with him?"

I hastily shake my head because the truth of the matter is that I still can't remember a single detail from last night.

Nervously licking my lips, I whisper, "I don't know." I shake my head again. "I can't remember anything."

Some of his coldness recedes. "How is that possible?"

"Gracie was upset when she showed up at my door last night." Dominic sends Matteo a hard look full of contempt. "She had a few glasses of wine to help settle her nerves."

"I only remember having one," I interject. It was half a glass at the most.

Matteo's narrowed eyes shift between Dominic and me as if he's trying to piece together the truth for himself.

"You can't deny that you woke up naked in my bed this morning," Dominic says.

My cheeks ignite with heat. Unfortunately, that fact *is* undeniable. "The last thing I remember is falling asleep on the couch and then waking up in his bed this morning. Whatever happened in between that is blank."

Absently stroking his cheek, Dominic muses, "It was such a heat of the moment kind of thing that we didn't use protection."

The blood rushing through my veins turns to ice. I thought the situation couldn't get worse.

I was wrong.

I'm not on the pill. Not yet, anyway. I have an appointment set up for next week. But that does nothing to solve my current predicament.

Strangely excited by the prospect, Dominic adds, "Nothing would please me more than if you ended up pregnant, Gracie. Your parents would have been ecstatic."

My fingers rise to my temples. "Stop." Nausea churns in my stomach. I'm going to be sick right here on the staircase. "Please, just stop."

Confusion threads through his voice. "Gracie? What's wrong? Did I say something to upset you?"

"You need to stop bringing my parents into everything." Anger roils through my belly as my voice picks up strength. "I have no idea how either one of them would feel about Matteo. And I certainly don't know how they would feel about this situation either. You keep throwing Mom and Dad in my face and I'm tired of it."

Sometimes I think Dominic is trying to manipulate me into doing what he wants by bringing them up in conversations. It needs to stop. I haven't said anything before because Dominic is family. The only family I have. He wants the best for me. But I can't listen to it anymore. It hurts too much.

His face falls. "Gracie, I never meant-"

"I think you did."

I straighten my shoulders. My anger continues to grow as I think about the last two months and all the times he's used my parents to herd me in a specific direction. I didn't want to see it before. I didn't want to believe it was purposeful. I've never lashed out at Dominic. There's never been any reason.

Until now.

Matteo kisses the top of my head. His eyes stay trained on Dominic's as if he doesn't trust him. "I have a car waiting out front. I want you to wait inside the limo. There are a few things I need to clear up with your godfather."

I step out of Matteo's arms and turn to face him. Does he think he can just send me to the car like an errant child while he and Dominic have at each other?

I don't think so.

"No. I'm not leaving the two of you alone together," I say firmly.

Dark eyes meet mine. "Bella," he cajoles, "you have my word that I won't touch him. But there are words that need to be said and I would prefer them to be discussed in private."

"Does it have something to do with me?" I ask even though I know the answer.

He eyes me wearily. "Yes."

I fold my arms across my chest, the overnight bag still hangs from my shoulder. "I'm not leaving. If you have something to say to Dominic, I'd like to hear it."

My refusal exasperates him. He's not used to me fighting him. All he usually has to do is flick his obsidian gaze in my direction or trail his fingers over me, and I fold like a house of cards, eager to do whatever he wants.

Well, not this time.

"Bella-"

Brows drawn together, I repeat in a sharper tone, "I'm not leaving."

He watches me for a long moment and then shrugs. In a soft voice, he admits, "I don't want you to hear this."

"I'm staying."

Pulling me into the protective shelter of his arms, he holds me close. I can't imagine what he could possibly have to say to Dominic that needs to be kept from me.

Matteo turns, glaring at Dominic from where we stand on the staircase. "Did you think I would leave the welfare of my woman up to the police?" His gaze turns lethal. My heart stutters at the vicious gleam in it. "That I wouldn't use every damn resource I had at my disposal?"

Uncertainty flashes across Dominic's face. My mind scrambles to understand what Matteo is alluding to.

Why is he bringing up yesterday's accident?

Matteo chuckles when Dominic remains silent. It's an ugly, harsh sound that grates against my ears. It sends a cold frisson of discomfort skating down my spine. A dangerous rage lurks under Matteo's thick coat of ice. I don't understand why it's directed at Dominic, though. My heartbeat kicks up as I wait for Matteo to continue. I realize as dread washes over me that there must be more.

"Rest assured, Grimaldi, I'm just as concerned about Grace's welfare as you claim to be. Which is why I made sure she had protection whenever she left the building. No one is going to hurt my woman." Eyes blazing, his voice turns deadly. Another shiver races over my spine. "You'll be pleased to know that we found the driver who tried to hit her."

Dominic folds his arms across his chest. Again, his expression falters for a second. If I didn't know him so well, I probably would have missed it.

"That's wonderful news," he says evenly. "Is the bastard in police custody?"

Matteo's lips slowly twist into a chilling smile. "No. I took care of the interrogation myself. There was no reason to involve the police in this matter."

My eyes drop to the hand resting against my shoulder. Drawing in a sharp breath, I notice the bruised and bloody knuckles.

"It didn't take much coercing to extract a confession. Within fifteen minutes he was begging for his life, ready to spill every transgression his own mother had committed."

Unimpressed, Dominic mutters, "A beaten man will say just about anything to save himself.

"Yes," Matteo muses, "that is so true. Although I have to say, most men, once they grasp the severity of the situation they find themselves in, have no compunction about ratting out whoever paid them to commit a crime." He flashes another menacing smile at Dominic. "Trust me, it didn't take much encouragement before this particular man was eager to hand over whatever details I asked for. Even though he never met with the man who paid him to scare some woman by almost striking her on a busy street, he knew details that only someone close to her could provide." Matteo pauses before adding in a silky voice, "He was given her schedule in advance so that he would know where to find her at different times of the week."

Stunned into silence, my eyes stay riveted to Dominic's face.

No.

The picture Matteo is painting isn't possible.

Dominic would never do something so awful. He loves me. We're family. Why would he want to hurt me? A whimper of pain escapes my lips. My godfather takes a step toward me and Matteo lets loose a vicious growl.

"You touch her ever again, and I'll kill you myself, Grimaldi. Do you understand me?"

Dominic's fists clench at his sides. "You can't do that! You have no right to keep Gracie from me!"

Matteo's barely leashed anger continues to bubble beneath the surface. I've never seen him like this. His demeanor should frighten me, but it doesn't. He's done everything in his power to protect me, even when I didn't want it.

His deep voice cracks like thunder, and I wince. *"You paid a man to scare her! For all you know, something could have gone wrong and she could have died!"*

A wave of dizziness crashes over me. I shake my head to clear it and whisper, "Why would you do something like that?"

What Matteo has accused Dominic of is true. I see it in his eyes and in the stricken look on his face.

"Gracie, please. Just listen-"

Matteo cuts Dominic off. "Tell her the rest, or I will." He waits a beat and adds harshly, "You've had me investigated? Just know that I returned the favor."

Dominic pales. Whatever Mateo has discovered is worse than Dominic hiring someone to scare me with an attempted hit-and-run.

How is that possible?

How is *any* of this possible?

"Tell her!" Matteo's voice whips out, cracking the charged air. *"Or I will!* Either way, she's going to find out what a bastard you truly are."

The man I've known my entire life, the one I trusted above all others, deflates. His shoulders sag as if the weight of the world has been dumped on them. Moistening his lips, he clears his voice and admits, "I'm broke, Gracie." His eyes beseechingly stare at me. "It's all gone."

"Finish it," Matteo snaps.

I rip my eyes away from Dominic to the man holding me. His face looks as if it has been carved from granite. No mercy will be given. Whatever Matteo dug up in the darkness will now be dragged into the light of day.

"I've had to dip into your inheritance to pay the bills."

My brows pinch together in confusion. *"What?"*

He clears his throat again. "I've been borrowing from your accounts. It was-"

Matteo cuts him off. "He has siphoned three million dollars from your trust fund, Grace. It's gone."

"It's not gone. I was going to pay her back!" Dominic plows a hand through his hair giving it a wild, disheveled look. A panicked note I've never heard before creeps into his voice. "I needed to get everything under control. You have to believe me! I was just borrowing it. You wouldn't have ever known it was missing," he rambles.

Brimming with disbelief, I shake my head as his excuses roll around in my mind like marbles. "I don't understand how you could pay someone to *hurt* me." I thought Dominic loved me. He was my father's best friend. He's known me since infancy. He was there while I grew up. And then when the unthinkable happened.

How could he pay someone to *hit me with a car?*

I feel as though I'm being repeatedly stabbed in the heart with a butcher knife. I can't breathe without pain filling every recess of my body.

"He was only supposed to scare you, Gracie. He assured me that you wouldn't get hurt." Desperation floods Dominic's eyes. He looks like he's about to become unhinged. For the first time, I feel as if I don't know this man at all. "You have to believe me! I love you! I would never do anything to hurt you!"

Tears threaten as I shake my head. "But I *was* hurt. Whoever you hired jumped the curb. He could have killed me."

Dominic looks devastated by my words.

Matteo's deep voice cuts through the thick air. "You wanted her to think that it happened because of me." His words are razor-sharp. "Because my family is dangerous, right? You were hoping she would break off our relationship and come running back to you."

Dominic snarls, "You're nothing but a criminal! A mobster! The scum of society!"

"And yet, you're the one who paid some low-life, petty criminal that you represented a few years ago to hurt the woman you were supposed to protect. You gave him all her information so that he would be able to track her down." Matteo tilts his head and asks, "And what if he'd gotten ideas of his own into his head, hmm? What if he'd decided that he was going to throw in a few things free of charge?"

Dominic blanches.

Once I realize what Matteo is alluding to, fresh nausea swirls in my already upset stomach. So much more could have happened.

What the hell had Dominic been thinking?

"He almost hit me," I whisper hoarsely as bits and pieces from yesterday morning flicker through my mind like a picture show. "If I hadn't jumped out of the way, he would have run me over." More hot, angry tears prick my eyes. "You did this because you didn't want me with Matteo?"

"He wanted you for himself. He wanted total control over your inheritance. Your godfather owes quite a bit of money," Matteo says.

"No! That's not true. I love you, Gracie!" Dominic holds up his hands. "Yes, the money would have made life easier, but I've always loved you. We're family. Just you and me. Remember? It's been that way for the last two years. I've taken care of everything. I've been there during the most difficult period of your life. That has to mean something, doesn't it? I know what I've done is wrong, but it was the only way to get you to open your eyes and see how dangerous the Valentinis can be! They're criminals! Part of the mafia! You can't be with a lowlife like him."

Tears streak down my cheeks. Dominic's right, I couldn't have gotten through the last two years without him. "All Matteo has done is protect me while you stole from me." My voice grows and gains strength. "And then you hired someone to scare me into leaving him."

"Gracie, please try to understand-"

Not willing to hear any more excuses, I swipe at the errant tears. "I understand perfectly." My mind is struggling to keep up with every-thing that has happened within the last twenty-four hours. As all the pieces fall neatly into place, another thought occurs to me. "We didn't sleep together last night, did we?"

Shifting from one foot to another, Dominic's eyes stay locked on mine. "No."

Relief sweeps through me. I give voice to the suspicions that have nagged me ever since waking in his bed. "You drugged me."

I may have a glass or two of wine every so often, but I rarely drink enough to get intoxicated. And certainly not enough to pass out. It made no sense that I wouldn't be able to remember going to bed last night. Or anything else he claimed that happened.

"You'd had such a difficult day. It was just a little something to help you relax. That's all."

Oh my God...

Matteo's fingers bite into my arms as he hauls me closer. I wince. He's holding on to his temper by a ragged thread. I feel it in his taut posture. Every muscle is whipcord tight. I don't want him to unleash his fury because it would be deadly.

Staring into his eyes, I whisper pleadingly, "Please, take me home." It feels like my entire world is crumbling around me. First, I lost my parents and now I'm losing Dominic. He was like a second father to me. I thought I could trust him implicitly.

I was wrong.

Dominic rushes forward as Matteo leads me down the staircase.

"Gracie, please! You have to listen to me! I did all this for you! For us! So we could be together!" His voice grows shriller with each word. "You never gave us a chance! Your parents wouldn't want you with some scumbag mafia prince!"

Something snaps in me.

I'm tired of him using my parents against me every single chance he gets. Constantly manipulating me with their memory. How did I not see it sooner? I'd thought he wanted to remember them like I did, to keep their memory alive, but that wasn't the case. They were nothing more than a tool to keep me in line.

Throwing off Matteo's arms, I fly toward Dominic and pound on his chest in a blind rage with my scraped-up hands. *"Stop talking about them! Don't you dare speak of them again!"* Fresh tears pour down my cheeks. *"How could you have ever loved them if you were able to steal from their legacy and hurt me like this?"*

"No," he cries, "that's not true! I loved them. You know I did! Your father was like a brother to me."

I'm crying so hard now that I can barely see or speak. "No! You stole my money, you tried running me down, you drugged me, and then you lied about us sleeping together! You couldn't possibly have loved them or me!" Sucking in a shaky breath, I expel it slowly from my lungs in a feeble attempt to get ahold of myself. I need to finish this. "You've been lying to me this entire time. I never want to see you again."

He begins to cry. If I didn't feel so dead inside, the sight of Dominic with tears running down his face would break me. "Gracie, please. I'm sorry for everything. I... I should have been up front with you about what was going on with my finances. You have to know how much I love you."

I step away from him, swiping at more tears. Matteo stands silently a few feet behind me. He's there if I need him, but he's willing to let me fight my own battles. He's willing to let me say my piece without whisking me away and taking care of everything for me.

"Gracie... please. Just give yourself a few days to calm down. Maybe then we can sit and talk. I'm sorry, it was never supposed to be like this."

"No." Once I walk out that door, I'll never see him again. He needs to understand that. "We're done, Dominic. I want what's left of my inheritance released to me immediately. If the paperwork isn't delivered by tomorrow morning, I'll go to the police and press charges for embezzlement, the hit-and-run, and drugging me."

He pales, but doesn't say a word.

There are no more arguments.

Matteo's hands settle on my shoulders. "Let me take you home, bella."

Knowing this will be the last time I see him, my eyes lock on Dominic's forlorn blue ones for a moment before I turn my back on him. Fresh air slides across my tear-stained cheeks when I step outside. Victor is there, holding open the door as I climb into the limo. Matteo slides in after me. Once the vehicle pulls out of the circular drive, I look out the back window to find Dominic standing in the open doorway.

The enormity of what has transpired slams into me once more, and I burst into noisy sobs. Matteo pulls me as close to him as possible, gathering me into his arms.

"Please don't cry. You're safe now. Everything will be okay, I promise."

His softly spoken reassurances do little to alleviate the burning ache in my heart.

CHAPTER THIRTY-SEVEN

With my eyes closed, I sit between Matteo's long, muscular legs as he gently rubs a sudsy washcloth over my back. Ironically, I feel like I've been hit by a Mack truck after what happened with Dominic earlier.

I'm emotionally drained.

I'm more broken and battered on the inside than on the outside.

Matteo has been at my side ever since storming into Dominic's house. He's taken care of me, treating me with kid gloves as if I've been crafted from glass and are infinitely precious.

I was uncertain as to what the future held for us last night. I wasn't sure if I could accept his family being involved with the mafia. Or Matteo being part of it. But after everything I've been through in the last forty-eight hours, I've realized that none of it matters.

Not because I'm alone in the world and *someone* is better than *no one*. It has everything to do with how much this man cares for me. And how much I care for him. The irrepressible chemistry that exists between us.

It's undeniable.

Magnetic.

Impossible to resist.

I doubt I could walk away from Matteo even if I wanted to.

He breaks into my pensive thoughts by pressing a kiss against my shoulder blade, his warm breath ghosting over me as he lingers. Delicious shivers dance across my flesh.

"I'm sorry about Dominic," he says softly.

The entire situation continues to baffle me. I still can't wrap my mind around everything my godfather set in motion.

"He did care about you, Grace. Still does."

My chest tightens. But I'm tired of tears. I refuse to release the little buggers. I force out a laugh, but it's a weak attempt and one that's full of sadness. "Well, he has a strange way of showing it."

Matteo says in a low voice, "If I hadn't been involved, I doubt Dominic would have hired someone to scare you. I think us being together is what pushed him over the edge."

Swiveling my head so our eyes can meet, I growl, "Don't you dare make excuses for him. He didn't have to do any of it." Hot licks of anger bubble up inside me. "I could have been hurt far worse than I was." I don't add *killed*. But we both know it's the truth.

Matteo's voice softens. "I know, bella. It makes me sick inside to think about it." He lays another kiss against the nape of my neck.

"He was quite willing to pin the blame on you and your family," I remind him. Matteo is all too aware of what Dominic tried accusing him of. It doesn't escape me that without Matteo's involvement, I might not have ever found out that Dominic had been stealing from me.

"That was never going to happen. I wasn't going to rest until I knew who tried hurting you."

"Thank you for that."

"You don't have to thank me." A hard glint enters his dark eyes as they hold mine. "I told you before that I take care of what's mine."

I smile as desire sparks to life and burns in the bottom of my belly. "Are you trying to tell me that I'm yours?"

He snorts. It's the cutest sound imaginable. "Was there ever any doubt?"

I shrug, suddenly feeling shy. "Just making sure."

We've never sat down and had a big heart-to-heart about our feelings. That's why his next words take me by surprise.

"I love you, Grace."

My eyes widen at the unexpected declaration. "I love you, too," I whisper in return.

He leans forward and kisses me, gently turning my body until I'm lying across him. His erection presses against my belly, and my body awakens despite how tired I felt seconds ago.

It's always like this between us.

He groans when my fingers wrap around his hard cock and begin stroking him. "Not tonight. You need to rest."

My body is sore, but another part is beginning to ache as well. It's an ache only Matteo can relieve. I playfully bat my eyelashes and pout. "Don't you want me?"

His voice turns raspy as if he's battling his own urges. And I love that. Love that I can drive him to the brink of distraction. "Of course I do, but you need a few more days to heal." That doesn't stop his lips from crashing into mine. From claiming my mouth and branding me as his. "Then I'll take you exactly how I like best. Hard."

A delicious thrill bolts straight down to my center. The ache between my thighs intensifies and grows into a steady, pulsing beat. A demand for more.

"I'm not going anywhere, Grace. I'll always be right here with you."

His promise takes the sharp edge off my desire, filling me with a tenderness I didn't think was possible.

"I love you," I whisper against his lips. I don't want him to ever doubt me. "I don't care who your family is. I don't care what you've done in the past. I only care about you." My eyes meet his. "*You're* all that matters."

The darkness hiding in his eyes disappears. A smile spreads across his face. My belly flips because he's the most gorgeous man I've ever seen and I can't imagine there coming a time when I'm not affected by him.

At least, I hope there won't be.

The same love coursing through me fills his espresso-colored eyes. He reminds me, "Just know that you are mine, bella. You will *always* be mine."

EPILOGUE
Matteo

Five years later

I throw open the door as the bell rings. George has a guest list at the front desk and is sending people up. It's been a steady stream of family and friends arriving for the last hour. There are already about thirty people milling around the living room. The condo is open, airy, and spacious.

It fits the three of us perfectly.

I've been doing my best to convince my wife that we should take over my parents' compound in the country. It would be the perfect place to raise Caterina.

Along with the rest of the kids we plan on having.

I shake Jonathan's hand. "Hey, man. Good to see you."

Jonathan and Grace have been friends since she started at The Art Institute five years ago. Jonathan volunteers on a weekly basis. Grace will finish up her doctorate program next spring. She's already been offered a permanent position as a curator with the museum.

Can you believe that?

Dr. Grace Valentini, PhD.

Damn right it has a nice ring to it.

Although I can't deny that Mrs. Grace Valentini has a damn fine ring to it as well.

I sprung the question on her about six months after the attempted hit-and-run incident. I knew how our relationship would play out before I stormed over to Dominic's to claim her. By that point, Grace was already my woman. She may not have known it, but that doesn't make it any less true.

I wasn't lying when I told her godfather that I protect what's mine.

I do.

I give the two-year-old bundle of energy in my arms a kiss on her cherub-like cheek. I've been protecting what's mine for five years now and that's never going to change.

Jonathan grins. "We wouldn't miss it for the world."

Jamie hands over a six-pack of Corona.

I nod appreciatively. It's one of my favorite beers. "Thanks for bringing the good stuff."

He gives me a wink. "Anything for you."

Jonathan holds out a bottle of white, which I happen to know is one of Grace's favorites. She won't be partaking in any today, though. The three of them love getting together and indulging in a few glasses of wine while gossiping about what's happening at the museum, which is kind of mind-blowing because you would expect it to be dull and mundane in a stuffy place like that.

Apparently not. The art museum is a hotbed of love, scandal, and intrigue.

I almost snort at that thought.

"And this is for my most favorite girl in the world." Leaning toward me, Jonathan tickles Caterina's belly. She squeals and holds out her chubby arms.

"That's right, baby girl, come to Uncle Johnny."

Caterina shrieks with excitement as Jonathan lifts her high above his head. Jamie smiles at her while making silly faces. I keep waiting for them to pop the news that they're adopting. They've been talking about it for a couple of years.

"Every time I see you, beautiful, you look more and more like your daddy."

I roll my eyes. "Yeah, I wouldn't mention that to Grace. It's kind of a touchy subject. Every time someone makes a comment, I end up getting an earful about how she's the one who carried her for nine months and gained all the weight." I shrug and add, "With any luck, this next one will take more after her." Everything in me softens as I think about a little girl or boy with my wife's looks and coloring.

Both of their heads whip toward me.

Realizing I just let the cat out of the bag, I wince. "Shit. I wasn't supposed to mention anything yet." I want to bellow it from the rooftops, though. "Grace wants to wait a few more weeks before we make an official announcement."

"*Oh my God!*" Jonathan shoots a triumphant grin at Jamie. "See! I told you there was another bun in the oven. In fact, I was just saying the other day that the girls were looking more bodacious than usual."

I give him a deadpan look. "Yeah, I don't want you discussing my wife's *girls*. Or how *bodacious* they look." I'm the only one allowed to discuss my wife's breasts. The *girls* belong strictly to me. Bodacious or otherwise.

Jonathan rolls his eyes. "*Please*. We all know that I am most definitely *not* a breast man."

Jamie laughs his ass off, and I can't help but smile. Not that I'll tell him this, but he's right. Grace's breasts are bigger. Bodacious is the right word to describe their newfound lushness.

And I fucking love it.

I love when my wife is pregnant. Knocked up with my kid is a good look on her. I'm gunning for at least two more. Maybe three. I want a whole houseful of Valentinis running around.

My gaze locks on my beautiful wife. She's surrounded by my parents and siblings. Chloe is right beside her. After what went down with Dominic, the two women are tighter than before. Chloe may not be blood to either one of us, but she's family.

Just like Jonathan and Jamie.

That means everything to a man like me. And I know it means everything to Grace. She may not have parents, siblings, aunts, uncles, or cousins, but she has all the people in this room. Every single one of them would do anything for her and at the end of the day, that's all that matters. Some of these people are family, bound by blood. Others are friends that have been pulled into our tight-knit inner circle. They are the family we've chosen to walk with us.

As our eyes continue to cling, I want to stalk over, sink to my knees, and run my hands over her bulging belly. Sometimes I catch sight of her when I'm not expecting it, and she literally steals my breath away.

How the fuck did I get so lucky?

How does a woman as amazing as Grace end up falling for a guy like me?

I don't know.

And furthermore, I don't give two fucks.

Her lips curve into a radiant smile as if she knows what's running through my head. As if, from across the room, she feels the need I have for her.

A need that eclipses almost everything else.

A love that continues to pound through me, growing stronger, running deeper, and encompassing more of my world, with each passing day.

A love I wasn't looking for but nevertheless found in an elevator on the way to the thirtieth floor.

See that woman across the room?

The gorgeous blonde with big blue eyes that can bring a grown man to his knees?

That has already brought this man to his knees?

Yeah, that woman is mine.

That woman will *always* be mine.

And just like I told her five years ago, I protect what's mine.

Roman

Present

I'm beginning to lose myself.

I feel it happening more with the passing of each day, and it scares the shit out of me. During rare moments of self-reflection, doubt creeps in, and I question objectives that should be irrefutable.

For a man like me, this is a precarious situation.

Over the last three years, I've done everything in my power to keep her at a distance. I've been a bastard. I've been rude. I've tried ignoring her. I've withheld my friendship. Most days, I'm barely civil to her, because I know all hell will break loose once the floodgates open.

None of my tactics douse the spark that flares to life when we're in the same room. I'm a moth dancing too close to the twisting flames.

One of these days, I'm going to get burned.

Or end up with a bullet in my head.

A solitary image of her flickering through my brain is enough to make me grow unbearably hard.

I've found myself on the verge of reaching out to slide my fingers through the glossy strands of her dark hair too many times to count.

Because I'm a sick and twisted fuck, I often fantasize about wrapping the thick, rope-like length around my palm and pulling it taut. I want her lush, naked body bowing like a supple tree branch and bending to my will. I want her rendered incapable of doing anything other than submitting to my dominance.

The thought of her on bent knees, ass high in the air, cheek and chest pressed against the mattress as I hold her pinned, puts me on the brink of blowing my wad.

Sofia can't figure out why I act like such a bastard. I see the silent questions lingering in her eyes. If I were a lesser man, I'd fall to my knees and beg for absolution. But that's an impossibility.

I know the truth, even if she doesn't.

You'd think she would grow to despise me because of my churlish behavior. But she hasn't. Not yet. She may have learned to stay away from me, but she doesn't always abide by what she knows is best for her.

Sofia doesn't understand the feelings I stoke to life inside her. Nor does she understand the attraction vibrating in the air between us. But I do. I recognize it all too well. She wears her emotions across her heart-shaped face. And she doesn't realize that I feast upon them like a starved monster lurking in the darkness.

They're much too tempting for me to resist.

Something primitive inside me enjoys the way her body reacts to mine. Without meaning to, she displays her sexual desire for me. She flushes when our eyes meet. Her nipples harden under clothing. Her breath hitches, causing the pulse in her neck to beat erratically like the wings of a trapped bird.

I want nothing more than to claim her and make her mine.

But that will never happen.

Sofia Valentini will never belong to me.

I can't get her out of my head. I've tried losing myself in dozens of other women over the years. It isn't difficult to find a willing woman in this city. Not when you work for the Valentinis. Our reputation precedes us wherever we go.

And the pussy flows freely in response.

It makes no difference how high or low you rank in the organization. Name recognition is more than enough to get you whatever you want. These women want to live vicariously through you. Money, drugs, blood, and violence are powerful aphrodisiacs.

It's surprising how drawn some of these women are to a dangerous lifestyle. They want to singe their wings without getting burned. They want to dance close to the fire without getting torched.

But Sofia is different.

She's a princess who was born into this lifestyle, and now that she's free to make her own choices, she wants nothing to do with the Valentini empire. She would prefer to come from average, middle-class parents. Not one of the most well-known crime families in the United States, whose power and corruption dates back generations. And not one that resides in a multi-million-dollar compound on twenty sprawling acres of prime real estate along the shore of Lake Michigan.

Sofia Valentini is an exotic bird trapped in a gilded cage.

I've tried fucking women with the same olive-toned flesh. Big-breasted, generously-hipped, angelic-faced women I pretend with in dark rooms as I empty myself into their welcoming bodies.

But it's no use. No matter how hard I try, I can't forget that these women are nothing more than a poor substitute for the one I really want.

I've gone the other route, too, and screwed females who look nothing like her. Blondes. Redheads. Brunettes. Ones who are slim as reeds, with no tits to speak of. And ones who are tight and athletic and limber as hell.

You'd think a woman who strokes and plays with my balls as I slam into her from behind would be enough to make me forget Sofia.

It's not.

When Sofia should be the last thing occupying my mind, she pushes her way inside. Then I ejaculate in a blind outrage with a roar of frustration. Instead of providing relief, the release fuels the fury and lust boiling within me.

It also forces me to acknowledge and accept that I have no fucking control over my own thoughts, feelings, or body where Sofia is concerned, which pisses me off more than anything else. I take pride in being able to turn my emotions off as if they were a light switch. I couldn't do my job if I didn't have that kind of self-control.

But that capability is rendered useless with Sofia.

She's my weakness

While I might not be able to possess her, I'll be damned if another man lays claim to what's mine.

Sofia
   Three years ago

"Well, hello there, handsome." My sister cranes her neck. "Who do we have here?"

At twenty-five, Francesca is already married and living in Philadelphia with her husband. I don't get to spend as much time with her as I'd like. Since we're two years apart, and she's my only sister out of four siblings, we're thick as thieves. I'm always excited when she comes home for a visit.

Our mother has arranged a shopping excursion on Michigan Avenue, along with two dinner parties with friends and family while Frankie's here. If there's time, we'll head up north to spend the weekend at our cottage in Door County, Wisconsin. Escaping the frenetic energy of the city is always a welcome change. I could spend days wandering around the quaint little towns dotting Lake Michigan's eastern shores. Like the family compound which lies north of Chicago, the cottage has been in our family for generations.

I don't bother glancing in the direction where Frankie's eyes are focused. I already know what—or who—has captured her attention. My skin prickled with awareness as soon as he stepped outside.

"That's Roman. He works for Papa," I tell her, ignoring the nerves dancing at the bottom of my belly.

Frankie snorts. "Of course, he does." Still staring at him, she states the obvious. "Damn, but he's hot."

The appreciative tone of her voice makes the edges of my lips curl into a smile. Clearing my throat, I admonish, "Have you forgotten that you're a married woman?"

Francesca and Dante have enjoyed marital bliss for two years, and Frankie is the happiest I've ever seen her. They were high school sweethearts and have known each other since they were children. I can't imagine my sister with anyone other than Dante, who has mastered the art of reining her in when necessary while allowing her to spread her wings and soar. Not an easy feat for any man. Frankie can be a handful. There's no doubt in my mind that the two of them were made for one another.

"Please." She rolls her eyes. "I can appreciate a good-looking male when I see one."

"Uh-huh," I tease, recalling how she threatens her husband with bodily harm whenever she catches him looking at other women. "Can Dante appreciate a good-looking female when he sees one as well?"

"Not if he enjoys having balls."

I burst into laughter. Francesca has nothing to worry about. Dante loves her beyond reason and would do anything for her.

How can I not envy them?

It's difficult to imagine having a relationship like theirs since my past is riddled with courtships that fizzled out around the six-month mark. Of course, being hung up on a man who wants nothing to do with me doesn't help my love life either.

Those thoughts viciously circle through my brain as my gaze settles on Roman. Looking deliciously sweaty, he makes his way into the yard from the basement gym where my father's men work out. I've unintentionally memorized his schedule. Every day like clockwork, Roman spends an hour lifting weights before taking a four-mile run along the trails bordering the wooded property.

I like watching him when he's unaware of my presence. Then I can look at him as much as I want without the fear of getting a glare in return.

I don't know why he doesn't like me.

But he doesn't. You'd have to be blind not to notice his disgust. He doesn't even try to hide it.

I sensed his disdain the first time we met. Each subsequent

encounter has only intensified those feelings. I'm not sure what I did to cause this reaction in him, nor do I know how to alter his perception.

What I have learned in the time I've been acquainted with Roman is to give him a wide berth. And yet, knowing his feelings, I still gravitate to this spot at the same time every morning. I just can't help myself.

I must be a glutton for punishment, because I live for these fleeting glimpses of him. I file them away in the back of my mind to take out when I'm alone in my room.

Roman is one of my father's men. His disposition toward me shouldn't matter. But it does. I've racked my brain to come up with a rational explanation for his behavior, but can't find one. As much as it troubles me, I refuse to confront him and ask about it.

That would indicate I give a damn and that his opinion matters.

Which isn't the case.

All right, maybe it is.

I can pretend all I want to the outside world, but I can't lie to myself. I have a sick obsession with the man. I have no idea why he fascinates me.

No one would ever accuse Roman of having a sparkling personality. The man is surly to the extreme. At least toward me, he is. Every time he glowers at me, my breath catches, and my pulse runs rampant. My panties dampen whenever I imagine his big, rough hands stroking my naked body.

I'm not under any illusions that Roman would be a tender lover.

There doesn't seem to be a gentle bone in his body.

He's the strong, silent type, with eyes that constantly assess his surroundings to look for threats. I've never seen him kick back and relax. I'm not even sure if he knows how to smile.

His complexion is dark and swarthy. My guess is that he's of Italian descent. His body is hard. Strong. Honed for violence. A thin veneer of civility masks the explosive personality I sense lurking beneath the surface.

My sister and I silently watch as Roman moves through a series of stretches. I'm held prisoner by the sight of his muscles contracting and lengthening. Since he hasn't glanced in our direction, I assume he's unaware of us ogling him from the screened-in porch as we enjoy steaming mugs of coffee.

Roman's dark head angles toward us. His gaze collides with mine, and I realize that he's been aware of us the entire time. Our interest has not gone unnoticed.

The hairs on my arms rise as he stares at me.

"Well, well, well," Francesca murmurs, her voice full of amusement. "What do we have here?"

I try to look away, but can't. I'm transfixed by the sight of him. Other than the long black athletic shorts sitting loosely around lean hips, his sun-kissed skin is gloriously bare. His muscular chest glistens with perspiration in the early morning sunlight. His cheeks are flushed from his exertion in the gym. Dark stubble covers both chin and jawline.

This man is the epitome of tall, dark, and sinfully sexy. I'm not alone in my appreciation. I've seen the way other women watch him. He may not want it, but he attracts female attention without even trying.

My sister elbows me in the ribs. "Have you been holding out on me? Is there some kind of illicit flirtation going on between you and one of Papa's henchmen?"

Without acknowledging our presence, Roman severs eye contact and releases me from the captivity of his stare. Air rushes from my lungs, and my legs turn to jelly as he takes off at a fast clip toward the dense woods bordering the side of the property. I track him until he passes through the tree line.

I shake my head to clear it of the random thoughts that have accumulated. "Of course not. There's nothing going on between us."

"Are you *sure* about that?" she sing-songs teasingly, letting me know that I'm not fooling her for a minute.

Now that Roman has disappeared into the forest that comprises three-fourths of the property, my heart rate returns to normal and coherent thought floods through my brain.

"He can barely tolerate the sight of me, Frankie." The bitter truth of the words rings harshly in my ears and tastes bitter on my tongue.

Her brows pinch together. "Why do you say that?"

I shrug and murmur under my breath, "You saw the way he stared at me, right?"

"Yeah."

I glance at my sister. Our gazes catch and hold. We've always been adept at silently communicating with one another. It's a childhood trick that came in handy when we were trapped in a roomful of adults.

For the first time in my life, I don't want that mental connection with Frankie. If she looks too closely, she might see the feelings I have for Roman. And I'm not comfortable with owning up to something that scares and confuses me so much.

I casually wave a hand in the air. "He always looks at me that way. It's like he's angry that I'm breathing the same air as him."

"Hmm." She presses her lips together in a thoughtful manner. "Interesting."

None of my father's men have ever made me feel uncomfortable or unwelcome in my own home. But Roman does.

I console myself with the fact that school begins again in less than a month. I'll return to my apartment in the city, where I can immerse myself in classes and forget all about Roman Santori.

For a while.

I'm in my second year of a master's program in Educational Psychology. Most of the people I know who are my age don't spend their summer breaks living at home with their parents, but Mama and Papa are overprotective. They worry about my safety. We have an understanding. I stay at the compound during breaks in exchange for freedom during the academic year.

I really don't mind spending time at home.

Let me rephrase that—I never minded before Roman began working for my father.

I've been uneasy in his presence from the get-go. I've tried being polite and friendly. Not overly so, but enough to pass one another in the hallway or kitchen with a cordial greeting.

My attempts at civility were repeatedly met with cold, emotionless looks and a handful of muttered words that barely passed for conversation. I now go to great lengths to stay out of parts of the house I know he'll be in to avoid any more forced interaction.

As much as Roman intimidates me, I'm still drawn to him. His masculinity appeals to something infinitely female in me. My senses go haywire whenever he's in the vicinity. I don't understand my visceral reaction to him since he's the opposite type of guy I usually find attractive.

"I don't know," Frankie speculates, snapping me out of my musings. "I get the feeling there's more to it."

"You're crazy. I know when someone doesn't like me." My heart clenches as I add, "And for some reason, I rub this guy the wrong way."

ABOUT THE AUTHOR

Jennifer Sucevic is a USA Today bestselling author who has published nineteen New Adult and Mature Young Adult novels. Her work has been translated into German, Dutch, and Italian. Jen has a bachelor's degree in History and a master's degree in Educational Psychology. Both are from the University of Wisconsin-Milwaukee. She started out her career as a high school counselor, which she loved. She lives in the Midwest with her husband, four kids, and a menagerie of animals. If you would like to receive regular updates regarding new releases, please subscribe to her newsletter here- Jennifer Sucevic Newsletter (subscribepage.com)

Or contact Jen through email, at her website, or on Facebook.

sucevicjennifer@gmail.com

Want to join her reader group? Do it here -)

J Sucevic's Book Boyfriends | Facebook

Social media links-

www.jennifersucevic.com

https://www.instagram.com/jennifersucevicauthor

https://www.facebook.com/jennifer.sucevic

Amazon.com: Jennifer Sucevic: Books, Biography, Blog, Audiobooks, Kindle

Jennifer Sucevic Books - BookBub

https://www.tumblr.com/blog/jsucevic

https://www.pinterest.com/jmolitor6/